LANCASHIRE
Lass

Libby Ashworth was born and raised in Lancashire, where she can trace her family back to the Middle Ages. It was while researching her family history that she realised there were so many stories about ordinary working people that she wanted to tell. She has previously written historical novels – *The de Lacy Inheritance* and *By Loyalty Bound* – as well as local history books.

Libby currently lives in Lancashire with her son.

Also by Libby Ashworth

The Cotton Spinner

A
LANCASHIRE
Lass

Libby Ashworth

arrow books

1 3 5 7 9 10 8 6 4 2

Arrow Books
20 Vauxhall Bridge Road
London SW1V 2SA

Arrow Books is part of the Penguin Random House group
of companies whose addresses can be found at
global.penguinrandomhouse.com

Penguin
Random House
UK

First published in Great Britain by Arrow Books in 2020

www.penguin.co.uk

A CIP catalogue record for this book is available from
the British Library

ISBN 9781787463592

Typeset in 11.5/15.7 pt Palatino
by Integra Software Services Pvt. Ltd, Pondicherry

Printed and bound in Great Britain by Clays Ltd, Elcograf S.p.A.

In memory of Susannah Smithson.

Acknowledgements

Thanks to both my editors – Cassandra Di Bello and Jennie Rothwell, for their tireless work on this book and their welcome advice. Thanks also to all the rest of the team at Arrow – my copy editor, for her attention to detail, the cover designer for the beautiful image, and everyone who has worked so hard to make this book a success.

Thanks to my agent, Felicity Trew, and to Caroline Sheldon and everyone at the Caroline Sheldon Literary Agency for all their support.

Thanks once again to Blackburn Library for their Cotton Town website, which is an amazing resource for anyone who wants to study the history of Blackburn. And also to the Tuesday Reading Group for their interest and patience when I talk too much about my books.

Thanks to all my other friends, both readers and writers, who always offer encouragement. I hope you enjoy the story.

Chapter One

'Gone? Gone where?' asked Hannah.

Sally, the scullery maid, shrugged her shoulders. 'I came down to set the fires and get the water on to boil, but Cook never showed up and when I knocked on her door there were nobody there. All the bedrooms are empty. Upstairs and down.'

Mary hurried in, pushing her hair into her cap. 'What's to do?' she asked when she saw their faces.

'Sal says everyone's gone.'

'Don't be daft,' said Mary, glancing at the row of bells high on the wall as if she expected them all to start tinkling at any moment. 'We'd best get started on making some tea and toast before Mrs Slater gives us a telling off. I'll scramble the eggs.' She reached for a dish and the bowl of eggs and began to break them one by one, whisking as she went.

'Sal says the family's all disappeared as well,' said Hannah, reaching out to stay Mary's hand as she picked up another egg.

Mary hesitated and then gave Sally a fierce look. 'Hast tha been to look?'

'Aye. I crept in to lay the fires, but their beds weren't slept in and their drawers were left open and nothing in 'em. And I can't find Mr Cox or any of the footmen. I thought I were all alone until Hannah came down.' A sob caught in her throat and she sat down on Cook's chair and pulled a rag from her sleeve to wipe her nose. 'I didn't know what to do.'

'Let's go to look,' said Mary to Hannah, setting down the whisk. 'There's bound to be an explanation,' she added as they hurried up the corridor past the housekeeper's room and the butler's pantry. Both were deserted. 'Folk don't just disappear in the middle of the night,' Mary continued as they walked through the breakfast room, and glanced into the dining room where the table had been cleared and reset after last night's supper. They went into the drawing room. The blue cushions were all plumped, but the blinds were still pulled down and Sal had neglected to clean out the hearth. All three rooms were empty.

'Where can they be?' asked Hannah as they crossed the main hall with its cabinet of stuffed exotic birds and looked into the billiard room where the only sign of life was the score from the last game still chalked up on the board. They went up the main staircase, normally forbidden to them except for the early-morning dusting, and tapped on the bedroom doors before opening them. No one was there. It was as Sal had said. Drawers and wardrobes were left open and the beds were untouched with the covers still folded back for bedtime.

'Moonlight flit,' said Mary.

'No.' Hannah knew of people who'd done that. But they were poor folk who couldn't afford to pay their rent, who disappeared in the middle of the night with a few belongings piled on to the back of a cart, to avoid their debts. 'People like the Sudells don't do that.'

'What other explanation is there?' asked Mary and Hannah had to admit that she couldn't think of one.

They went down the stairs and back to the kitchen to find Robert, the hall boy, sitting at the table with Sal drinking tea and eating buttered toast.

'They've gone,' he said.

'We can see that,' Mary told him. 'Dost tha know why?'

'Aye,' he said. 'I woke in the night with all the kerfuffle from the yard and went to see what were

3

afoot. Old Cox shoved me back inside and told me to keep my trap shut. He said Mr Sudell has lost all his money and wanted to leave afore he were found out because of the shame of it.'

'Lost his money?' said Hannah. 'How could he lose his money?' It wasn't like a sixpence slipping out of his pocket, she thought. They said that he had a million pounds.

'Bought too much cotton,' said Rob. 'He had it stockpiled, but now that the price has fallen he can't make his money back. He's bankrupt. There's nowt left.'

'But what about all this?' asked Hannah. 'The house alone must be worth a fortune.'

'It'll have to be sold to pay off his debts.'

'What about us?' said Hannah, suddenly realising that this was her problem too.

Rob shrugged. 'They took some of the staff – them as had been with 'em for a long time. But the rest of us are out of a job. I suppose we'll be expected to clear out afore the bailiffs come.'

Hannah sat down at the table and reached for a piece of the toast. It was unthinkable. This was her home now. She loved this place. She'd thought that leaving her job in the mill in Blackburn and coming to work for the Sudells was the best decision she'd ever made. The air was clear up here on the hill, away from the smog and the smoke and the grime. She'd had no intention of ever going back, but now she wondered what other option there was.

Mary went back to scrambling the eggs. 'We may as well eat these,' she said. 'Who knows when we'll get another meal? There's bacon too. Get it on to fry.'

'How long dost tha think we have before they throw us out?' Hannah asked her friend. They'd gone to sit in the drawing room to pretend that they were gentry.

'Not long,' said Mary from her cushioned seat at the window. She nodded her head to where a cloud of dust in the distance betrayed the approach of horses up the long winding driveway. Hannah groaned. She was enjoying lying full length on the blue damask couch and she'd hoped that they would have longer before they were forced to leave.

'It's all right for thee,' complained Mary. 'Thy parents or sister will take thee back, but there's no way I'm going back home. I'd rather starve.'

'It won't come to that. Lots of the mill owners are building themselves big houses. They must need staff.'

'I doubt we'd stand much of a chance without a character reference. We were lucky here,' Mary reminded her. 'But things have changed. No one gets taken on now without a letter from their former employer. And it doesn't look like we'll be getting one.'

'Or the wages we're owed,' said Hannah as she reluctantly swung her feet to the floor and bent to lace her boots. The horses had arrived outside the main door and men were surveying the front of the house. It seemed that they would barely have time to pack their belongings before the house was secured and they were sent on their way.

Half an hour later Hannah and Mary were walking down the long drive towards the road with their bags in their hands. It didn't seem that long since they'd walked up it with such high hopes. Hannah had been so happy. She'd been overjoyed when the Sudells had agreed to employ her as a maid at their new country house, and after she'd been promoted from a scullery maid to a parlour maid she and Mary had talked excitedly about the possibility of becoming a lady's maid, with all the excitement and glamour of looking after Mr Sudell's daughters, being responsible for their lovely dresses, doing their hair, hearing their secrets and maybe even meeting someone special. Hannah longed to meet someone special. She'd seen such handsome men arriving at the Sudells' door in their carriages for visits and parties. Men who wore silk cravats, and whose hands were soft and clean and who looked as though they'd never had to weave a length of cloth in their lives. How she'd wished that one of them would notice her as she crept about the house with her dustpan and brush. She knew that it was silly and that she ought to resent those who didn't have to do a turn to earn their living. She knew she should set her cap at some hardworking lad, but it didn't hurt to dream, she told herself. After a long day wasn't she allowed at least a few minutes of imagining what her life could be like before she fell into an exhausted sleep?

Now a very different future beckoned. There was no point going home to her parents at Ramsgreave. There was no work for her there and she needed to earn her keep. So, if there was no chance of another position as a maid, she supposed that she would have to go to her sister, Jennet, and her brother-in-law, Titus, and ask if they would take her back as a boarder. Then she would have to go to the mill and try to get her job back. It wasn't what she wanted, and she silently damned Henry Sudell for having ruined her life.

When they reached the end of the drive, the bailiff pulled the tall iron gates closed behind them and began to secure them with heavy chains.

'That's it then,' said Mary. 'I suppose we'd better start walking.'

'Where will tha go?' asked Hannah as they took the lane that led down the hill towards the Preston to Blackburn road. 'I could ask our Jennet and Titus if they'd take thee in. They don't live on Paradise Lane any more,' she added, knowing that Mary wouldn't want to live next door to her own family. 'They moved on soon after I left.'

'I don't blame them,' said Mary. 'I wouldn't want to live next door to my father either after what happened. Where are they now?'

'On Water Street, next to the river. Come home with me for today at least,' said Hannah. 'I'm sure tha'll be welcome to stay for a night or two until tha finds summat else.'

She tried to sound hopeful and positive, but the truth was that she wasn't entirely sure of her own welcome. Things had been difficult before she left. When Titus was in prison and it had been just her and Jennet and little Peggy, things had been all right. They'd struggled, of course, but they'd managed. But when Titus had come home and found Jennet pregnant with another man's child, he'd been upset and difficult and they'd done nothing but argue. In a way she couldn't blame him. It must have been hard for him and it hadn't been entirely his own fault that he'd been

8

sent to the House of Correction in Preston – or so he said. His story was that he'd been to a Reform meeting on the moor and got caught up with some loom breakers afterwards and been arrested. He'd been lucky not to be transported and it was when Jennet thought she would never see him again that she'd slept with George. She was going to go to America with him, but when Titus got the prison sentence instead of being shipped off to Australia she'd decided to wait for him and George went on his own. It was only after George had gone that she found out she was having his child. She'd expected Titus to understand and forgive her, and he had in the end, but even Hannah could see that the love they'd once had for one another had taken a harsh blow. And so she'd left them to themselves, to try to mend their marriage, and now she had no idea what sort of reception she'd receive when she turned up unannounced on their doorstep.

They walked on, keeping to the side of the busy road as the traffic clattered past them, stirring up the dust. It was July and it had been dry since the beginning of June. Out in the countryside the dust had been bearable, but as they approached the town Hannah could see the low-lying haze clinging to the mills and the rows of terraced houses that lay in the valley. The noise increased as well.

Birdsong was replaced by the thumping of the engines that drove the looms, the shouting of the carters as they unloaded the bales of raw cotton at the warehouses and took away the lengths of calico to the mills up at Darwen where they would be bleached and printed to make the pretty dresses that the daughters of the gentry wore – dresses that clung to their bodies in the breeze and showed every curve – dresses that Hannah had wished she could wear rather than the stiff black gown she'd been given to work in up at Woodfold. She'd left it behind on the bed. It wasn't really hers and she had no intention of wearing it again. Although she could have cut it up to make something else. It could have been sewn into a little jacket, she thought as she regretted her hasty decision. Time was a luxury they'd not been granted that morning and she'd had no idea when she got up and dressed that she'd be back in Blackburn, with no job, before dinnertime.

The river Blakewater was low with the lack of rain and in the heat a stench rose from it that made her feel nauseous. She wondered why Jennet and Titus had come to live here. Such bad smells weren't healthy and she knew that her sister worried about Peggy since she'd had the scarlatina as a baby.

Number six was the only house with the door ajar and Hannah knocked and called. 'Jennet?'

There was no answer so Hannah stepped into the parlour to be met by a damp fug. Every rung of the airer was filled with drying underwear and more was arranged on a maiden set in front of the fire where a kettle boiled, adding steam to the already hot and damp atmosphere.

'Jennet?' she called again, going through to the back kitchen and out into the small walled yard where she found her sister, surrounded by bed sheets flapping on the clothes line.

'Hannah! What's tha doin' here? What's happened?' she asked, glancing over Hannah's shoulder at Mary.

'We've been put out.'

'Why? What's tha done?'

'Nowt!' protested Hannah. 'Sudell's lost all his money and run off in the middle of the night.'

'No!' Jennet stared from one to the other, not able to believe what they were telling her. 'Tha's havin' me on.'

'We're not, Mrs Eastwood,' said Mary. 'It's true. Bailiffs have been. They've turned us out and chained up the gates.'

'Good Lord,' said Jennet. 'How come he's lost it? He were that rich. What's he spent it all on?'

'Cotton. Or so we were told. Paid too much and can't get his money back. He's left on the quiet because of the shame.'

'So tha's lost thy job?' she said, drying her reddened hands on her apron.

'Aye. That's the top and bottom of it,' said Hannah. 'We had nowhere else to go.'

'Come inside,' said Jennet. 'Come on,' she added to little Bessie, who was playing in a tub of water. 'I'll make a pot of tea. Hast tha eaten?'

'Aye,' said Mary. 'We breakfasted in style, though it'll be a while before we have another meal like that again.

'Oh, I don't know.' Hannah put the parcel she'd been carrying down on the table for her sister to unwrap.

'Bacon?' said Jennet. 'There must be a couple of pounds of it!'

'Well, it would've been a sin to let it go to waste.'

'I'll get it in the pan. Titus'll be home for his dinner soon and it'll be a rare treat for him.'

'How's things?' asked Hannah as she sat down on one of the familiar bentwood chairs at the table and unfastened her bonnet.

'So so,' said Jennet as she spooned tea into the pot. 'I've started takin' in a bit o' washing to help make ends meet.'

'So I see,' said Hannah as her sister moved the maiden from in front of the fire and poured the boiling water from the kettle into the dark brown teapot. 'Where's Peggy?' she asked as Jennet got down a towel to dry off Bessie.

'She's been given a place at the Girls' Charity School on Thunder Alley. She's learnin' to read – doing champion at it an' all.'

'Really?' said Hannah.

'Aye. She's a clever lass. She must get it from Titus. I were never any good at that sort of learnin'.'

'Hast tha ever tried?' asked Hannah. Some of the servants at Woodfold had been able to read – the butler, the housekeeper and the cook, Mrs Slater, who used to read to them in the evenings from the penny novels she bought when she went to market. Hannah had loved those stories and she longed to be able to read them for herself, but she'd always worried that it would be too hard.

'Titus tried to teach me,' said Jennet as she turned the bacon. 'It made no sense, but our Peggy's taken to it well.'

'Is Titus still working on the road building?' asked Hannah.

'No. He's back in the mill.'

'Not t'Dandy Mill?'

'No. They'll not take him back there. He's a weaver at Water Street, just across the way. That's why we got this house.'

'It stinks though,' said Hannah.

'Aye it does, especially on days like these.'

'Is tha not afraid of the bad miasmas?'

'Of course I am. But we were lucky to get it. And we had to get away from Paradise Lane.' She glanced at Mary. 'Thy father were doin' all in his power to make it difficult for us.'

As Jennet poured tea the mill hooters began to go off. First one and then another until the whole town was filled with their wailing. Then the clatter of clog irons on the cobbles began and a few minutes later Titus came in the door, stopping in his tracks when he saw them all sitting round the table and smelled the bacon frying.

'What's all this?' he asked. 'What's tha doin' ere?' he asked Hannah with a suspicious glance at Mary. 'How do?' he said to her. 'What's goin' on?'

'Sudell's gone bankrupt and done a runner,' Mary told him.

'Bloody hell!' Titus hung his cap up on the hook behind the door. 'There were some talk at t' mill, but I didn't think it were true.'

'Gone in the middle of the night,' said Hannah. 'We knew nowt about it until we got up this morning.'

'And what's tha plannin' on doin' now?' asked Titus as he tucked into the plate of bacon.

'We'll have to get mill work again, I suppose. I was hopin' as tha'd let me board with thee for a while.'

'Aye, all right,' said Titus. 'We could do with another wage comin' in. And what about thee, Mary?' he asked. 'What'll tha do?'

'I'll have to look for lodgings, I suppose.'

'Can she not stop here?' said Hannah. 'I don't mind sharing a bed.'

Titus pushed the last of the bacon into his mouth and chewed. 'There's not room,' he said. 'I don't mind thee stayin' for a while, but Mary'll have to find somewhere else.'

'I'll be on my way then!' said her friend, standing up and reaching for her bonnet.

'Don't go, Mary! Sit thee down,' pleaded Hannah.

'No. I knows when I'm not welcome. Thanks for the tea,' she said to Jennet.

'Where will tha go?'

'I'll take a room somewhere. I have a few shillings put by. I'll let thee know where to find me.'

Hannah watched as her friend went to the door and closed it behind her. None of them spoke as she passed the window. Hannah was tempted to run after her, but she knew it would achieve nothing. Mary would be able to look after herself, she thought, although she was disappointed and embarrassed that Titus had been so blunt in his refusal.

'Tha could have let her stay for a day or two,' she told him. 'It were a bit mean to send her on her way like that when she's nowhere to go.'

'She could go to Paradise Lane,' he replied. 'If I let her get her feet under t' table here, we'll never get rid. It's different wi' thee. Tha's family. But her folks have caused us too much trouble for me to be doin' her any favours.'

'None of it were Mary's fault!'

'Aye, well …' he remarked, draining his cup and reaching for his cap. 'I'd best be gettin' back. I don't want my pay dockin' for bein' late. I'll see thee later,' he said, kissing his wife.

'If it had been up to me I'd have been soft and let her stay,' said Jennet after he'd gone. 'But Titus is right. We can't afford to keep folk who aren't family.'

'She would have worked and paid her way.'

'Aye, she would have been willing to work, I know that. But work's still not that easy to come by,' said Jennet. 'Mills have taken some workers back on but it isn't like it was when we first came. Trade's still poor, and if we'd let her stay it would have been even harder to ask her to go. I'm sure she'll find somewhere. And she does have a home of her own.'

'Aye, but she'll not go there. She told me stuff whilst we were away – about her father. Bad stuff,' said Hannah.

'I can't say as I'm surprised,' replied Jennet as she began to fold the washing she'd taken down from the rack. 'Folk think that what goes on behind closed doors is private, but nowt's private when tha lives cheek by jowl wi' folk like we do in this town. He's a bad lot is that Joe, and Nan's no better. I'd hoped that Mary might make summat of herself once she got away from them. It's a cryin' shame tha's had to come back.'

Chapter Two

Mary walked out of the house on Water Street with her head held high. She didn't even bother to slam the door behind her. She was angry, but she wasn't sure that she wanted to live there anyway. Jennet was all right and she felt sorry about the trouble that her parents had caused her. But she didn't like Titus.

She paused as she reached the corner of King Street. It would take her down to Paradise Lane and she was tempted to go and have a look. There would be nobody in at this time of the day. She found herself walking down the hill without having made any conscious decision. It was as if her feet were leading her home, except that it wasn't her home any more.

The row of cottages facing the mill wall looked just the same. She walked down to number eight and pressed her face up to the window. The chairs were pushed back from the table where her family had left in a hurry to go back to work after their dinner. The fire was banked up ready to be rekindled into a blaze when they got home, and her father's chair was still by the hearth with the same cushion on the seat, flattened from use. She no longer had a key and when she tried the door it was locked against her. It was futile anyway, she thought. Her father hadn't wanted her to leave and it had taken all her courage to face him and say that she was going to work for the Sudells. And it had been such a relief to get away and be free of him. She could never go back.

Mary looked around as she heard footsteps coming down the cobbled street, hoping that whoever it was hadn't seen her peering in through the window. The young lad who was walking towards her looked familiar, but it was a moment before she recognised him as her brother. John had grown much taller since she'd last seen him and he looked older too. He'd been little more than a child when he'd been sent away to the prison, but the person who warily approached her now seemed on the verge of adulthood.

'John?' She wasn't sure if he'd recognised her and the thought made her feel bereft. He had been like a babe to her. She'd nursed him and brought him up almost single-handedly whilst their

19

mother and her elder sisters had been at work. She'd carried him to the mill every dinnertime, baby in one arm and her mother's dinner in a dish in the other, striving not to drop either, so that her mother could sit down and feed him whilst she ate.

'Mary?' His voice had deepened.

'Aye,' she said. 'I didn't think to see thee. I thought tha were still at Preston.'

'They let me go a week back,' he told her.

'I'm glad to see thee.' She wanted to hug him, but he looked so fragile and she wasn't sure whether he would welcome such an open show of affection, so she just reached out and rubbed his arm with her hand. He was all bones.

'They're not in,' he said, nodding towards the door.

'I didn't really want to see them.'

'But tha'll come in for a minute?' he asked, taking a key from his pocket to unlock the door.

'Aye. Of course.'

Mary followed him into the small parlour, breathing in its familiar smell. John took off his cap and she saw that his head had been shaved; the scar from where he'd once banged it on the fender was clearly visible. He sat down on their father's chair, pulled off his dirty boots and rubbed at his feet.

'They're too small for me.' He grimaced and she saw the weeping blisters on the backs of his heels and the red marks on his toes. 'I need some new clogs.'

'Aye. And socks,' she told him. 'Hast tha no money?'

He shook his head. 'I'm not earning much but they still expect me to pay the same for my keep as Susan and Esther do.'

'That's hardly fair. They both earn a good wage as weavers.'

'Aye. But tha knows what Father's like. He says it's only right.'

'Here.' She fished a shilling from the savings she had in her purse and put it in his hand. 'For thee,' she said. 'Not a word to Mam and Dad.'

'Thanks.'

'What was it like?' she asked, sitting in the chair opposite. 'I've worried about thee day and night.'

'It were all right,' he said. 'We got fed.'

'But did they treat thee well? What did they make thee do?' His sentence had been hard labour and she'd spent many nights crying into her pillow and worrying about him. He'd always been such a slight little boy and she'd been terrified that the work would be too much for him.

'They had this big wheel', he told her, 'that raised the water from the well. It takes four or

21

five men walking on it to make it turn. They called it a treadmill. We were made to walk on it for hours a day.' He stared at his hand, the one that he'd caught in the mule at the mill. Although the surgeon had saved the fingers, they weren't much use to him. He could barely move them and so struggled to do any fine work. He would never be a spinner like their father. 'They wouldn't teach me weaving. Said there were no point to it. They did teach me to read a bit, though, and add up. I managed to hold a pen in my other hand even though it were frowned upon.'

'And what now?' she asked. 'What work is there tha can do?' She was about to tell him that he mustn't go back to thieving again, but she held her tongue. If that Sam Proctor hadn't come to live next door with Titus and Jennet Eastwood he would never have been persuaded into it in the first place. But with his damaged hand and no work, she could understand that the temptation of acting as a distraction whilst Sam picked the pockets of the gentry had been too much for him to resist.

'I'm doin' a bit at the stable yard on Thunder Alley, but it's only when they need me,' he said. 'That's why I'm finished for today. I were hopin' to get summat where I could use my numbers. They said I were quite good at it, but folk know me in this town. They know I've been in prison and they'll not risk giving me employment in their offices – especially not when I'd be handling their cash.'

Mary nodded. She could see that it was going to be hard for him.

'Dost tha know what happened to Sam?' he asked her. 'Mam and Dad'll not speak about it. Did he get ... tha knows ...'

'Hanged? No.'

'Transported then?'

She shook her head. 'He got clean away,' she told her brother. 'They never caught him.'

'How did he manage that?'

'It were summat to do with Titus Eastwood. He spirited him off somehow, though nobody knows how. Mam were that angry it were just thee that took the blame she vowed she'd get her own back on him and Jennet. That's why they moved from next door. They're on Water Street now.'

'What's tha doing here anyway?' he asked. 'They said tha'd gone away with Hannah Chadwick.'

'I did,' she said and told him about the Sudells.

'So will tha not stop here now?' He sounded hopeful but she disappointed him.

'No. I must be gone afore they get home. I've to find lodgings somewhere. I can't live here.' She didn't tell him why not.

'But I'll see thee again?' he asked.

'Of course! I'll not lose thee a second time,' she told him.

She hugged him before she left and bid him not to say a word to their parents about seeing her. They were bound to find out soon enough, but for the time being she'd rather they didn't know she was back in town.

There were plenty of inns and pubs where she could get a bed for a night or two until she found a job, she thought, but she needed one that wasn't too expensive, especially as she'd just parted with a shilling. Not that she regretted it. She wouldn't see her brother unshod whilst she had money in her purse.

She turned into Shorrock Fold. It was one of the oldest parts of town and the buildings had gables that jutted out into the street, making it too narrow for anything wider than a small cart. The Star was down here. She thought that it was fairly respectable – or as respectable as a beer-house could be. The tenant was a woman too, a Mrs Hall, and Mary felt more comfortable asking for lodgings here than somewhere that was run by a man.

She opened the door and stepped inside. It smelled of stale beer and smoke and yesterday's hotpot.

'I'm not serving,' said Mrs Hall. 'I forgot to put the sneck down on t' door. I'm open again at six.'

'It's not beer I'm after. I'm after a room for a day or two.' The woman gave her a shrewd look. 'I can pay,' Mary added, taking out her purse and showing the landlady a florin.

Mrs Hall wrung out the cloth she'd been using to wipe her counter and hung it up to dry. 'Right,' she said. 'Where's tha come from?'

Mary decided it was probably best to be honest. 'I were working as a parlour maid for Mr Sudell.'

'I heard he's done a runner.'

'Aye. In the middle of the night. Took some staff with him. Rest of us have been thrown out.'

'It's a rum do,' said the woman. She studied Mary again. 'How will tha manage wi' no wages?'

'I'll get work,' said Mary. 'I was in the mill afore so I can always go back to that, and I have a bit put by in the meantime.'

'Three and six a week – up front,' said the woman.

Mary counted out the coins on to the counter, thinking that she would only have enough for a few weeks if she didn't get work. 'Does it include meals?' she asked hopefully.

'Aye, there's always summat t' eat,' said Mrs Hall. 'Tha can lend a hand in th' evenings if tha likes, until tha gets a proper job. I'll knock a shilling off for that.'

'All right,' said Mary, relieved that she'd found somewhere so easily and didn't have to risk sleeping on the streets.

She followed Mrs Hall up the steep stairs at the back of the building, up two flights to a small room under the eaves. It wasn't so bad. Not as nice as the room she and Hannah had been given at Woodfold, but it looked clean. The walls were plain white but the floor was covered in patterned oilcloth. Under the tiny window with its small panes of thick glass there was an iron bed with a flock mattress and a pillow, a washstand with a flowery jug and basin, a chair and a small cupboard.

'Blankets and sheets are in here,' said Mrs Hall, pulling open the cupboard door. 'I'll leave thee to make up t' bed. Tha can come down about five and have summat t' eat and then give a hand servin' until we close at eleven.'

'Aye. That's all right.'

'Lass in t' other room is Alice. I think she might be having a nap now, but tha can knock and introduce thyself later. She'll show thee t' ropes.'

When Mrs Hall had gone, Mary sat down on the chair. Unexpectedly she found herself unable to hold back tears, though whether she was crying from relief or sadness or anger she wasn't sure. It certainly wasn't how she'd expected her day to turn out when she'd got up that morning.

After a while, she pulled herself together, wiped her eyes and made up the bed. Then she went back down the stairs to ask about the privy.

'Bottom o' the yard,' said Mrs Hall. Mary hesitated. 'What's to do?' asked the woman.

'Canst lend me a rag?' she asked. 'I've started my monthlies and I forgot to pack mine, what wi' leavin' in such a rush an all ...'

The landlady sighed. 'Right. Wait there,' she said before going upstairs and returning with a couple of cloths in her hand. 'Keep 'em. I don't want 'em back.'

Mary thanked her and went to find the privy. When she was done she went back inside and saw from the clock in the kitchen that she had a couple of hours to spare before five o'clock. She wondered if it was worth going to enquire about work at the mills. She supposed she might as well go and ask. The sooner she got a job, the sooner she would feel more secure.

Mary decided not to ask at the Dandy Mill on Paradise Lane. There was too much risk of running into her family there, and for another reason she'd been glad to get away from the groping hands of Mr Hargreaves, the overlooker. The man was a menace and all the lasses loathed him. He'd even tried it on with Hannah. She'd said that one night after all the other lasses had gone he'd had her pinned against a wall upstairs and would have forced her if she hadn't screamed and Jennet hadn't come running up the stairs and got him off her.

Mary walked down to the King Street Mill instead and went in the main door. She'd forgotten how noisy the mills were. The pounding of the looms seemed much worse than she remembered, though it may have been because the factory was running at full power. Nothing stood idle and the women were dashing between one loom and the next, changing the bobbins and mending the threads as the cloth pooled on to the floor.

'Can I help thee?' asked a man. He was wearing fustian britches and an open-neck shirt made from Blackburn Check.

'I need work,' she told him.

He shook his head. 'I've nowt at t' moment,' he said. 'Try Brookhouse.'

Mary spent the rest of the afternoon trailing from one mill to the next, with no luck. Nobody seemed to be taking on. She hadn't thought that it would be so difficult to get work and by the time she arrived back at the Star she was seriously worried about what she was going to do if there were no jobs.

It was almost five o'clock so she washed her face, tidied her hair as best she could and went down the steps to the kitchen to see what her duties would be.

'Is that all tha has to wear?' asked Mrs Hall when she saw her.

'Will it not do?' she asked. She'd thought that the dark skirt and white blouse would serve her well.

'It's a bit plain.'

'Plain?' repeated Mary, surprised.

'Aye. The gents that come in 'ere like to see a prettily dressed lass bringing their drinks,' she told her. 'See, here's Alice. She knows how to dress.'

Mary looked at the girl who'd just come in. She was wearing a flimsy cotton frock that reminded Mary of the dresses that Mr Sudell's daughters wore. Her hair was piled up on her head with ringlets hanging down around her ears. Her shoulders were almost bare and Mary thought that she looked more like she was going to a dance at the Assembly Rooms than to work.

'I've nowt like that,' she said, wishing that she had. She'd only ever had enough money to buy serviceable cloth to make plain clothes.

'Well, tha'll do for now,' said Mrs Hall. 'If tha decides to stay on we can get thee sorted out wi' summat more fitting. Right, this is what tha's to do. It ain't hard,' she said as she showed Mary how to pour the beer into the pots and where to wash them up when they'd been used. 'Main thing is to smile and be polite. That's what t' customers like. And as long as tha fetches 'em what they asks for and gets the right money for it, tha'll not go far wrong. Now we'll have us tea and then we'll be ready to open.'

Mary followed her back into the kitchen where Mrs Hall doled out hotpot into dishes and set them on the table. 'Eat up!' she told them and Mary perched on the edge of a stool and tucked into the meal. She was hungry, which was surprising when she considered how much she'd eaten earlier, but it had been a long and trying day.

Mrs Hall sat down with them, shook out a napkin and tucked it into the top of her low-cut frock so that she wouldn't splash any food on it. Mary watched in fascination as her ample bosoms quivered as she chewed the meat from the lamb chops, holding them between her fingers and licking her lips. 'Is tha walkin' out wi' anyone'?' Mrs Hall asked her.

'No.' Mary followed suit and picked up the chop from her basin to eat it with her fingers. 'There wasn't much chance to meet up with anyone at Woodfold.'

'Right.' She seemed strangely pleased. 'Hast tha had an admirer in t' past then?'

'No, not really,' said Mary. She didn't think that Hargreaves counted as an admirer even though he had spent a lot of time staring at her as she leaned over the looms. 'I were too busy working, and my father kept an eye on me.'

'Right. How old is tha?'

'Nineteen.'

'I thought tha might be younger.' She continued to study Mary as she chewed, making her feel as if she were being judged, although she wasn't sure what for.

'So hast tha never been with a man?' asked Alice.

'Been with ...?' It seemed an odd line of conversation from someone she'd only just met.

'Aye. Been to bed with. Tha knows.'

'Aye. I know what tha means. At least I think I do.'

'Well?'

'No ...' She felt her cheeks flushing.

'Take no notice of Alice,' said Mrs Hall. 'She means no harm. Right,' she added. 'Let's get this lot cleared away and open the door. I bet they're already waiting.'

Mary lingered in the kitchen, washing the bowls, listening as the bolt was drawn back on the door and men's voices spilled inside.

'Come on. Get a shift on. There's thirsty customers out here,' Mrs Hall called to her and she went out into the parlour aware of a sudden pause in the conversation as several pairs of eyes took a good look at her.

'Tha's new,' observed one man. 'What's thy name?'

'Mary.'

'Well, Mary, what about fetching a pint for me and my mates here?'

'Yes, sir.' She gave a slight curtsey and laughter rang around the room as she hurried away to draw the beer.

'No need for that,' hissed Mrs Hall. 'Tha's not at Sudell's fancy house now.'

Mary flushed with anger as she got the beer. She didn't like to be laughed at and she wondered whether coming here had been a good idea after all. But, she told herself, once she got a proper job she could find better lodgings and in the meantime, serving beer was saving her a shilling a week off her rent and she'd be a fool to turn it down to go and sit upstairs on her own in the little attic room.

'So, where dost tha come from?' asked the man when she returned with the beer.

'Ireland, originally. We came here for work in the mills.'

'But tha's not a mill lass.'

'Not recently. I've been working for the Sudells, up at Woodfold.'

'I heard it's all been locked up,' he said before taking a long drink and wiping his mouth on the back of his hand.

'Aye. We were turfed out this mornin'.'

'Tha's done well to find another job so quick,' he observed.

'I'm only doin' this until I can find summat better,' she told him.

'Summat better! Is that true, Nellie?' he called. 'Are we not good enough for this lass now that she's worked for *Mister* Sudell?' He emphasised the *mister* and all the men around the table laughed again.

'Don't tease her, Fred,' said Mrs Hall as she served some newcomers. 'She's only just started and she'll not last if tha doesn't treat her nice.'

'Oh, I'll treat her nice,' he replied with a knowing look.

'Leave it,' Mrs Hall told him.

'All reet,' he said, lowering his gaze.

'Don't let Fred bother thee,' said Mrs Hall. 'He's all talk and he means well. But tha'll have to learn how to handle the banter if tha's going to work 'ere. It's no place for shy lasses,' she warned her.

'I can look out for myself,' replied Mary.

Chapter Three

Hannah woke with a start when the knocker-up rapped on the front window, and a moment later she heard Titus going down the stairs. She turned over and came face-to-face with Peggy.

'Why are you sleeping in my bed?' demanded the child.

'Because I've come to live here for a while.'

'I don't like sharing a bed,' said Peggy. 'Look the other way. I need to use the pot.'

'I'm going down now,' said Hannah, pushing back the covers and reaching for her clothes.

Peggy had grown up so much in the time that Hannah had been away that she barely recognised her – and she'd become such a lady. It must be the school, she thought. The child spoke so well she could almost have passed for gentry.

Hannah went down and helped Jennet to make the breakfast.

'I can take Peggy to school,' she offered. 'Then I'll go round the mills to see what work there is.'

'That'd be a big lift,' said Jennet. 'Tha can fetch some buckets of water from the spring later an' all, if tha would.'

'Aye, of course,' said Hannah. 'Tha knows I'll pull my weight.'

After breakfast she took her niece by the hand and they walked up to Thunder Alley where the girls' school was situated in a long low building, tucked in next to the boys' national school. The street was filled with children of all ages, from little ones like Peggy to the ones who looked old enough to be in work and were causing a nuisance kicking a ball in and out of the younger children as they waited for the master and mistress to open the doors and let them in. Some of the younger ones were crying, but Peggy was watching the older children with a look of disdain at their rowdy behaviour. She seemed wise beyond her years, thought Hannah as she heard the little lass sigh when the ball bounced off the wall with a thud, bringing the schoolmaster to his door. He was wearing dark trousers and jacket and an unfastened grey cravat hung loose around his neck as if he'd been disturbed whilst still dressing.

'Bring that ball to me!'

Hannah watched as he held out a hand and one shamefaced boy slunk forwards and placed the ball on top of his outstretched palm. The master tossed the ball into the air and caught it again easily. 'Line up!' he ordered and the unruly boys began to jostle themselves into a queue that writhed down the street and around the corner, the bigger ones elbowing the smaller ones to the back. She admired his control. He was only young, but the boys did what he bid. He put the ball down, resting one foot on it, and stood fastening his cravat on the street; then, conscious of being watched, his eyes sought hers and he grinned at her, making her cheeks flush. She saw that his eyes were an unusual green, contrasting with the curly hair that flopped over his forehead. He pushed it back and picked up the ball and held it under his arm before standing to one side and sending the line of boys into the schoolroom, snatching off a cap here and cuffing the back of a head there as they passed him. Then, with a last glance at Hannah, he closed the door behind him, shouting for silence as it thudded to.

'We're going in now,' said Peggy, tugging on her hand. Hannah turned her attention to the girls who were filing into the school next door under the eye of a young woman in a dark skirt and cream blouse. Her hair was swept up into a plain style, but her face was plump and soft and Peggy ran to her eagerly to be greeted by a caress to her head as she disappeared through the door. Hannah exchanged a smile with the schoolmistress and then found that she was suddenly alone on the quiet street. She stood for a moment, looking at the windows of the boys' school and trying to imagine what was happening inside. And as she walked away a smile twitched at her lips as she remembered the schoolmaster's grin.

Hannah made her way down to the Brookhouse Mill where she'd worked before going to Woodfold. The overlooker remembered her and said that she was a good worker, but he was sorry there was nothing at the moment. She told him where she was living and he promised to send word if there was a vacancy, but somehow she didn't think he would.

She made her way to the other mills, but met the same reply everywhere. The mills had all the workers they needed.

She went back to Water Street for some dinner and then took the buckets up to the spring to fill them, leaving Jennet to her ironing. It was busy now that there were so many people and only the one well, and she had to wait. On the way back she saw some people filling their buckets from the Blakewater to save time and she wondered how they could bear the smell of it. There was a green mass floating on the top of the slow-flowing river and she thought she'd rather stand an hour at the spring than take that home.

In the afternoon she went to some of the shops to see if they needed any assistants, but they all turned her down when they found she had no experience. Towards teatime she walked back to Thunder Alley to collect Peggy. Her pace increased as she turned the corner from Northgate, hoping that she might catch a glimpse of the schoolmaster again, but the door to the girls' school opened first and when Peggy came out she was eager for home and Hannah was forced to leave, disappointed, before the boys were dismissed for the day.

'What did tha learn?' she asked Peggy as they walked along. She'd never been to school herself and she was intrigued by what went on behind the closed doors.

'Reading and writing this morning, then knitting this afternoon,' said Peggy.

'Is that right? What does it say on that shop?' she asked, wondering if the child really could read.

'Mercer's,' Peggy told her, although, not being able to read herself, Hannah had no way of knowing if it was right.

*

'Hast tha been to every mill?' Titus asked her at teatime when she told him that she hadn't been able to find work.

'Aye, all of 'em – Brookhouse, King Street ...' She began to name them.

'Not Dandy?' he asked.

'She's not goin' back there,' said Jennet. 'Not with that Hargreaves.'

'He's all talk.'

'No, he isn't. He tried to take advantage of our Hannah – would have an' all if I hadn't gone back to look for her.'

Hannah exchanged a glance with her sister, but knew not to say what had really happened in front of Titus. It was bad enough that her sister had gone with George Anderton. If she admitted that Hargreaves had raped her, Titus would kill him, and having her husband hanged as a murderer wouldn't help anybody.

'Well, she'll have to pay her way if she's to stay. Otherwise she'll have to go home,' he said.

'I've put two and six in the kitty,' Hannah told him, annoyed that he was talking about her as if she wasn't there. 'That should be enough for a week or so.'

'Aye, I suppose so.' He pushed back the chair, scraping it across the floor, and reached for his cap. 'I'll see thee later.'

'Where's he off to?' asked Hannah as she watched him pass the window.

'It's the Reform meeting on a Tuesday night.'

'Is he still involved with that? After what happened?' she asked as she began to clear the table.

'He's been very keen since he came back,' said Jennet. 'They meet at one of the beerhouses and set to tryin' to put the world to rights. I hate it when he goes. I worry as he'll end up back in the prison again if he doesn't learn to mind what he says.'

'But I thought it was all over and done with now that the town's getting members to send to Parliament.'

'Aye. So did I. But Titus says it'll make no difference because ordinary folks still have no say in the matter. He says that if we don't keep pushing for change then we'll be made fools of by the gentry for ever.'

'Or at least them as don't make fools of themselves by losin' all their money,' remarked Hannah.

Chapter Four

'It'll be busy tonight,' Mrs Hall had warned.
'There's a Reform meeting.' So Mary wasn't
surprised when Titus Eastwood walked in. He
frowned when he caught sight of her, but had the
manners to say 'How do' and to thank her when
she brought his beer to the table. Mary knew that
he was a Reformer. It was how he'd ended up in
prison, but it hadn't deterred him. In fact, he
seemed to be in charge of the group of men who
gradually filled up the benches and the stools,
supping their beer and lighting their pipes and
filling the parlour with such a fug that Mary could
barely see to put the cups on the tables.

When everyone had been served, Titus rapped
on the table with his knuckles and the men fell
silent to hear what he had to say.

Mrs Hall ushered her into the kitchen.

'We'll take the chance to have a sit-down whilst yon lot does their talkin',' she told her.

'What do they talk about?' asked Mary, lingering in the doorway, wishing that she could stay to listen. At Woodfold she'd been interested to hear the discussions around the servants' table at dinnertimes. Mr Cox in particular had had firm views on the rights of the working man and had lectured them at length on the coming Reform of the Parliament.

'I expect they'll be talking about Sudell,' said Mrs Hall. 'Everyone else is.'

It was true. Wherever Mary went to ask for work she was told there was none, but when she mentioned that she'd been a maid at Woodfold the questions came thick and fast. Mr Sudell's flight had caused quite a stir.

'Let's get this supper on,' said Mrs Hall after a while. 'They'll be hungry and thirsty again when they're done. I might not have much interest in Reform, but it's good for business.'

'Where's Alice?' asked Mary as she prodded at the potatoes in the hotpot to check that they were soft all the way through.

'Upstairs,' replied Mrs Hall.

'Is she poorly?'

'No.' Mrs Hall's tight lips warned her to say nothing more. Mary stirred up the hotpot and put the lid back on. She wasn't stupid and she suspected that Alice had taken a man upstairs, and done it with Mrs Hall's blessing. The sooner she got herself some other lodgings, the better, she thought.

'Will tha tell Hannah where I'm stayin'?' she asked Titus later as she served the food.

'Aye. Hast tha got work?'

'Only helpin' out here.'

'Aye, well, mind what tha gets mixed up in,' he warned her.

'I'm all right,' she replied, thinking that he could easily have saved her from the situation if he'd allowed her to stop at Water Street. She moved away to put a bowl down in front of the man sitting next to him. He smiled up at her and said, 'Thank you.' He seemed a cut above the usual customers and she wondered who he was. There were all different sorts in for the meeting. Even the schoolmaster had come and she wished the usual customers were as clean and polite as him.

When she went back to the kitchen with some empty cups she saw that Alice had come down. She was counting some coins into Mrs Hall's hand and neither said a word to her. She washed up the cups and went back into the parlour where Alice had joined a man who hadn't been at the meeting but had somehow managed to get himself a good seat near the fire – his legs stretched out as if he owned the place. He was well dressed, as if he had money, but he didn't look like gentry. His hastily knotted cravat was too bright and although the other customers treated him with respect they didn't treat him with deference.

'Who's the new lass?' she heard him ask Alice.

'Mary,' she told him. 'She's only here to help serve. Nothing more!'

'Jealous?' he asked with a grin.

Alice didn't reply but started to gather the used cups as the men began to say their goodnights.

'Tha can get to bed now,' Mrs Hall told Mary. 'Alice'll finish up.'

As she climbed the steep steps to her room, Mary wondered if they all thought she was a complete innocent. She could see full well what was going on, although she wanted no part in it. The man had had the same look in his eyes that her father used to get when he came home after drinking in the pub.

It had begun when she started to stay up a bit later, after everyone else had gone to bed. The house was peaceful at that time and it gave her the chance to be alone for a half an hour – a rare luxury. When she heard her father's clogs

44

coming unsteadily up the street she knew that the peace was over and that it was time for her to get off to bed, if she could push her sisters up far enough to make room for her. At first she'd thought he was being affectionate when he'd come in and put his arms around her and kissed her. She'd liked it because he was never much of a loving father when he was sober. She'd been flattered by his attention, craved it, and kissed him back and let him hold her even though she knew it wasn't right for a father to touch his own daughter like that. But it had felt nice, so she hadn't pushed his hands away and nothing much had come of it until one night when she'd been sitting by the embers, straining to see the frock that she wanted to finish sewing because the next day was Sunday. The weather had turned fine and she'd wanted to wear something nice.

He'd come in and greeted her with a smile. Then he'd come across and kissed her, full on the lips, and she'd felt his tongue pushing into her mouth. He'd gripped her arms so tightly that she'd tried to wriggle away because he was hurting her, but it seemed to get him more excited and he'd pulled her down from the chair, on to the rag rug in front of the dying fire, and he'd touched her breast through her blouse.

'Don't,' she'd told him.

'But tha's my little Mary,' he'd said. 'Tha doesn't mind bein' nice to thy dad, does tha? We don't need to say owt to thy mother.'

She'd known it was wrong, but he was her father and her mother had always told her that she had to respect him because he was the head of the family – that she had to do as she was told and not be such an uppity madam. Besides, she couldn't push him off. He was strong and although she knew he shouldn't be touching her leg up under her skirts, she'd liked the feel of it and it awakened something in her, and when he'd rolled her on to her back and got on top of her there was nothing she could do but let him have his way. It had hurt and she'd called out, but he'd clamped his hand tight over her mouth until she felt like she couldn't get her breath. Her heart had been pounding and she'd wanted to cry, but she'd been trapped there whilst he thrust and grunted until he shuddered and let her go. And when she'd struggled to her feet, shocked and alarmed, there'd been wet running down her leg and she'd thought she'd pee'd herself in fright but it was sticky and there was blood.

'Did I hurt thee?' he'd asked as she gazed at the mess on her fingertips. 'I didn't mean to.' He'd reached out and caressed her cheek. 'Tha's a good lass. Don't tell thy mam. It's our little secret.' Then he'd reached into his pocket and fished out a sixpence. 'Buy thyself a nice ribbon to go with thy new frock,' he'd told her before staggering up the stairs to his bed.

Chapter Five

Hannah watched Peggy as she wrote her letters on a slate with a piece of chalk, then showed them to Bessie, and asked her to say what they were. Every time Bessie replied she pronounced '*Correct!*' in a voice that sounded remarkably like that of her teacher, Miss Parkinson.

'Will tha teach me to read?' Hannah asked Titus.

'I thought tha weren't interested,' he said, looking up from the pamphlet he'd spread across the table. It was Sunday afternoon and the rain was pouring down outside.

'I've nowt else to do,' said Hannah, hoping that he wouldn't refuse.

'Maybe tha should get our Peg to teach thee,' said Titus as he watched his daughter move on to spelling out a simple word.

'C ... a ... t.'

'Pussy cat!' called out Bessie.

'No! No! No! Not *pussy* cat. Just cat!' Peggy reprimanded in her best teacher's voice. 'You have to read the word!'

'Just listen to her, givin' herself airs and graces.' Titus laughed. 'She's a clever lass is our Peggy.'

Hannah tended to agree, but her heart ached for little Bessie, who had grown bored with the game and had picked up her rag doll to nurse on her knee. Although Titus heaped love and praise on Peggy, he rarely said a good word about Bessie. He seemed indifferent towards her, although that wasn't surprising, given that she wasn't his child.

'Give it 'ere,' said Titus to Peggy, holding out his hand for the slate. 'Let's see whether Auntie Hannah's any good at it.' Peggy passed him the chalk and he began to make marks with it, faster and with more ease than the child. 'These are vowel sounds,' he said. 'Tha can begin with them.'

Hannah pulled out the bentwood chair and sat down beside him, staring at the marks as he told her the sounds they represented. It wouldn't really matter if she found she couldn't do it, she told herself, but she really wanted to try. She wanted to learn to write too. In fact, it was the writing that interested her most because she longed to save the stories that she made up in her head. When she was little, they'd been childish tales about the sprites and elves that lived in the brook

49

at Ramsgreave. As she'd grown they'd changed and become about animals and then about people. When she'd come to live with her sister in Blackburn, the stories had become darker as she witnessed the hardship and the starvation of the people who had no work, but as things improved her imagination had taken a new turn and now the stories in her head were mostly about romance. Her latest one was about a handsome and wealthy young mill owner who visits one of the grand houses up on Revedge and falls hopelessly in love with one of the maids there, becoming determined to marry her and give her a life of wealth and privilege. Hannah thought that she had never liked one of her stories better.

She stared at the letters that Titus had drawn, trying to commit to memory the sounds that they represented. He'd gone back to reading his pamphlet. He was always reading something in his spare time. And when he wasn't reading he was talking about what needed to be done for the working man. He hadn't been the same since he'd spent time in the House of Correction and Hannah sometimes wondered if she didn't prefer the old Titus: the one who'd teased her when he was courting her elder sister; the one who'd given no thought to reading or writing or what went on in London and the Parliament; the one who'd been content to weave on his loom and tend his patch at the back of the cottage at Pleck Gate. But everything had changed when the mills came and he'd moved his family into town, and although she'd thought it was exciting at the time she knew now that working in the mills wasn't the life she wanted. She'd seen the wives of the gentry with their lovely clothes and beautiful houses and she thought that she'd like a bit of that for herself.

'Shall I put t' kettle on for tea?' she asked after a while as she guessed it was nearing five o'clock.

'Hast tha somewhere to go?' asked Titus.

'I thought I might go to evensong,' she said. 'The rain seems to have eased off now.' It wasn't that she was particularly keen to sit through one of the Reverend Whittaker's tedious sermons in the parish church, but it was one place she could meet up with Mary without raising any eyebrows.

Hannah filled the kettle with water from the bucket in the back kitchen and put it on the hob to boil. Then she began to set the table. There were oatcakes for tea and treacle to spread on them. Bread was still too expensive and without a patch of land to cultivate there were no eggs or jam to supplement their diet, just what they could afford to buy from the market.

After they'd eaten, Hannah went upstairs to get her best bonnet and coat. The church bells were ringing, cutting across the peace of Sunday when the absence of the noise of engines and machinery provided a faint echo of the little market town Blackburn had once been before all the workers came.

'See thee later!' she called as she pulled the door closed behind her.

'Don't be late, our Hannah!' called her sister. She knew that it was a warning not to linger after church and it annoyed her. Granted she was living with them, but her sister and brother-in-law weren't her parents to tell her what she could and couldn't do, yet they'd quickly fallen back into the habit of treating her like a child.

'Mary!' Her friend turned and waited for her to catch up. The ribbons on Hannah's bonnet had come unfastened and she retied the bow as they crossed Darwen Street to reach the church door, joining the men and women going in to worship and avoiding those who were thronging the streets, worse for drink, even on a Sunday. It was no wonder they were ragged and barefoot, thought Hannah, when they spent their wages on gin and beer rather than food and clothing. It was surprising that the gentry were still willing to hand out charity to them when they did nothing to help themselves.

As they settled into seats near the back of the church she watched Mr and Mrs Feilden walk down the aisle to their pew at the front. She almost sighed as they went past. He was such a good-looking man – tall and athletic, and he wore the most wonderful, fashionable clothes. His wife was dressed in pale blue with a matching bonnet and a dark jacket. She had a velvet reticule swinging from her wrist and bestowed a smile on those she thought worthy as she passed by. It seemed that now the Sudells had fled they thought themselves the most important people in the town.

Hannah nudged Mary and pointed to the man who had followed them in. 'That's the schoolmaster!' she whispered. He always wore the same jacket and trousers, but today he had a silk cravat – his Sunday best – and his wayward hair was carefully brushed. He took a pew and put his hat down beside him and Hannah was relieved to see that he was alone.

'He comes into the Star,' Mary told her. 'Just for the Reform meetings,' she added to reassure her.

There wasn't the opportunity to say more as the organ played a fanfare and the congregation stood to sing the first hymn.

Hannah found her eyes straying towards the schoolmaster time and again as the service went on. She hardly heard a word of the sermon and at the end she lingered, just to watch him walk down the aisle and to try to follow him out of the door. She hoped that he might recognise her, but he was chatting with the Feildens when she got out into the churchyard and Mary had already linked an arm through hers and was asking if she wanted to come back to the Star with her.

'We can sit in my room for a while and talk,' she said. 'Mrs Hall doesn't need me on a Sunday.'

With a final glance back, Hannah allowed herself to be led away. She knew that she was being ridiculous. Just because he'd smiled at her once didn't mean that there was any chance he was interested in her.

'I wish Titus had let thee stay with us,' said Hannah, not for the first time, as they reached the beerhouse and Mary held the door open for Hannah to follow her in. The place stank of beer and tobacco. She followed Mary up the steep steps and into the small attic room. It was nicer than she expected. Too nice for a lass to have all to herself, she thought as she heard voices talking outside – a man and a woman – and a door opened and closed, muffling the laughter.

'Tha can't stop here,' said Hannah, realising what was going on. 'It's not respectable.'

'And where does tha suggest I go?' asked Mary. 'It's not as if folk are fallin' over themselves to take in a non-paying house guest.'

'But there must be other lodgings?'

'Aye, for them as is in work. If tha knocks on the door and tells them tha has no money comin' in and little prospect of things changing then tha gets sent on thy way.'

'But this is a ...'

'A brothel. Aye. I weren't born yesterday.'

'But tha hasn't ...'

'No, of course not! I've been payin' rent.'

'But what'll tha do when thy money's gone?'

'Well, if I can't find owt else, I'll be on the street. There's no way as I'm doin' that,' she said, nodding her head towards the other room. 'That's Alice. She entertains the gentlemen.'

'Oh Mary. This is horrible. I wish there was something I could do. Why doesn't tha go home? It can't be any worse than this, can it?'

'It can,' said her friend. 'I told thee what my father did. I'd rather sleep under t' bridge than go back there.'

Chapter Six

'I've heard as Mr Feilden is looking for a new parlour maid,' said Titus one evening a few weeks later when he came back from his Reform meeting.

'Out at Feniscowles?' asked Hannah, looking up from the sheet of paper where she'd been practising her writing. Jennet had gone out to take back some laundry and Peggy and Bessie were in bed.

'No, for the King Street house. The lass who's there now is gettin' wed next month. Why doesn't tha go and enquire after it?' he asked her.

'Because I don't have a character reference,' she told him. 'Nobody'll take a maid on now without a letter of recommendation and because Sudell went off like he did, I don't have one.'

'What sort of thing would it need to say?' asked Titus.

'That I'm honest, hardworking, that I wasn't dismissed for any reason. I don't know really.'

'I don't suppose anyone does. I suppose as long as tha has a letter then they'll be happy with it.' He sat down and pulled a clean sheet of paper towards him.

'What's tha thinking? Tha can't write it!' protested Hannah.

'Why not?' he asked. 'I can say as tha's a hard worker and honest and goes to church every Sunday.'

'But it has to be from Mr Sudell because he was my last employer.'

'And that's impossible.'

'I know! That's why I'll never get another job as a maid. It isn't fair.'

'Things are rarely fair, our Hannah,' said Titus. 'I found that out the hard way. But some good came of me being sent to that place. I had the chance to learn to read and write. So maybe now it's time for me to use that learnin' to make sure that tha doesn't get dragged down by what's not fair.'

'But it's dishonest,' she said, surprised at him. He was always harping on about fairness and what was right and wrong so why was he so keen to do this – except that if she got the job she would be living in, and she'd be out from under his feet. Was he that desperate to get rid of her?

'It's not entirely dishonest,' he said as he took the pen and dipped into the inkwell. 'I'm not sayin' anything that's not true.'

'But it needs to be signed by Mr Sudell.'

'Well, I'll just write his name. It's not as if he's here to do owt about it and it's worth a try. If they sends thee away then tha's no worse off,' he reasoned.

Hannah watched as he began to write, following the words as he read them out loud:

> *To whom it may concern:*
>
> *I can recommend Miss Hannah Chadwick as an honest and hardworking maid who has left my employment as my house at Woodfold Hall has been closed up and her services are no longer required there.*
>
> *Henry Sudell*

Titus signed it off with a flourish and blotted the ink dry before handing it to Hannah. 'Go and show them that,' he said.

'But tha might get sent back to prison if anyone finds out.'

'No one'll find out. Go tomorrow and get the employment,' he told her, leaving her in no doubt that it was what he expected her to do.

*

Next morning, Hannah wondered whether she dared do what Titus had told her. She also wondered whether she should go down to the Star and tell Mary that there was a job going. The trouble was there was only one job and they would be in competition for it – and Mary would want to know where she'd got a character reference from. If she told her that Titus had written it, she might ask if he would write one for her as well. Hannah knew that he would refuse and it would make things awkward. Better to say nowt, she thought. Besides, if she told Mary and Mary got the job instead of her, Titus would be livid. She felt guilty though. Mary had always been a good friend to her and she didn't like going behind her back. She half hoped that she wouldn't get the job, even though she would be glad to get out of Water Street.

She put the letter in her pocket before taking Peggy to school. They reached Thunder Alley just as the schoolmaster came out to ring his hand bell for the boys to line up. Since she'd seen him in church she'd asked Jennet about him and now she knew that he was called James Hindle and that he'd come from Bolton to teach here. He lived in the little cottage that adjoined the school, next door to the one that Miss Parkinson lived in. There was a rumour that they were sweet on one another. Hannah hoped it wasn't true and she reassured herself that she'd never seen them give one another so much as a glance.

His cravat was tied today and his hair was combed and slicked down, though how long it would remain tidy Hannah couldn't guess. It was never so neat at the end of the day when the boys came running back out, shouting to one another and jumping about the street like the lambs on the hills in their relief to escape the confines of the classroom. She watched as they lined up for the day to begin. She hoped that Miss Parkinson wouldn't come out just yet so that she could stand and watch him for a while, but the schoolmistress was never tardy and the girls were going in.

Once the door to the girls' school had closed, Hannah began to walk slowly down Thunder Alley. It would have been obvious to keep watching and embarrassing, too, if he'd noticed her, but she could savour the last of his voice as he called out to the latecomers to hurry or they would be sorry.

As she turned the corner she was almost trampled by two carriage horses, tossing their heads and pulling on their reins. Between them a young boy was struggling to keep them under control.

'John?' she said, not sure that it really was him.

He glanced at her and nodded his head, but the horses were on the point of dragging him away so she stepped well back to let them pass and turned to watch as he pulled them into the stable yard.

She'd always felt sorry for John. Even before the accident at the mill he'd seemed a down-trodden sort of lad who was always being shouted at by his father. She'd cringed sometimes at the language that had echoed through the walls from their neighbour's house on Paradise Lane. To listen, anyone would have thought that John could do nothing right. And even after the accident in the spinning room, she'd had the impression that John's father blamed him for his carelessness. It had been horrible. She remembered the sight of his hand, all mangled, after it had been caught in the machinery. It was what had caused the beginning of the trouble between them and Jennet. Hargreaves had given Nan's looms to Jennet to run whilst Nan had been at the surgeon's with John and when she'd come back she'd accused Jennet of stealing her job. There'd been such a row and it had ended with the neighbours being at daggers drawn, with her and Mary caught in the middle of it, which is partly why they'd left to go to Woodfold, to get away from it all, because Mary's father had forbidden Mary to have anything to do with her. It was after that that Sam had turned up and got John into trouble and when Sam had got clean away and John had been sent to prison, his parents had made life so intolerable for Jennet and Titus that they'd had to move away. None of it had been John's fault and she was glad to see him back, though he didn't look happy and she still felt sorry for him.

Turning her thoughts back to her own problems, Hannah walked towards King Street. It was where the big houses were, where the gentry lived. The Feildens' house was at the bottom of the hill, on the outskirts of the town, where they had a view of the surrounding moorland. It was recently built and the bricks still glowed, unsullied by the filthy air that was always filled with soot from the chimneys of the mills and cottages. The house stood back from the street, in its own garden surrounded by a stone wall and railings. The entrance was through a high wrought-iron gate and beyond it a path led to a flight of steps that rose to the front door.

She patted the letter to make sure she still had it. What would she do if they looked at it and saw that it was a forgery? Would they send for the constable? Her heart was racing and she lingered on the busy street, not daring to approach the door, but not daring to go home either and admit that she hadn't enquired.

At last Hannah took a deep breath to steady her nerves. The latch clicked as she raised it and the gate squeaked a little as it swung open. She was sure that there must be a servants' entrance, but she couldn't see where it might be, and she was still hesitating when the front door was opened and Mrs Feilden came out with one of her daughters and stared at her.

'Horrocks!' she said to the butler, who was holding the door. 'Find out who that girl is and what she wants.'

'You!' called the man. 'What are you up to?'

Hannah curtseyed and apologised. 'I was looking for the servants' entrance,' she said. 'I heard that there was a vacancy for a maid.'

'She's here to enquire about the maid's position.'

'Tell her to come back later – at eleven o'clock,' instructed the woman. 'I'll see her then. Does she have a character reference?'

The butler raised an eyebrow at her.

'Yes,' said Hannah. 'Yes, I do.'

'Come back at eleven then.'

'Yes. I will. Thank you.' She curtseyed again and hurried out on to the street, almost running into the path of the Feildens' carriage in her eagerness to get away.

She had a couple of hours to fill before she went back – if she went back. She could go home and help Jennet with the laundry, but that would mean changing out of her best clothes and then back into them again and she didn't feel she could be bothered. She could go to see Mary, but she knew that if she did she would tell her about the job. So she walked back towards Church Street and wandered in and out of the market stalls. After a while, she'd seen everything and some of the stall-holders were watching her suspiciously so she moved away and stared at the door of the Old Bull. She wished that she dared to go in and sit down and order a drink, but such places weren't for a woman alone, not if you valued your reputation, and so she wandered down towards the bridge at Salford and sat there a while, watching the carts and carriages coming and going until she thought that it must be near to eleven.

She made her way back to the Feildens' house and once more lifted the latch on the gate. The butler must have been watching out for her. He appeared, as if by magic, and called to her. 'This way!'

She went down the side path and in through the back door where she found herself in a modern kitchen where a cook was preparing the dinner, assisted by a scullery maid. The cook gave Hannah a brief smile as she replaced the lid on a pan. 'Sit thee down,' she said. 'Tha looks a bit peaky.'

'I'm fine thanks,' she said, sitting on a chair at the table.

'Here. Cup of tea,' said the cook, putting a cup and saucer down in front of her. It looked like china, patterned with tiny flowers and seemed too good for servants. She hardly dared to pick it up and drink from it in case it broke. 'Everything's new,' Cook told her. 'We're spoiled here. Hast tha come about the parlour maid's job?'

'Aye. Yes. I heard the present one is gettin' wed.'

'That's right. She's finishing at the end of the month.'

'Has anyone else enquired?' asked Hannah.

'Aye. A couple. I don't think Mrs Feilden were much impressed by 'em though.'

Hannah wondered if she should press the matter to discover what the other applicants might have been lacking, but before she had a chance, the butler came back and told her to follow him. He led her up a flight of stairs and they came out in the hallway from where a more splendid staircase rose before splitting into two to reach both wings of the house.

'This way,' said the butler and held open the door of a morning room to the east of the house where the sun was slanting in through the high windows. Mrs Feilden was sitting at a small desk with some letters spread in front of her and Hannah felt herself blush as she remembered the one in her pocket and wondered whether it would pass muster.

'Your name?' asked Mrs Feilden.

'Hannah Chadwick, ma'am.'

'No need for that. You can call me Mrs Feilden.'

'Yes, ma'am, Mrs Feilden.' Hannah found herself curtseying again and cursed herself for her lack of social skills. The Sudells had insisted on old-fashioned formality, but Mrs Feilden seemed to want to embrace modernity both in her house and in her dealings with her servants.

'Have you worked as a maid before, Hannah?'

'Yes, Mrs Feilden. I was employed by the Sudells at Woodfold Hall, but ...' Hannah hesitated.

'Yes. It was an unusual thing to do, to disappear like that. It's caused so much talk. Did you receive a character reference?' she asked.

Hannah felt her cheeks burn and was sure that she would be found out. She considered turning and running away, except that she wasn't sure of the way out. So she fumbled in her pocket and then held out the letter that Titus had written. Mrs Feilden unfolded it, glanced at it and put it on her desk. 'What were your duties at Woodfold?' she asked.

'Setting the fires, making the beds, dusting, helping a bit in the kitchen.'

'Good. We're not so grand here as Mr Sudell, so you'll need to be able to turn your hand to most things, and even help me as a lady's maid on occasion.'

'I'm sure that won't be a problem, Mrs Feilden. I'd like to be a lady's maid.'

'Good. Where are you living at the moment?' she asked.

'With my sister and brother-in-law on Water Street.'

'What are they called?'

'Eastwood.'

'Titus Eastwood? The Reformer?' she asked.

'Aye. Yes,' said Hannah, wondering if Mrs Feilden was about to change her mind.

'My husband knows him,' she said. 'He says he's a good man.'

'It was Titus that told me about the job.'

'Then it must have been my husband who mentioned it to him. I'm sure he'll be very pleased. Would you like to come on Monday? At nine o'clock? You can spend a couple of weeks with Jane showing you what's what before she goes – if you don't mind sharing a room with her.'

'No ... no, I don't mind,' said Hannah, amazed at how easy it had been, and Mrs Feilden seemed nice. She thought that she was going to enjoy working for her.

The butler showed her the way out and told her to come to the back door when she returned. Hannah thanked him and stepped out of the gate on to King Street. It didn't seem real. She knew that she should get home so that she could tell Titus when he came in for his dinner. And she would have to tell Mary too, but she couldn't face that just yet.

'I've got a job,' Hannah told her friend as they walked through the market on Saturday afternoon.

'Which mill?'

'It isn't in a mill. I've a job as a parlour maid again.'

'How did tha manage that without a character?'

'A friend of our Jennet's spoke for me,' she lied.

'Where is it?'

'King Street. The Feildens' house.'

'I suppose it were that Mrs Whittaker, the vicar's wife, as put 'em on to thee. Jennet always were tight with her.'

'Aye,' said Hannah. The vicar's wife had helped her sister out when Titus was away, but there seemed to have been a cooling between them since he'd come back. Jennet had told her that Mrs Whittaker had been cross that Titus had refused the road-building work at first. Hannah could understand why. It wasn't work for a skilled weaver, but he'd taken it in the end – out of desperation, she supposed, but she knew that her sister wasn't as friendly with Mrs Whittaker any more. They said 'Good morning' at church, but it was always a bit strained. Still, if Mary thought that Mrs Whittaker had spoken for her, it was better than having to explain where her character reference had really come from.

'Was there just the one job going?' she asked.

'Aye. I'd have told thee if there'd been two.'

'But tha didn't tell me about this one.'

'No. Like I said, I didn't have much choice. Titus wants me out of the house.'

'I thought tha were my friend, Hannah Chadwick, but tha's played a dirty trick on me with this.'

Hannah was stunned by the anger on her friend's face. She knew that Mary might be a bit upset about it, but she'd never thought she would glare at her with such animosity.

'But there were only one job.'

'Aye. And it could have been mine.'

'I'll tell thee if another one comes up.'

'Will tha?'

They stared at one another, facing each other in the middle of the busy marketplace as the crowd thronged around them, pushing them this way and that in annoyance that their way was being blocked.

'Tha's not been much of a friend after all,' said Mary at last and Hannah watched as she turned sharply away and began to walk towards Fleming Square. It was clear that she wanted nothing more to do with her – not at the moment anyway – and Hannah couldn't blame her. She would probably have felt the same if she'd been in Mary's position and she knew that the Star was not a fit place for her to be living. But once Mrs Feilden had told her that Mr Feilden knew Titus, she'd realised that she could never have gone home and pretended that she hadn't got the job. She'd had no choice, and even if she'd told Mary, it wouldn't have made a difference. Not that she'd ever be able to convince Mary of that. She'd seen the hatred in her friend's eyes and it made her hate herself for what she'd done.

Mary was furious. Hannah could at least have told her about the job. She could have given her the chance to go for it as well. It would have been the fair thing to do and she was sure that Mrs Hall would have given her a character. What

Hannah had done was selfish, and underhand, and she began to wonder how good a friend Hannah was after all. She would have loved that job, and she really needed it. She was running short of money and she feared that she would find herself out on the street before very long.

'What's tha lookin' so glum about?' asked Mrs Hall when she went in and began to stomp up the stairs to her bedroom.

'My friend – well, I thought she were my friend – Hannah's got herself a job as a maid at the Feildens' house.'

'And why's that made thee so cross?'

Mary came slowly back down the stairs. It seemed as good an opportunity as any to be honest. 'If I can't get work I won't be able to afford to stay here for much longer,' she said.

'Come in the back,' said Mrs Hall. 'Let's put t' kettle on and have a brew. Everything seems better with a brew. I'm sure as we can work summat out.'

Mary followed her into the back, her clogs clattering on the stone-flagged floor.

Mrs Hall filled the kettle from the barrel of rainwater she kept near the door and set it to boil. 'Now then,' she said as she spooned a generous amount of tea into the pot. 'Let's have a think about how tha can earn a bit more money.' She sat down in her rocking chair and studied Mary for a moment. 'Dost tha like stoppin' here?' she asked.

'Aye. It's well enough,' said Mary, sitting down on one of the stools by the table.

'There's not many places where tha'd get a room all to thyself,' Mrs Hall told her.

'I know. I'm not complainin' about the rent. I just don't have the money.'

'Alice makes a bit extra,' said Mrs Hall, leaning forward to poke the fire. 'Some of t' better-off customers can be generous if tha knows how to keep 'em sweet.'

'Aye. I've seen her with that man – the one with the nice clothes.'

'Dost tha know who he is?'

'No. But he doesn't favour a mill worker,' replied Mary.

'He isn't. He's Mr Starkie, the pawnbroker. One of the few professions that can turn a tidy profit in a town like this when folks are quick to pawn their best clothes on a Monday morning to get a few shillings to see 'em through to the end of the week. He's gettin' a bit bored with Alice though. Lookin' for summat fresh,' said Mrs Hall. 'He might help thee out a bit if tha were more friendly to him.' She poured the boiling water on to the tea leaves and set the pot to brew. 'Dost tha know what I'm gettin' at?' she asked.

'Aye. I do. I'm not simple,' Mary told her. 'But that weren't the sort of employment I were thinkin' of.'

'Well, I don't like to turn thee out,' said Mrs Hall. 'But I'm not one of these charitable organisations like the ones run by the lady do-gooders of the town who have nowt else to do with their time. If tha stays, tha needs to pay thy way.'

'Could I not work more hours in the kitchen?'

'Not without costin' me money,' said Mrs Hall, pouring the tea and passing a cup to Mary. 'Like I said, I'm not here to be charitable. I've done my best to accommodate thee by givin' thee the reduced rent in exchange for servin' in t' parlour, but I can't create work where there is none any more than t' mill owners can. And tha'll find as bein' sweet to t' gents is easier work than fourteen hours a day mindin' looms. It's mostly done lyin' down!' She laughed. 'Think about it,' she said. 'Yon Mr Starkie would be a good start for thee. Tha needn't be afraid of him.'

'I'm not afraid of him!'

'Good. Like I said, think about it. And if tha wants any advice, I'm here to help. Right, best get on,' she said putting her cup aside and grasping the edge of the range to haul herself up from the chair. 'These taties won't peel themselves.'

Chapter Seven

Hannah paused outside the iron gates on King Street and shifted the weight of her bag from one hand to the other. She was looking forward to this job but the thought of the forged character letter was still hanging over her like a pall of smoke. She was terrified that she would be found out. Yet there was nothing else to do but open the gate and go in. She had no alternative.

The cheerful red-headed lass who opened the door to her introduced herself as Jane and almost pulled her into the kitchen in her enthusiasm, telling her to take off her coat and bonnet and make herself at home.

'Don't mind her,' said Cook with a smile. 'She's that over-excited about getting wed that there's nowt we can do with her.'

'It's not because I'm glad to be leaving,' Jane told her. 'Don't think that. It's a good place here and tha'll like it, I'm sure.'

'Aye, tha'll be all right here,' said Cook, putting down a cup of freshly brewed tea in front of her. 'They're good employers are the Feildens. Very fair.'

'Come and see the bedroom,' said Jane.

She carried Hannah's bag up to the room in the attics. There was a good-sized bed that she would be sharing with Jane until she left, but after that it would be all hers and Hannah looked forward to the luxury of spreading out in it. Even at Woodfold she'd shared a bed with Mary. She pushed the guilty thoughts about her friend to the back of her mind. There was nothing more she could have done, she told herself. If she heard of another job she would let her know, but in the meantime, Mary would have to cope as best she could.

'I've managed to make some space,' Jane said. 'But I've got that much tackle as I've collected for my bottom drawer I needs a dozen bottom drawers!' She opened one to show Hannah what she had: two sets of white cotton sheets, three tablecloths, towels, tea towels and a fine embroidered nightie that she held up for inspection. 'For the wedding night!' she giggled.

75

'It's beautiful!' said Hannah. 'Did tha do the embroidery?'

'Aye. It's made my eyes and head ache for weeks, but it's been worth it.'

'Who's the lucky chap?'

'His name's Eddie Cottam. Works at Eanam Mill as an overlooker. He's not badly off either. We're going to rent a house on Clayton Street and I've a mind to set up as a seamstress once I'm finished here. Anyway,' she went on, 'unpack thy things and then come down and I'll show thee what thy jobs will be.'

Hannah lifted her clothes from her bag and laid them in the drawer that Jane had emptied for her. They didn't fill it. Then she hung up her coat and put her best bonnet carefully on the shelf before slipping out of her best frock and putting on the blue and white striped one that was laid on the bed for her. It wasn't new and was too big. She suspected that it had belonged to Jane. When she got a moment she would take in the seams. Meanwhile, the apron she tied around it pulled it into place. She peered into the little mirror as she fixed the cap over her hair and then went back down the stairs to the kitchen. Everyone seemed very kind and friendly. She thought she was going to be happy here.

*

'Dost tha mind finishing off by thyself?' Jane asked Hannah the following weekend, after the family had eaten their Sunday dinner and the pots had been cleared away to the kitchen.

'Is tha meeting Eddie?'

'Aye. We're going to the Reform meeting. Mrs Kitchen will be there. She's such an inspiration.'

'Mrs Kitchen? I'd like to see her!' said Hannah as she scraped the plates before stacking them to the side of the sink for washing.

'Come with me then,' said Jane.

'But ...' She stared at the washing-up.

'We'll do it when we come back. Tha doesn't mind, does tha?' she asked Cook. 'Just this once. As a favour?'

'Go on. Get thee gone,' sighed Cook. 'But tha doesn't need to think tha can go off every week,' she warned Hannah. 'Not when there's work to be done.'

Hannah ran to change into her best dress and get her bonnet before going with Jane out of the side entrance and down the path on to King Street. It was busy already with both men and women making their way to the meeting.

'Look!' exclaimed Jane. 'There's Dr Bowring's carriage. He must be going to speak too.'

Hannah watched the brougham, pulled by two handsome bays, pass them, throwing up dust as it went. A young man was peering out at the crowds, his face intense behind round spectacles. She'd heard talk about John Bowring. He had put up as a potential MP for the town and was popular with the working people because of his support for Reform and the rights of the working man. Titus said that he was the only one amongst the candidates who knew what he was talking about and that the town would do well to return him as a member as he was sure to speak up on their behalf.

'There's Eddie,' said Jane, waving to a man who was standing on the corner, smoking a pipe. 'Eddie!' He looked up and smiled when he caught sight of her and she grasped Hannah firmly by the arm so as not to lose her in the crowd as they pushed forward.

'Aye up!' He puffed smoke from his mouth before removing the stem of the pipe and leaning to kiss Jane. 'Who's this tha's got in tow?'

'This is Hannah, who's takin' over from me at the Feildens' house. This is Eddie,' she said to Hannah as she brushed a speck of dirt from his jacket.

'Hannah Chadwick.'

He reached out and shook her hand. 'I'm pleased to make thy acquaintance, Hannah Chadwick.'

'Come on,' said Jane. 'I want to get a spot at the front where we can see the speakers.'

Eddie tucked Jane's arm through his and Hannah followed them as the throngs of people filled the narrow streets until they were spilled out on to Lower Tacketts Field where a rickety stage had been set up using crates and boxes covered with planks of wood.

Hannah was surprised to see how many women had come out with their menfolk. She wondered if Jennet was there, but it was impossible to look at everyone who had gathered. Besides, it was taking her all her time to stay on her feet as she was pushed this way and that as people fought for a better spot.

The speakers climbed up a set of ramshackle steps on to the stage and Hannah caught sight of Titus near the front. He looked as if he was helping to create some order out of the chaos and she knew that he was never happier these days than when he was in charge of something.

At last the crowd quietened down as a group of women approached the stage.

'There's Mrs Kitchen,' Jane told her. The woman was younger than Hannah had expected and was beautifully dressed in a calico printed gown, short jacket and a bonnet with a green favour prominently displayed. The chairman on the stage waved her forward as she hesitated and she was handed up the wobbly steps until she stood there with the men. The crowd hushed and hardly a breath was drawn as the women raised themselves on tiptoe to see Mrs Kitchen standing up there beside Dr Bowring.

'Sir,' she said, addressing the chairman, Mr Knight, 'we, the Female Reformers of Blackburn shall consider it a favour if the address, which I confer into your hands, be read out to the meeting. It embraces a faint description of our woes and may apologise for our interference in the politics of our country.'

As Mrs Kitchen descended from the stage there was a huge burst of applause and Hannah clapped her hands together until they hurt. She felt so proud of the women who had dared to involve themselves in politics.

The chairman appealed for silence and when it was quiet once more he studied the paper in his hand for a moment and then began to read Mrs Kitchen's words.

'"We can speak with unassuming confidence that our houses, which once bore testimony to our industry and cleanliness, are now robbed of all their ornament. Even our beds, which afforded us health and sweet repose, are now torn away from us by the unfeeling hand of the relentless tax gatherers, who are reposing on beds of down whilst we have nothing more than a sheath of straw. And behold our innocent, wretched children and their appalling cries for a crust of bread! Come to our dwellings and behold our misery and wretchedness, for language cannot paint the feelings of a mother when she beholds her naked children and hears their cries of hunger and approaching death!"'

Hannah knew that Mrs Kitchen was right. She'd seen the half-naked children in the street. They looked no more than skin and bones. And when she went to the spring she heard talk of families who'd lost their homes because they had no money for the rent. It was bad enough now, but there would be deaths when the winter came and no mistake.

The end of the speech was met by another outburst of applause and even some cheering from those at the front. Hannah glanced around and saw that all the women who had attended were nodding their heads as they clapped enthusiastically.

'So true!'

'It needed saying!'

'We can't just leave it to the men. Not when it's about the childer,' said another.

'We should have rights too!'

As the other speakers came forward for their turn, they all thanked Mrs Kitchen for her courage and her words.

'We are all in this together. Men and women,' said Dr Bowring. 'The government needs to hear our concerns. Why should our children starve when they have wasted all their money on fighting in France? Is it because they would rather see us browbeaten than risk us rising up against them to claim our rights as the French did? The sop they have offered us in Parliamentary Reform will not give us justice! Nothing will change until the voices of the working men are heard through the vote!'

More applause and cheering followed each speaker and, as the atmosphere grew livelier and Hannah was surrounded by people who jostled and closed in around her, she felt a moment of fear. She suddenly understood how Titus had been swept away in the Luddite riot the night he was arrested. If a riot followed this meeting she wasn't sure how she would escape and get back to the safety of the Fieldens' house. But when the speeches were done people began to drift away, chatting in groups about what they had heard, and the threat of violence dissipated. Hannah thought that it was due to the number of women in the crowd who pulled on their husbands' sleeves and reminded them that it was time to go home. No matter what had been said, the hooters would still sound at six the following morning and those who had work would have to go to earn what money they could to try to feed their families.

'Will tha be all right gettin' back?' asked Jane as space began to open up around them.

'Aye. I'll be fine,' said Hannah. In truth she was anxious, but she could see that her friend wanted to go off with her husband-to-be and she was loath to say that she would have preferred someone to walk back with her.

She followed the crowd as it dispersed from the field. As she walked, she caught sight of a familiar face and her heart thumped as she recognised James Hindle. For a moment she thought that he had recognised her, but he seemed lost in his own thoughts and almost bumped right into her as she hesitated.

'Sorry.'

'Hello!' she greeted him. She cursed herself for sounding so enthusiastic as he looked at her with a puzzled expression, obviously thinking that he should know her but unable to place her. She felt a red blush flame her face. She wished that she could turn and hurry away, but they were hemmed in by the crowd and she felt compelled to offer some explanation.

'You're the schoolmaster on Thunder Alley,' she said, knowing that it sounded ridiculous. Of course he knew who he was. He didn't need her to tell him. Why could she never think of anything interesting to say in real life when the characters who peopled her stories were always so articulate?

'Aye. I am.' She could tell that he was still trying to place her by the way that he was looking at her so intently.

'I used to bring my niece to the girls' school.'

'Of course. I knew I'd seen you before. Did you enjoy the meeting?' he asked as they joined the queue to thread their way on to Tacketts Street. 'I thought Mrs Kitchen's speech was particularly evocative.'

'Yes. I enjoyed it. And it was pleasing to see so many women here.'

'It was. Reform is for everyone, not just men,' he agreed. 'Are you headed home now?'

'Aye. I have work to do.'

'On a Sunday?' he asked.

'I work as a maid,' she told him.

She was hoping that he might say something about himself. But he only nodded and said that it was nice to see her again as he was swept away from her by the movement of the crowd.

Back on King Street, the washing up was still stacked beside the sink waiting for her. She ran upstairs to get changed and put on her coarse apron, then filled the sink with hot water from the copper and began with the glasses and delicate items before moving on to the heavy pots and pans that had been left to soak. As she worked she told Cook about the meeting and Mrs Kitchen's speech.

'That woman would be better off stoppin' at home and lookin' to her childer instead o' gallivantin' around and interferin'. Politics is nowt to do with womenfolk. Best leave it to men.'

'But her speech was so heartfelt,' Hannah told her. 'It was about how hard it is for women to see their children hungry. And Dr Bowring said it was up to women as well as men to force changes.' She didn't mention that James Hindle had said the same thing. Her conversation with him had been a precious thing that she didn't want to share.

'Aye, well, best not say too much about that here,' Cook warned her. 'Mr Feilden's a good man and he has the best interests of folk at heart, but he doesn't talk daft like that Bowring does. No good'll come of lettin' all and sundry make the laws. Mark my words.'

Hannah scrubbed at some stubborn marks on the roasting pan without replying. She didn't agree, but knew that Cook was right when she said that it was best to keep her thoughts to herself whilst she was here. She'd hardly had this job a week and she didn't want to lose it. She wasn't sure that Titus would take her in again and she didn't want to be left like Mary with no job and nowhere to go.

Chapter Eight

Jennet watched as Molly Chambers from next door leaned over the wall, lowered her kettle into the Blakewater and then hauled it up again on a string.

'I hope tha's not thinkin' of drinkin' that,' she said.

'What's it to thee?' asked Molly as she grasped the kettle by the handle and came towards her own front door.

'Well, it ain't clean.'

'Looks clean enough to me,' said Molly. 'And it's a sight easier than trailin' down to yon pump with three little childer in tow. Tha wants to mind thy own business.'

'I were only tryin' to help,' said Jennet. 'Tha doesn't want to be makin' thyself and t' little 'uns poorly. Not when there's talk of the typhus fever at the Eanam Mill.'

'It's fine,' Molly told her as she went in. 'I've been drinkin' it for years and it's never done me any harm.'

Jennet went into her own house with Bessie. It was a boiling-hot day and she was glad to get back from the market and out of the sun. At least the sheets she'd pegged out earlier had dried on the line and she would be able to fold and press them after dinner. She went through to the back kitchen to put her shopping away. Molly had a point, she thought. It was a chore having to walk down to the pump to fill up buckets. She usually relied on her barrels of rainwater for laundry but it hadn't rained in weeks and they were empty. She'd sometimes used water from the river in the past, but it was so low now, and had so much green slime floating on its surface that it was no good for washing. It had been a huge help whilst Hannah was at home, she thought, but now that her sister had gone to the Feildens' house she had to fetch water herself and take Bessie with her.

She missed her sister. It wasn't just the help she'd given in the weeks since she'd been back, it was her company. It had been good to have someone to talk to. Titus never seemed to be at home these days. Once he'd finished work he would gulp his tea down without even tasting it and then go off to some meeting or other, only coming back at bedtime. It sometimes seemed like they barely exchanged a word from one Sunday to the next. And when Sunday came he was always reading some pamphlet or meeting up with friends to discuss the coming election. He was very excited about it, though Jennet wasn't sure what difference it would make because all the politicians were gentry and none of them really understood the struggles of ordinary working folk.

The mill hooter broke into her thoughts and moments later Titus came in and hung his cap behind the door.

'I've been run off my feet all mornin',' he complained, 'doin' the job of two men. Billy Ratcliffe's sent word that he's sick.'

'What's to do with him?' asked Jennet, knowing that it must be serious. No one stayed away from work and got their pay docked unless they were at death's door.

'They're sayin' as it's the typhus.'

'No!' Jennet heard the clatter and realised that she'd dropped the serving spoon on to the hard flagged floor. 'I thought that were just workers at the Eanam Mill?'

'Aye, well, it seems to be spreading. Papers are saying that it serves folk right for going out in the night air to listen to Dr Bowring – that they've caught cold and not looked after themselves.'

'What nonsense,' said Jennet. 'It's all the filth in this town that makes people ill. And we're too near the bad smells from the river here!' She could hear her own voice rising in panic as Titus stooped to pick up the spoon. 'I saw Molly Chambers from next door filling her kettle from it.'

'Yon's a daft lass,' agreed Titus. 'Don't thee be tempted, our Jennet. Not even for the laundry. Get clean water from the spring.'

'Aye, I will. I've to go this afternoon,' she said, wondering if he realised how hard it was.

Titus wiped the spoon on a cloth and handed it back to her. 'We need to be careful,' he said. 'We mustn't let our Peggy get ill again. Keep her away from the river. Make her cover her mouth if needs be.'

'I will,' said Jennet, noting that he made no mention of Bessie.

When he'd gone back to work and she'd washed up, she took her two big buckets and, giving Bessie a small one to carry and bidding her to stay close, she set off down to the Hallows Spring. There was only a short queue to use the pump at this time of the day, but the talk amongst the women who were waiting was also about the illness that was creeping through the town.

'My Bert reckons as it could be the cholera,' said one. She sounded as if she enjoyed being the voice of doom, thought Jennet, but the words sent a shiver through her and she hoped and prayed that the woman was wrong. The typhus fever was bad enough, but cholera was a threat that was terrifying. They'd had it up at Newcastle where it had come in on a ship and it had spread as far as London and Oxford. Blackburn had remained unscathed so far, but people were always afraid that it might take hold and spread like fire through the cramped streets and crowded housing.

'They say that drunkenness brings it on and there's plenty of that around here,' said another woman as she pumped the handle to flush water into her buckets. 'Stay sober, that's my advice. We've taken the pledge.'

'What? Tha's given up drinking altogether?' asked the first woman.

'Aye. There's not a drop passed our lips since we went to hear Mr Livesey speak about Temperance.'

'I couldn't do that. I needs a drop of summat after a long day, and my Bert enjoys his pint. There's nowt wrong with a drink as long as tha knows when to stop.'

'There's too many as doesn't know when to stop though,' the other woman told her as she picked up her filled buckets by the handles. 'Tha only needs to look around to see that.'

'Aye. Well, stick to thy water then,' said the first woman. 'And good luck to thee!' She shook her head as she began to fill her buckets. 'Lot of nonsense in my opinion,' she told Jennet. 'Folk deserve a bit o' fun when they've worked hard all day and I wouldn't be surprised if it's water and not beer as is spreadin' disease.'

'Aye,' agreed Jennet. 'I warned my neighbour about takin' water from t' river. The smell's that bad down there it can't be healthy.'

She filled her own buckets, putting a little into the small pail that Bessie carried. There was no point overfilling it because she would spill most of it before they got back home. The heavy load pulled on her arms as they walked in the heat and she was glad to get back. The sun had gone off the yard now, but it was still warm enough to get another load hung out to dry before she had to go and get Peggy from school. Perhaps it was time to let her walk home on her own, she thought. Most of the other children did because their mothers were at work in the mills. But she worried so much about Peggy. She knew that she was overprotective of her ever since she'd come down with the scarlatina as a baby. They'd so nearly lost her and Jennet was always afraid that illness would strike again in this filthy town. Titus was right when he said that they had to protect her, but Bessie needed protecting too. Although she'd had such a difficult birth, Bessie had thrived and was rarely ill, but Jennet had heard talk about how cholera could strike a child down in the morning and by teatime they could be dead. It was a horrifying prospect.

Back at home, Jennet watched as Bessie plunged and scrubbed some of the smaller items of clothing in the dolly tub. She was wet through again but her frock would soon dry as they walked up to Thunder Alley. Bessie squeezed the items together and plunged them again, copying the way that Jennet washed. It was still a game to her and Jennet hoped that she would never have to do it as a living. She had ambitions for both her daughters and although Titus always talked about how clever Peggy was, Jennet knew that Bessie was clever too. She wasn't as talkative as her sister, but she watched and listened and it saddened Jennet to know that she had begun to understand that Titus always favoured Peggy. It would have helped if she looked less like George, thought Jennet. But she was the image of him and even if she'd tried to keep it secret she could never have passed her off as Titus's daughter. Perhaps it was as well that George had gone, though on days

93

like these, when she struggled to get all her work done and the tea on the table in time for Titus coming home, she wondered if she might have had an easier life if she'd gone to America.

As soon as the next lot of washing was on the line she went to meet Peggy. Not many mothers were standing outside the school door but she was familiar with the ones who were there and they exchanged greetings.

'Hast tha heard about the fever?' asked one. Talk of illness seemed to have replaced the speculations about Henry Sudell as the main topic of conversation in the town.

'Dost tha think it might be cholera?' asked another.

'I heard it were typhus.'

'That's bad enough. Whatever it is, it's spreading.'

'Aye. My husband said there's folk off sick at his mill on Water Street,' Jennet told them. The frowns and worried glances abounded as the mothers grasped their children's hands and hurried home. An air of fear was beginning to pervade the town as people waited to see who would fall sick next.

'They're startin' to say it's cholera,' said Titus when he came in.

'Aye. That's what I've been hearin' too. Though it could be that folk are a bit hysterical.'

'Aye, happen so,' he said. 'But they say as Billy Ratcliffe's proper poorly and t'doctor from the Dispensary has been out to him and he's recommended that the house is limewashed.'

'Probably just a precaution,' said Jennet as she poured the tea. 'It does no harm to be careful.'

'Dost tha think we should keep Peggy home from school?' he asked.

'I'm not staying here doing washing!' piped up their daughter.

'Tha'll do as thy father says,' Jennet reminded her, knowing that the child could twist Titus around her little finger and always got her own way. 'I don't think there's need for her to stay away,' she said to Titus. To tell the truth she was more worried about him if the sickness had spread to the mill.

A couple of days later, Jennet came back from taking Peggy up to Thunder Alley and saw Molly Chambers taking water from the river again. She gave an inward sigh. There was no telling some people. She took out her key to let herself into the house and start on the pile of laundry that was waiting for her, when she heard Molly come up and put down the bucket outside her own front door.

'Our Kitty's poorly. I've had to stop home,' she said. Jennet heard the fear in the woman's voice and bit back a stinging reply. 'I'm goin' to have to wash all the bedding,' she said.

'Well, it should dry. It doesn't look like rain.'

'It'll take a while when it's all drippin' wet.' Molly hesitated. 'I were wonderin' if I could have a lend of thy mangle?'

So that was what she was after, thought Jennet. But she knew it would be churlish to refuse. The woman did look worried.

'Tha'll have to wait until I've finished my work,' said Jennet.

'Aye. I will. Give me a shout when it's free then?'

'Aye, all right.'

Jennet went inside and pulled an apron over her head. Today's work wasn't so bad – mostly underwear and shirts and blouses from one of the better-off houses on Richmond Terrace. It wasn't such heavy work as sheets and blankets. Most people had taken advantage of the hot weather to get their bedding done, and though it had paid well, Jennet was glad to see the last of it.

She added some more small coals and cinders to the fire under the copper in the washhouse. The washhouse had been the reason they chose this cottage. Even though it was so close to the Blakewater and its bad miasmas, it meant that Jennet could work as a laundress without having to find care for Bessie.

It would take a while for the water to heat up so she went down to the pump to fetch more spring water for the rinses. Once again, the talk there was of illness. A child had died on Clayton Street and the rest of the family were ill. Notices were being put up, said one woman, warning people that this wasn't ordinary English cholera, but Asiatic cholera – a much more deadly disease.

'Folk turn blue just before they dies. That's how they know,' she told Jennet.

Jennet carried her buckets home with worry snapping at her heels. She didn't usually heed the talk she heard at the pump or on the market. There were always doom-mongers who enjoyed spreading their tales, but this seemed different. She'd seen men putting up the posters and she wondered about little Kitty from next door.

When she'd finished wringing out the clothes and hung them up to dry she went and knocked on Molly's door. As soon as her neighbour opened the door she could smell the sickness.

'Tha can use t' mangle now,' she told her. 'How's Kitty?'

'It's comin' from both ends,' said Molly. 'As soon as I've cleaned her up she starts again. I've just put another lot to soak and I need to get these dry afore I can make up the bed again.'

She came through Jennet's parlour with her arms full of the wet sheets and began to put them through the mangle, turning the rollers to squeeze as much moisture as possible out of the washing before it was pegged out.

'Dost tha think it's the cholera?' asked Jennet, hardly daring to say the dreaded word out loud. 'Has the doctor been?'

'Not yet. He's too busy. I've just been told to give her a purge and then starve her for a day to see how she is. If she's no better he'll come and take a look.'

Jennet nodded. She wanted to say that she'd warned her about the river water, but it was too late for that now. She just hoped that the child got better and that Molly would take more care in the future.

When Titus came in for his dinner she asked him what the posters said.

'Just common sense really. Telling folk to wash every day and take their rubbish away. But there's more off ill,' he said. 'Might be best if tha walks up to Mr Wraith's chemist's shop and gets some tincture of rhubarb and castor oil, just in case.'

'Aye. And I'll get plenty of chloride of lime,' said Jennet. 'If folks need their bedding done again, it'll have to be disinfected.'

Chapter Nine

After her conversation with Mrs Hall, Mary had climbed the stairs to her room to think about what had been suggested. She'd wondered how it had come to this. She'd worked so hard all her life – first in the mill and then at Woodfold. She'd never taken a day off sick, never stolen a thing that wasn't hers, never told lies. She'd handed her wages over to her mother when she lived at home to help feed the rest of the family, and at Woodfold she'd tried to save a little – not that it had done her any good because it was all gone now.

It wasn't what she wanted. She wanted a proper job, like the one Hannah had got, not be forced to earn a living by being *nice to gentlemen*. But it seemed that there were no proper jobs to be had, not without a letter of character or an influential friend to speak up for her.

The only alternative she'd been able to see was being turned out and ending up in the workhouse. The thought of that terrified her. She'd heard such terrible stories about that place. And at least it was clean here, she'd thought, running a hand over the counterpane. She'd heard rumours of illness taking hold in the town and seen a cart taking a body away from a house on Clayton Street. Perhaps it was better to be sweet to the men than be dead. Alice seemed to thrive on it. And if she earned a bit extra she'd be able to help John and give him money to buy warm clothes that fitted him before the winter came. She'd seen him the other day, fetching the coach horses from the stables to one of the inns to harness them up. He'd looked as thin as ever and his trousers were even shorter. And would it really be that bad? It wasn't as if she was an innocent. Not after what her father had done.

Mary had been unable to come to a decision but as the days went by and the money in her purse dwindled to nothing she'd had to acknowledge that she wasn't left with much choice.

On the Saturday night as she brushed out her hair and began to pin it up again, she left a few strands hanging loose to curl around her ears and the nape of her neck. There was no one here to tell her to tuck it into a cap and no danger of it getting caught in a loom as there had been when she was in the mill.

When she went down to the kitchen, Mrs Hall gave her an approving smile.

'Tha looks nice,' she said. Mary didn't need to say that she'd eventually decided to heed her words. 'And remember to smile,' she advised, squeezing Mary's cheek. 'Gentlemen don't want to see a sad face. They want someone to give 'em a bit of pleasure and take their minds off their troubles for a while. The more tha cheers 'em up, the better they'll reward thee. Now, let's 'ave us tea and then we'll get started.'

'Where's Alice?' asked Mary as Mrs Hall dished up the hotpot. She'd seen them whispering to one another after she'd come down.

'I've given her the night off.'

Mary didn't reply. She knew why. It was so that when Mr Starkie came in he wouldn't be able to go upstairs with Alice. He would have to choose her instead.

'I've been savin' summat for thee,' said Mrs Hall when they'd finished eating. She took a small brown paper package out of her pocket and put it down on the table. 'Go on, open it!'

Wondering what it could be and what she'd done to merit a gift, Mary carefully unwrapped it. She stared at the small sponge with a ribbon attached, wondering what it was.

'This 'ere's white vitriol,' Mrs Hall told her, laying a small paper envelope beside it. 'Dissolve six grains in an ounce of water and then soak t' sponge in it before puttin' it up thy Mrs Fubbs. Once t'gentleman's finished tha can pull it out and it'll wash everything away. It keeps thee clean and prevents a babe. Wash it out after. Don't go usin' it again without washin' it and hangin' it up to dry. Dost tha understand?'

'Aye,' said Mary, staring at the object. It made her decision real. This was what she was expected to do. This was her job.

'Now,' said Mrs Hall, 'go and lift the sneck and let's see who comes in tonight.'

There was already a queue at the door. The mills were closing and it was pay day and the men who rushed in to put their pennies down on the bar were mostly the regulars who always said they'd come in for a quick drink on their way home, but who stayed for hours until they were too drunk to know any better or until their wives sent one of their children to find them and fetch them home.

Mary served up the pints of beer and tried to chat as if there was nothing wrong, but inside her stomach was churning. Every time the door opened her innards leaped as she looked up to see if it was Mr Starkie. She was just beginning to think that he wouldn't come and that she would have a reprieve for tonight at least when a draught blew across the parlour and there he was, framed in the doorway, his wavy hair tossed about by the breeze. He smiled when he saw her and made his way to the seat beside the fire.

'Evenin', Mary. Tha's lookin' pretty tonight.'

'Ta very much. What can I get for thee?'

'Pour me a pint.'

'Owt else?' she asked. Mrs Hall was insistent that she always try to sell a portion of the hotpot as well.

'What's tha got?' He grinned up at her.

'Hotpot.'

'Nowt else?' His eyes locked with hers and she felt a blush rising to her cheeks. 'Aye, well, get me a bowl of hotpot to be going on with then. Where's Alice tonight?' he asked, glancing around.

'Mrs Hall's given her the night off.'

'Really? Is that true, Nellie?' he called across the noisy parlour. 'No Alice tonight?'

'She's havin' a little rest.'

'She's not poorly, is she?' He sounded concerned. 'There's been some posters going up about avoiding the cholera.'

'There's no sickness here,' said Mrs Hall, putting the dish down in front of him. 'I just thought tha might welcome a bit of a change.'

'Really?' He glanced at Mary and then back at Mrs Hall. 'Really?'

'Aye. Mary likes it here, so she's decided to stop on. I thought tha might like to spend some time with her rather than Alice.'

Mrs Hall went back to the kitchen and Mary stood, staring down at Mr Starkie, ignoring all the other customers who were trying to catch her eye to get a refill.

'Well, this is a turn-up,' he said. 'I thought tha were too hoity-toity to be nice to a chap. What's changed thy mind?'

Mary shrugged. 'Needs must,' she told him.

He took a drink of his beer, put it back on the table and picked up the spoon to stir the hotpot. 'Tha doesn't sound as if tha's so keen.' Mary didn't reply and he glanced up at her. 'Sit thee down,' he said, pulling out a stool for her. 'Tell me a bit about thyself.'

'I've got other customers to serve.'

'Nell has it in hand,' he said. 'Sit down.'

Mary perched on the stool and watched as he blew on a portion of the hotpot before putting it in his mouth. 'Get thyself a beer. Charge it to me,' he told her. Mary poured the drink and took a couple of gulps, feeling the warmth spread through her, down to her toes. She took another mouthful. It was bitter and she didn't really like the taste, but she hoped it would help her to feel more obliging.

'So what were tha doin' afore tha came here? I heard tha worked for Sudell.'

'Aye. It's true. I were a maid up at Woodfold but they turned us out.'

'Did tha not want to be a maid any more?'

'I did, but Mr Sudell never gave me a character. No one'll take me on without one. I tried to get my job back at the mill, but they're not takin' on.'

'Tha doesn't want to be workin' at a loom for fourteen hours a day, does tha?' he asked. He put the spoon down in the dish and looked at her, holding her gaze. 'I can help thee,' he told her. 'Tha can have nicer clothes than those.' He nodded towards her plain blouse and skirt. 'I'm sure tha'd like a pretty calico dress to wear in this warm weather, and a bonnet wi' ribbons to go with it. I could get them things for thee,' he offered. She didn't answer. He drained his beer and glanced around. 'It's noisy in here,' he said. 'I can barely hear myself think and I'm strugglin' to hear thee an' all, with thy soft little voice. What say we go upstairs? I'd like to get to know thee better.'

Mary looked towards the door that led to the staircase and saw Mrs Hall nodding at her. If she refused she'd be on the street by morning. She knew that.

'Aye. All right,' she said.

Mr Starkie pushed the bowl away and stood up. 'Lead the way,' he said with a gesture that could have been mistaken for that of a gentleman.

Mary threaded through the crowd, telling the customers that their orders would be taken in a moment.

'Can tha manage alone?' she asked Mrs Hall at the kitchen door. 'It's very busy.'

'I can cope,' she told her. 'Go on up. Mr Starkie'll join thee in a moment.'

Mary climbed the stairs, carrying a candlestick. She picked up the sponge that was soaking in a bowl and put it inside her. After a few minutes Mr Starkie came in and closed the door. There was none of the laughing and giggling that she'd heard when he came upstairs with Alice.

She put the candle on the washstand although it wasn't quite dark outside and if she'd been alone she would have managed without its light.

Mr Starkie sat down on her bed and patted the mattress. 'Come and sit with me,' he said. Mary sat down and allowed him to take her hand. 'Tha's a lovely little thing,' he said. 'Tha's not afraid, is tha?' Mary felt her heart begin to thud as she was reminded of her father. He stroked her face with his fingers. 'Tha doesn't need to be afraid of me. I'll do nowt to hurt thee.'

He slid his fingers around the back of her neck and drew her face to his. He kissed her, gently for a while, then pushed her down and kissed her harder as his hand sought her breast and squeezed it hard. She tried to protest but his mouth was covering hers and she couldn't cry out. The gentleman that he'd been moments before seemed lost to the frenzy that overcame him as he roughly pulled her blouse open and she heard some of the buttons scatter across the floor. She'd need to get down on her hands and knees to find them and stitch them back on once he'd gone, she thought.

He pinned her to the bed with his weight and pulled at her skirt and clawed at her drawers, dragging them down around her knees before getting on top of her and struggling to unfasten his trousers with one hand. She wanted to offer to help. She thought it might slow him down, but he was in no mood now for conversation and growled at her when she tried to speak. So she let him do as he wanted and tried not to clench up too tight because she knew that it was more painful that way. All she had to do was think of something else – something nice – until he was done.

At last he rolled away from her, gasping and panting and lay on his back staring at the beams that crossed the ceiling. On the washstand the candle guttered and went out and Mary didn't dare move or say a word. When he regained his breath he reached out and grasped her wrist.

'I thought tha were a virgin? Tha didn't feel like one to me! Hast tha told a lie?'

Mary was alarmed by the anger in his voice. 'I never said,' she replied. 'Tha's hurtin' me,' she protested, trying to pull her hand free.

'Hast tha been with other men?' he demanded.

'I ...' Mary was unsure what to say.

'Hast tha?' There was an edge to his voice that made her afraid.

'When I were at home,' she began, hearing her voice shaking as she spoke. 'When I were at home Father sometimes forced himself on me.'

'I thought tha weren't!' he said, getting up from the bed. 'Nell charged me a premium for thee,' he said, fastening his trousers and tucking in his shirt. 'She won't be happy when I go down and demand my money back. Tha shouldn't have lied to her. Tha should have known tha'd be found out, or did tha think tha could just clench thy thighs and get away wi' it?'

'I never said …' began Mary, but then remembered the conversation she'd had the first night she'd come, when Alice had asked if she'd ever been with a man, and she'd said no because she didn't want to talk about what her father had done. She'd thought no more about it, but now realised that Mrs Hall must have thought she was a virgin.

'Well, tha were all right for sixpence,' he replied, 'but tha weren't worth two guineas of anyone's money!'

The door was pulled open and closed. A draught wafted over her as she heard his steps going down the stairs. She got up and wedged the chair under the doorknob, unable to hold back her sobs. She might as well have gone home as allow this to happen to her.

Mary woke to the sound of someone pounding on her door. For a moment she couldn't clearly remember what had happened, but the stains on the sheet when she pushed back the bedclothes reminded her.

'I know tha's in there! Open up!' Mary had expected it to be Mrs Hall demanding an explanation, but it was Alice's voice that rang out – and she sounded livid.

'Just a minute!' she called, wondering what was wrong. The tickle of the ribbon against her thigh reminded her that she'd neglected to follow Mrs Hall's instructions and remove the sponge immediately afterwards. She pulled it out and put it on the washstand. She'd rinse it in a minute.

The pounding came on the door again and she pulled a shawl around her shoulders before moving the chair. The door was flung open from the other side, narrowly missing her and hitting the wall.

'What's thy game?' demanded Alice, her eyes glittering with fury as she spat the words.

'What dost tha mean?' Mary stared at the other lass. Every inch of her seemed angry as she stood in the doorway with her eyes narrowed and a hand raised as if she was about to strike her.

'Tha knows full well what I mean! Stealin' my best customer when my back's turned. Tha little bitch!'

She seized hold of a hank of Mary's hair and pulled hard. Mary felt herself propelled towards the doorpost but could do nothing to stop it. Her nose took the brunt of it and she felt the warm wet blood gush out before she felt the pain of the blow. She tried to grab Alice's hand to free her hair from her grasp, digging in her nails as she screamed for help.

She heard Mrs Hall's heavy tread on the stairs and Alice released her. The front of her torn blouse was covered in blood and when she put her hands to her face they came away covered in it too. Pain throbbed through her head and she began to cry with the shock of it.

'What the dickens is goin' on here?'

'She started it!' accused Alice. 'She's been wi' my best customer!'

'And tha's done this to her? Get in thy room, tha silly little madam!' Mary heard the slap as Mrs Hall struck Alice. She heard Alice's howl of pain and the scuffle, followed by the slamming of a door. 'Come on,' said Mrs Hall, taking her arm. 'Sit thee down on t' bed and let's take a look at thee.'

She heard the sound of water being poured and then flinched away from the pain as Mrs Hall tried to bathe her face.

'Keep still!'

'Stop it!' she pleaded. 'It hurts too much.'

'What happened?'

Punctuated with her sobs and moans of pain, Mary managed to blurt out what had gone on.

'I never thought it would come to this,' said Mrs Hall. 'I've a good mind to put her out on t' street.' Mary heard her wring out the cloth again. 'Here. Hold this to thy nose until it stops bleedin'. Tha's going to have two shiners and no mistake. Tha'll be no use to anybody until they fade. I never thought she'd take on like this,' she continued. 'I'll give her a good talkin' to. Nowt like this'll 'appen again, I can promise thee that.'

There was no sign of Alice by the time Mary crept down the stairs. She'd heard the raised voices after Mrs Hall had called her down. She'd heard Alice's furious footsteps coming back up to her room and the slamming of the door a few minutes later. Alice had paused and Mary had picked up the candlestick – the only weapon handy – as she tried to wedge the chair under the doorknob again so Alice couldn't get in.

'Tha'll be sorry!' Alice had shouted before her steps thumped back down the stairs and Mary had sat on the bed, shaking and terrified.

'I've given her 'er marchin' orders. Tha'll not be bothered with her again,' Mrs Hall said as Mary stood at the sink, hands plunged into icy cold water, peeling the potatoes for the hotpot. 'She's let me down has that one. Got too high and mighty for her own good.'

'Where's she gone?'

'Don't know. Don't care. We're well shut of 'er. Now, who's that bangin' on t' door? Can't they see as we're not open yet?' She slammed down the knife she was using to cut up the scrag ends of meat and went into the parlour. 'We're not open!' she shouted, but a moment later she lifted

112

the sneck and Mary heard Mr Starkie's voice. He came into the kitchen and stared at her face.

'Has t' doctor seen her?' he asked Mrs Hall.

'She doesn't need a doctor. It'll heal up in a day or two.'

'It doesn't look like it will.' He stared at her again and Mary began to wonder how bad she looked. Mrs Hall had taken her little mirror away saying it was best not to dwell on it, but Mr Starkie's expression and the throbbing in her cheekbones told her otherwise.

'She needs summat for t' pain at least.'

'I've given her a sip or two of gin.' It was true and Mary wondered whether that was part of the reason the sink in front of her seemed to sway from side to side every time she moved her head.

'She could do with a few drops of laudanum. She needs to go to t' Dispensary. I'll take her. Get thy shawl, Mary!' he instructed her. 'And here, take this.' He gave her a brown paper parcel. 'It's a frock,' he said as she stared at it uncertainly, 'like I promised.'

'Who's payin' for this doctor visit?' she heard Mrs Hall ask as she went upstairs.

'I am,' he said. 'Tha doesn't need to fret.'

'What happened?' Mr Starkie asked her as they walked towards King Street. Mary had pulled her shawl around her head and face despite the warmth and was aware that people were staring at her as they passed. She told him about Alice.

'I'm sure she's sorry for it,' he said. 'I know she has a bit of a temper, but she's not a bad lass. Tha weren't thinking of making a complaint to the magistrate, or owt like that?'

'No,' said Mary. It hurt when she shook her head. She'd never even considered it. She'd been brought up to believe that it was best to settle your own scores and not involve the gentry.

'I think that's for the best,' he said. 'No need to tell everyone.'

There were a few other people waiting when they reached the Dispensary. Most looked deathly pale and one woman went out twice to throw up on the street outside the door. Mary hoped it wasn't the cholera.

They sat down on one of the benches to wait. Mary loosened the shawl and saw them stare at her and then at Mr Starkie. She knew that they all thought he'd done it and she was sorry that he took the blame in silence and was glad when it was her turn and she was called through to see Dr Scaife.

The doctor held her head gently and stared at the injuries, asking her about how much it had bled, whether she could breathe through her nose and if it had always been that shape.

'I think it could be broken,' he said at last. 'There's nothing I can do about that, but I can give you something for the pain.' Mary watched as he went across to his vast chest of small drawers and measured out various powders and tinctures into a bottle. 'Two drops every three to four hours – not in gin!' he told her. 'Do you have money to pay?'

'The gentleman said he would pay.'

Dr Scaife frowned. 'Did he do this?'

'No. It were another lass. She were jealous.'

She wasn't sure if he believed her, but he opened the door for her to go out into the waiting area.

'What do I owe thee, doctor?' asked Mr Starkie.

'A shilling,' he said and Mr Starkie fished into his pocket and pulled out the coin. 'Make sure she rests,' he said. 'No work for a week at least.'

'Aye. I'll make sure of that,' replied Mr Starkie.

When they got back to the Star, Mrs Hall mixed the drops into a cup of tea and then told her to go upstairs for a lie-down. In her room she saw that the sheets had been changed on the bed and her sponge had been rinsed through and hung up to dry. The package that Mr Starkie had given her was on the chair and she picked it up and put it on the bed to open it. The frock inside was cream, patterned with pale pink rosebuds and trailing green leaves. Mary held it up by the shoulders to shake out the creases and then put it against herself. She thought it would fit fairly well although some of the seams might need altering. She wished that she was still friends with Hannah. She was a much neater seamstress and would have made a better job of altering it, but the hatred she felt whenever she thought of Hannah was still raw. She'd pay her back for what she'd done one of these days, she thought. If Hannah had been fair with her, none of this would ever have happened.

She laid the frock over the back of the chair. The throbbing in her face was lessening but she felt tired and couldn't think straight. She stripped to her petticoat and lay down on the bed, listening to the sound of the mill engines throbbing in time to the blood pulsing through her ears, and eventually drifted off to sleep.

Chapter Ten

The Feildens were having a supper party and Hannah was busy helping Cook in the kitchen with the food. She was chopping vegetables for a salad and the aroma from the roast chicken and joint of beef that were cooling on the table was making her mouth water. Dishes of pickles, jellies and a sweet custard stood ready to be taken upstairs and Cook was making a salmon pie. It wasn't as lavish as the suppers that had been served at Woodfold, but the sight of so much food always made Hannah wonder how people could afford such excess when most ordinary folk struggled to buy enough oatmeal and potatoes to keep themselves fed. The image of young John, struggling with the horses on Thunder Alley, formed in her mind. He'd looked in need of a substantial meal, she thought.

'Mr Feilden's hoping to drum up support for his parliamentary ambitions,' said Cook. 'He's invited all the folk as he thinks will vote for him to see if they can be persuaded with some good food and fancy wine.'

'Titus says votes should be secret,' said Hannah. 'He says it isn't fair when votes can be bought with bribes.'

'I wouldn't call it bribery!' said Cook, sounding shocked at the notion. 'What's wrong with showing folk a little hospitality in return for their support?' she asked as she cut butter into portions and laid them on small plates, adding a sprig of parsley to each one.

'Titus says the members who go to Parliament should represent the best interests of all the towns-folk, not just them that has the vote.'

'Well, I'm sure Mr Feilden will. He's a good man and a fair one, and I've warned thee before that tha needs to mind thy tongue when tha's living under his roof.'

Hannah didn't reply. She knew she would only get herself into trouble if she kept repeating what Titus thought. She hadn't taken much notice of what he'd said when she was living with him, but since she'd been to the Reform meeting with Jane, she'd begun to take more interest, especially after seeing the schoolmaster there. She was trying to educate herself about politics so that she would sound interesting and intelligent, if she was ever lucky enough to get into conversation with him again.

'So does tha not think everyone should have a vote?' she asked after a while, unable to let it drop.

'What do ordinary folk know about what goes on in London?' asked Cook. 'It's none of our business.'

'But it is our business when one household has all this to eat and there are folk starvin' out there on the street.'

'Drunk, most of 'em,' said Cook as she lifted the pastry over her pie and began to trim and crimp the edges. 'They'd be better off if they weren't spending so much on drink. Now that Mr Livesey, he's got summat worth sayin' when he's telling folk not to touch it and to stay upright and sober. Tha'd be better off listenin' to him rather than the likes of Titus Eastwood who think that they're up on a level with the gentry. Anyhow, there's more important matters at hand than talking nonsense about votes. Tha'd best put a clean apron on. Mrs Feilden'll be ringing for thee to help her dress at any moment.'

As soon as the bell sounded, Hannah hurried up the stairs and tapped on the bedroom door. She was called in and found Mrs Feilden sitting at her dressing table in her petticoats with her hair hanging loose around her shoulders.

'Pin it up, Hannah,' she told her, 'and fix the feather.' She nodded towards the buff-coloured plume that lay in front of her.

'I'm no good at anything fancy,' Hannah admitted as she picked up the brush and moved the tray of pins within reach.

'I thought you had ambitions to be a lady's maid?'

'I do, Mrs Feilden. It's just that I haven't had the experience and I don't want you to be disappointed. I can do a simple style, but I've seen other ladies with such wonderful hair and I've no idea how they get it like that.'

'Artifice.' Mrs Feilden smiled. 'But don't worry. I'm not one for wigs and hairpieces. A simple style will suit me just fine.'

Hannah brushed out the strands of Mrs Feilden's fair hair and began to pin it up. She was used to doing her own hair and had often done Jennet's too, but touching her employer seemed too intimate and she found that her hands were trembling. However, in the end it didn't look so bad. She teased a few loose tendrils around Mrs Feilden's face and pinned the feather in place.

'Will it do?' she asked.

'It looks lovely, Hannah.' Mrs Feilden turned her head as she looked at herself in the mirror, making the fronds on the feather shimmer in the last of the evening sunlight. 'Now, help me get into my gown, will you?'

Hannah held the blue dress wide whilst Mrs Feilden stepped into it and then eased it up to her shoulders and fastened the row of tiny mother-of-pearl buttons that ran the length of the back.

'It's beautifully made,' she said, admiring the finish of the seams. She couldn't have done better herself.

She plumped out the upper sleeves and straightened the skirts. The fashion now was for a natural waistline and a full skirt and Hannah loved the new style, even though she would need to save up for much more fabric if she was to make something similar for herself.

'Thank you, Hannah. The guests will be arriving soon,' said Mrs Feilden, glancing at her clock. 'You'd better run down now and help Cook carry up the dishes to the table.'

Hannah could hear Mr Horrocks greeting guests at the door and ushering them into the drawing room as she approached the dining room with the joint of beef on a platter. She was terrified of dropping it. At Woodfold there'd been plenty of footmen to take food up to the table, but here she was a maid of all work and expected to turn her hand to everything.

She'd set the table earlier with a clean white cloth, a knife and fork and soup spoon for each person and a piece of bread by each knife. She'd placed a salt cellar and a pair of tablespoons at each corner and a carving knife and fork at the head of the table where Mr Feilden would slice the chicken and the beef for his guests. She'd brought up the jugs of spring water and tumblers and set them aside before drawing the curtains and lighting the candles to give an air of intimacy to the meal.

She placed the beef next to the chicken and then ran down the back stairs to fetch the other dishes. She had to be quick and make sure everything was placed correctly or she'd catch it from old Horrocks later on. He was a stickler and seemed to think she could do the work of two or three people all at the same time. It hadn't been so bad when Jane was still here to show her what to do, but on her own she found it impossible to be in two places at the same time.

But poor Jane wasn't having an easy time of it either, she thought as she hurried up the steps again with the salads. Eddie had taken sick and couldn't work so Cook was sending her food parcels to tide her over the worst of it until he got better.

'Be quick,' hissed Horrocks when he glanced in as he passed. 'I'm ready to announce supper and the table's still half empty.'

'There's only so much we can do,' panted Cook as she came up with the pie. 'Run down and bring up the soup tureen instead of standing there going on, and then tha can bring 'em through.'

Hannah had barely placed the last dish and slipped out of the dining room when the guests began to enter. Out of the corner of her eye she caught sight of a familiar face and her heart raced. James Hindle, the schoolmaster, was here. He was chatting away to the lady he was escorting into supper and he looked just as fine as any of the gentry who were present. Hannah wondered why he'd been invited. He didn't have a vote so couldn't influence the election. Perhaps he'd been asked because he was a Reformer – a gesture to the working classes. He certainly made a more suitable guest than Titus would have done, she thought as she went back to the kitchen. Titus would probably have banged on the table and lectured them loud and long about the errors of their ways.

The party went on until late and it was the early hours before the last guests went off in their carriages and they finally got to bed, but Hannah was up at her usual time to help Cook clear the table and to dust and tidy the house ready for

Mrs Feilden when she eventually rang for Hannah to help her to dress.

When Hannah got back to the kitchen Cook was packing a basket with some of the leftover food from the previous day.

'It's for Jane,' she told her. 'Will tha go? My back aches and I'm that tired today I could do with a sit-down. It's only on Clayton Street. Just across the way.'

'Aye. I'll take it,' said Hannah as she watched Cook fold a clean cotton cloth over the contents.

'Don't linger,' warned Cook. 'We don't want thee catchin' owt.'

Hannah put on her jacket and bonnet and let herself out of the gate. There'd still been no rain and as she crossed King Street dust blew up around her from the wheels of the wagons and carriages and clung to her skirt. It wasn't far to Clayton Street, although the small terraced cottages there had little in common with the Feildens' house. They stretched in a long row, all the same, each with a front door and one window upstairs and one down. It looked dreary in the heat. There was nothing green here and Hannah longed for the wide expanse of fields and parkland that had stretched around Woodfold Hall. She missed the scent of herbs growing in the garden, fresh vegetables and the aroma that rose from the ground after a longed-for rain shower. When it rained here in Blackburn, it just made the stench worse.

She reached the door of number twenty-six and knocked, wondering whether to wait or go in. After a moment she pushed the handle down and called, 'Hello?'

Jane appeared at the bottom of the stairs, her arms full of sheets. They looked filthy. 'Just let me put these to soak,' she said.

Hannah walked through the little parlour, admiring the soft furnishings, into the kitchen. The back door was propped open and in the yard Jane plunged the sheets into a dolly tub filled with water. The smell of lye was strong as she poked at them with a long posser.

'Is he no better?' asked Hannah.

Jane shook her head. There were tears brimming in her eyes as she glanced upwards towards the bedroom and then drew Hannah close so she could speak in a whisper. 'He's keepin' nowt down.'

'Has the doctor been?'

'Aye, briefly. He said to give him nowt to eat or drink until it stops, but he were pleadin' for a drink. He said he were that thirsty, so I made him a cup of sweet tea, but it all came back.' She prodded the soiled bedclothes again. 'I wish we'd spent less on curtains and bought ourselves a copper. It would have been easier to get this lot clean.'

'Our Jennet has a boiler. I could ask if she'd let tha use it.'

'Would tha? It would help. I'd ask thee to stay for a cup of tea, but I'm that busy ...' She paused. 'He's callin' again,' she said as a weak voice floated down from above them.

'I'll leave thee to it, then,' said Hannah. 'Mrs Feilden sent this,' she said, putting the basket down on the scrubbed table. 'It's leftovers from a do they had last night.'

'Aye. Thanks for comin' by and bringin' it. I wish tha could have visited in better circumstances.'

'He'll be better soon,' Hannah told her, feeling the urge to offer some reassurance, although the truth was that the cholera was taking lives all over town and it seemed there was nothing that could stop it.

She decided to walk down to Water Street before she went back. Cook wouldn't miss her for half an hour.

Jennet was in the parlour, pressing some starched cotton underwear.

'That's gradely stuff,' said Hannah, admiring the embroidery around the neck of a petticoat.

'Belongs to a woman up on Richmond Terrace.'

'I was wonderin' if tha'd do a favour,' Hannah said as she put the kettle on to make them a cup of tea whilst Jennet worked.

'Aye. What is it?'

Hannah told her about Jane.

'She's welcome to use it,' said Jennet, 'but it'll need to be tomorrow. I've another load to do myself after I've finished these.' She put the cool iron down on the range to reheat and picked up the hot one with a rag to continue. 'Everyone that has someone poorly is in the same boat,' she said. 'I've been lettin' Molly from next door use the mangle, but I can't let folk use it every day or I'll not get my own work done. What's needed is a common place where everyone can go with their soiled bedding to get it boil washed so as it's properly clean. It's no good just puttin' up posters to tell folk to keep themselves clean when there's no way they can manage it. I've seen folk soaking their sheets in the Blakewater and filling it with all sorts of filth and then lazy folk take their water from it rather than walkin' down to the spring. It's no wonder illness just keeps on spreading.'

She folded the ironed petticoats and took a moment to sit down and rest whilst Hannah poured the tea and made a cup that was mostly blue milk for little Bessie who was playing quietly with her doll.

'How's it going at the Feildens'?' Jennet asked and Hannah described the supper party and all the food that there had been. 'Tha's makin' me famished just thinkin' about it,' said Jennet as she stirred plenty of sugar into her tea. 'It sounds as if it cost a year's wages for just one meal.'

'Aye. It makes me think that Titus is right when he says things must change.'

'Siding with our Titus now?' Jennet laughed. 'I never thought I'd see the day. What's brought this on?'

Hannah told her about going to the Reform meeting, but she didn't mention the schoolmaster. She didn't want her sister to tease her about her growing infatuation with James Hindle.

'Did I tell thee that I saw John?' she asked. 'Mary's brother.'

'No. When did he get out of prison?'

'I'm not sure. He were on Thunder Alley. I think he's working at the stables.'

'How did he seem?'

'Older. Thin. His clothes looked too small on him.'

'What does Mary say about it?'

'I don't know. I haven't seen her. We had a falling out.'

'What? Tha's fallen' out wi' Mary?'

Hannah nodded. 'She were furious with me about getting the job. Said I weren't her friend no more.' She bit back the tears.

'Well, I'm surprised,' said Jennet. 'Titus said he's seen her at the Star, working as a barmaid.'

'Aye, but tha knows what sort of place it is?'

'I've heard,' agreed Jennet. 'I weren't happy when Titus said they were having meetings there. But I don't think he'd stray ... not that I could claim any moral high ground,' she added, glancing at Bessie.

'I'd best be getting back,' said Hannah, suddenly feeling guilty as Jennet began to pack away her laundry to get the dinner ready for when Titus came home.

She kissed her sister and hurried back across town. At the top of King Street she saw a woman in a pretty dress and a bonnet with a wide brim. There was something familiar about her and after a moment she realised that it was Mary. She called out her name, hoping that this might be her chance to make things right between them, but Mary either didn't hear her or didn't want to hear. She looked quite the lady, thought Hannah, as if she didn't have a care in the world. A stab of jealousy struck at her as she watched her former friend cross Darwen Street and disappear into Mr Wraith's chemist and druggist shop. She wished that she could walk about town in nice clothes with money to spend rather than having to go back to the Feildens' house and work hard. It didn't seem quite right that Mary, who had been so angry with her about the maid's job, looked as if she was doing very well for herself without having to lift a finger.

Chapter Eleven

After Hannah had gone, Jennet thought more about the idea of a place where women could take their clothes and bedding to lather them with soap and boil them in a copper. She was sure that it would help combat the cholera. If she'd still been on good terms with Mrs Whittaker, she would have had no qualms about raising the idea with her, but the vicar's wife had seemed cold towards her since the time she'd refused her any help from the Ladies' Charity because Titus wouldn't take work on the road-building scheme.

'Maybe I could catch her after morning service on Sunday,' she said to Titus after she'd asked him what he thought of the idea.

'I don't know that she'd be interested,' he said.

'No. But I could still ask. Summat needs to be done. Now that word's spread that I've been lending out my mangle and the copper, there's folk coming round at all hours askin' if they can use 'em. And whilst I know how desperate they are, I need to get my own laundry done. I hate turning 'em away, but the town should be doing summat for folk with all this illness goin' round. I shouldn't have to be providing facilities.'

'Perhaps it's time to start chargin' 'em,' suggested Titus. 'Run it like a proper business.'

'How can I start chargin' when they've no money, or barely enough money to feed and clothe themselves? Take Molly next door. She's had to stop work to look after her little 'uns. Three youngest are all sick now and she's washing day and night because she's havin' to change the beds that often. They've only got Harry's wages and that's not enough. She said she'd pawn bedding if she had any to spare, but she needs it all and everything else of worth has already gone to Mr Starkie. They're only left with a couple of boxes to sit on.'

After Titus had gone back to the mill, Jennet was waiting for her irons to heat up so she could finish pressing the laundry when she noticed how quiet it was. There was no noise coming from next door. It seemed that the children were all too poorly to even cry, and she thought she'd nip round and see if there was anything that Molly needed.

She left Bessie having a nap on the big bed upstairs and went round to tap on her neighbour's door. Molly was holding one of the children on her knee. The child was dozing, but her little face was white and she was whimpering.

'No better?' said Jennet.

'Worse, if anything. I've done all t' doctor said and not let a drop pass her lips. It's stopped the runs, but she's that lifeless I'm right worried.'

Jennet put the back of her hand to the child's forehead. She felt feverish. 'I'd take her back if she's no better by the time the Dispensary opens for evening surgery,' she said. 'I reckon she needs a few drops of summat to bring her fever down. I'll listen out for the others if Harry's not back.'

'I'd be grateful,' said Molly. 'The other two don't seem as bad. They're poorly, but not like little Annie here.' She shifted the child on her lap. 'Is that someone knockin' on thy door?'

'Aye. It'll be someone else wanting help with their washing,' sighed Jennet, knowing that she wouldn't be able to send them away even though she had a pile of shirts waiting to be starched. 'Shout out if tha needs me,' she told Molly.

She came out of the door to find a woman with a basket of wet washing waiting on her doorstep. 'I heard tha has a mangle that tha's lettin' folk use.'

'Aye,' said Jennet. 'Come through.' It wouldn't take long, she thought and she couldn't find the words to tell this desperate-looking woman to take her sodden bedding home again.

'I've three of 'em ill,' she told Jennet as she wrung out the sheets. 'I'm exhausted with it.' She looked it too, thought Jennet as she watched her place the folded sheets back in her basket. 'I just hope it stays fine long enough to get them dry.'

The congregation in church on Sunday morning was sparse. There were so many folk poorly and the gentry who lived on the outer edges of the town were keeping their distance for fear of falling ill themselves. Jennet probably wouldn't have gone to the service herself she was that tired, but she was determined to try to do something about providing folk with washing facilities and she knew that Mrs Whittaker was the best person to approach, although she found that her stomach was fluttering with anxiety as she lingered at the church door.

'Good morning, Jennet,' said the vicar's wife when she saw that she was waiting to speak to her. 'I hope you're well – and the children?'

'We're all well, thank you, Mrs Whittaker. But there's many that isn't.'

'Yes. The cholera is quite a concern,' she said. 'Mr Whittaker is busy with burials every day. He says he's never seen anything like it. But God works in mysterious ways and he must have his reasons.'

'Aye,' said Jennet. 'Mr Livesey's preaching that it's drink to blame.'

'He may be right, though the disease is taking the Godly as well as the sinners.'

'I were wondering ...' Jennet began.

'Yes?'

'I were wondering if it would be possible to make some provision for folk to do their washing. I've been lending out my boiler and mangle to a few neighbours, but it's not enough. I've my own work to do and there's that many coming now that I'm going to have to turn them away. There needs to be somewhere people can go, with hot water and soap and suchlike so's they can keep themselves clean.'

'It's an interesting idea,' said Mrs Whittaker.

'It's bad enough now when sheets can be pegged out to dry,' Jennet went on, 'but it'll be worse when the weather breaks and folk are stuck with sopping wet sheets and blankets in their houses.'

'Yes. I'm not sure how it could be done though,' said Mrs Whittaker. 'And it wouldn't be cheap.

But I'll mention it to Mr Whittaker and see what he thinks,' she promised before she bade Jennet 'Good morning' and moved on to speak to another parishioner.

'She'll do nowt,' said Titus when Jennet told him. 'They'll not spend money on summat like that, especially when they're not the ones to come up with the idea. A sack of potatoes here and there, and a roast at Christmas makes 'em look good and charitable, but when it comes to asking 'em to put their hands deep into their pockets they'll not agree. What we need is a good member of Parliament who'll speak up for us. Someone like Bowring. He talks sense. Tha'd be better off askin' him rather than yon vicar's wife.'

'Would he speak to me?' she asked.

'He often stops to speak to folk when he comes. Not just those with the vote. He'll be here this afternoon when the candidates are announced. Tha could come with me. We'll all go. Our Peggy'd like to go, wouldn't tha, Peg? Dost tha want to come and listen to Dr Bowring?'

Jennet had been hoping to have a bit of a sit-down and do the mending that had piled up in her work basket, but she was so disappointed at Mrs Whittaker's lack of enthusiasm for her idea that she thought she would go. Perhaps if Titus was right and this chap Bowring was going to be

136

voted in as a member of Parliament, he would be the one to appeal to concerning the welfare of the townsfolk.

Hannah was dusting in the morning room. It was early on a Sunday and quiet outside. The sun was barely peeping in through the window and Mrs Feilden was still upstairs. It was chilly, she thought as she flicked her duster across the surfaces of the tables and the mantelpiece. It wouldn't be long before she'd be expected to light the fires. The heatwave was over and in a few weeks' time the leaves would begin to turn on the trees – not that there were many trees in Blackburn, but there was a small beech in the garden that she could see, struggling to thrive in the drought and the fetid air.

She walked across to Mrs Feilden's desk. She always worried about disturbing anything there and took the trouble to place everything back exactly where she found it. There was a book. She picked it up and traced the letters on the spine with her fingers to see if she could read the title. *A New Book on Penmanship*, she read. Curious, she opened it and saw that there were pages and pages of examples of handwriting – bills of parcels, promissory notes, receipts and more, each showing the various styles of the formation of the letters of the alphabet. It must have been for Mrs Feilden's daughters to practise their writing, thought Hannah. The script was beautiful and she wished that she could form her own letters with such flair and style.

During the weeks that Titus had taught her how to read and write she'd made good progress and been surprised at how easy she'd found it to read. At first she'd delighted in reading the names above the shops and the street signs. Then she'd discovered that she could also read the words in the Bible that Titus kept wrapped in a small blanket in a drawer of the dresser. It had belonged to his father and was the most valuable thing he owned. She'd been flattered when he allowed her to look at it and turn some of the pages. Some of the longer words she would never have been able to decipher if she hadn't already known the passages off by heart, but she'd always loved the sounds of the words and the way they made shapes in her mind as she rolled them around on her tongue. But writing she'd found harder. She could form the letters but they looked more like printing and she wished she could learn how to write the flowing hands that were shown in this book.

She lifted it to her nose and breathed in the scent of it. It smelled of ink and other things she couldn't define. It reminded her of the precious sheets of paper and the pencils that she had in her little box upstairs in her room. She'd gone to Mr Tiplady's printing shop on Church Street for them. The purchase had made her feel guilty. There were more sensible things that she ought to have spent her money on, but the thrill of asking for them at the counter and seeing them wrapped up in a brown paper parcel had made her feel special, and clever, as if she was someone of importance because she knew how to read and write. She guessed that the shopkeeper thought she was buying them for her employer, but that didn't matter. It was better than being questioned about why she wanted them. She'd brought them back, clutched to her chest as if they were worth all the tea in China, and hidden them away, reluctant to use them at first, for fear of spoiling them and for fear of the words in her head looking silly when they were put down on paper in her shaky, unsure hand. But eventually she'd begun to write, unable to prevent the words from overflowing, and she'd sneaked a chopping board out of the kitchen, hoping that Cook wouldn't notice it was missing, so that she could use it to lay the paper on and kneel at the side of her bed, not saying her bedtime prayers in the last minutes of her day but writing down the story that was constantly forming in her head about the maid and the schoolmaster – the one to which she could give a happy ending.

Hannah put the book back on the desk and went to the shelf where Mrs Feilden kept her other books. She scanned the titles to see if she could read what they were. There were three volumes with the same title: *Ivanhoe* by Walter Scott. Glancing around to double check that she wasn't being watched, Hannah eased the first one off the shelf and opened it. The printing was close set and she brought it near to her face. She'd only meant to see if she could read any of the words but she found herself drawn into the story, turning page after page, until she heard the sound of Mr Horrocks's footsteps in the hallway and guiltily returned it to the shelf and picked up her duster.

'What are you still doing in here? You should have been finished long since,' said the butler. 'Mr Feilden's on his way down for breakfast so you'd better make yourself scarce.'

Hannah knew that her cheeks were burning, but the butler didn't notice, or else assumed that she'd been working hard. She hurried out as she saw Mr Feilden coming and paused to curtsey. He gave her a brief nod and she ran down the back stairs to the kitchen.

'Where's tha been?' grumbled Cook. 'Didst not hear Mrs Feilden ringing for thee? Tha'd best get up there sharpish.'

Hannah ran up the steep back stairs and arrived slightly short of breath.

'Ah, there you are, Hannah,' said Mrs Feilden. 'Will you fetch the blue dress, and I'd better wear the little jacket. It can be quite chilly in church.' Hannah fastened up the dress and helped Mrs Feilden to put on her shoes. 'Run next door and see if the girls need any assistance,' she said, 'and then tell Horrocks he can call for the carriage.' She stood up and reached for her bonnet. 'Will you be coming this afternoon?' she asked.

'To the hustings?'

'Yes. Mr Feilden will be speaking after the candidates have been announced.'

Hannah didn't know what to say. Two hours on a Sunday afternoon were supposed to be her time off. Sometimes she walked to Water Street to see Jennet. Sometimes she stayed in her room to write. At one time she would have gone out with Mary, although it would have been impossible to go to any lectures or classes or even the cheap seats at the theatre now that she was expected to be back to help clear away and wash the supper pots and then help Mrs Feilden get ready for bed.

'I'm sure you'll find it interesting,' said Mrs Feilden. 'Politics isn't just for the men, you know.'

'I know that. I went with Jane to see Mrs Kitchen.'

'Did you really? Jane always was very keen on that kind of thing. You'll come then?' she urged.

'Yes.' Hannah found herself agreeing as it dawned on her that the schoolmaster would probably be there.

So, that afternoon, wearing her Sunday best, Hannah joined the crowds making their way towards Tacketts Field. She looked about for Titus, knowing that he would attend, but as her eyes roved around the assembly she found it was a different face she was seeking – that of James Hindle.

As she threaded her way through the jostling throng to try to get nearer to the front she caught sight of Jennet – well, not so much her sister as the bonnet that she knew was hers. She was surprised that even Jennet had been caught up in the election fever. She'd expected her to stay at home, but, no, it was definitely Jennet with Bessie clinging on to her hand, wide-eyed and thumb in mouth.

She called out, but there was too much noise. So she began to elbow her way past people, until she was close enough to reach out and touch her sister's arm.

'Jennet!'

'I didn't think tha'd be here …' They both spoke at once; then they laughed and Jennet explained that she'd come to speak to Dr Bowring about a washhouse.

'Maybe I could mention it to Mrs Feilden,' suggested Hannah. 'If Mr Feilden is voted in, he might be willing to do something about it.'

'Aye. Tha could. But Titus is certain that Dr Bowring will win a seat. He says as everyone wants him to. Anyroad, they're about to begin,' she said as the officials got up on the stage and began to call for hush.

The candidates were announced and it turned out there were three in total who had their hopes pinned on being Blackburn's first members of Parliament. As well as Mr Feilden and Dr Bowring there was a Mr Turner who was a popular employer in the town. He was the first to speak.

'Gentlemen!' he announced. 'T ... d I wouldn't come, but I am come, an on the day of the election come r give me three cheers and if y the Old Bull Hotel there'll b

His speech was greeted with a loud cheer and once he'd got down from the stage, many in the crowd began to follow him back towards the town centre. Hannah saw Titus frowning.

'I didn't think he'd turn up,' he said. 'He's not shown much interest in politics up until now. Look how many of 'em are going off to get their free beer!'

Mr Feilden was next up and he told the crowd that he would represent their interests as best he could.

'I'm a local man,' he said. 'You know me and you know that I'm trustworthy. Vote for me!'

Then it was the turn of the charismatic Dr Bowring, who promised he would campaign for more reform, for votes for all, for equal rights for women and the abolition of slavery. When he mentioned equal rights for women, Hannah heard Mrs Kitchen and her union members cheer loudly and wave their banner. Hannah clapped enthusiastically and hoped that Titus was right when he said that this was their man. He was good-looking too, she thought. She almost forgot that she was supposed to be looking around for James Hindle.

People crowded around Dr Bowring when he came down from the stage. Some just wanted to his hand and wish him well, whilst others regaled him with their tales of woe, but he listened patiently and promised that he would do everything he could to help them if he was voted in. The pity of it was that most of those who spoke to him had no say in the matter. The decision would be left to those who were property owners or who paid more than ten pounds a year in rent. Hannah didn't see many of them lingering. They'd all gone off with Mr Turner.

She saw Titus approach Dr Bowring and introduce himself and shake him by the hand; then he turned to introduce Jennet. Hannah pressed closer to hear what they were saying.

'So if there was a washhouse that the women could use to wash the dirty bedding and clothes it would be easier for them to keep their homes clean and disease might not take hold,' she was explaining to him.

Dr Bowring listened intently with his head a little to one side and his eyes on Jennet's face. He nodded as she spoke.

'Yes,' he agreed. 'I will certainly look into that if I am successful. I'm sure it could make a big difference to your lives.'

'He's a good man,' said a voice from beside her. Hannah turned sharply to see James Hindle. 'I hoped you might be here again,' he said with a smile that made Hannah's stomach flip. 'Do you know the woman who's speaking to him?' he asked.

'Aye. That's my sister, Jennet Eastwood.'

'Titus's wife? I didn't know you were her sister.'

'Dost tha know Titus?' she asked him.

'I think most people in Blackburn do – well, those who want Reform anyway. Your brother-in-law is quite the radical.'

'Aye.' She was about to say that he'd spent time in prison for it too, but she wasn't sure whether or not that would impress him.

'James! Good to see thee!' Titus came over and shook the schoolmaster's hand. 'Dost tha know our Hannah?'

'We haven't been formally introduced. I'm James Hindle,' he told her and held out a hand. Hannah reached out, hers trembling, and allowed him to grasp it for a moment. He felt warm and his hand was soft, not callused from the mills.

'Our Jennet's been petitioning Dr Bowring about a washhouse,' said Titus.

'Yes, I heard. It's a good idea, especially with the cholera. My class has been decimated. There're so many boys ill or died and others that daren't come.'

'Aye. I keep wonderin' if we should keep our Peggy at home.'

'I like school,' remarked Peggy from where she'd been standing at his side listening to the grown-up talk. 'I want to go.'

Titus laughed. 'Aye, and what our Peg wants, our Peg usually gets.'

'Come and have a drink – my treat,' invited James. 'You haven't signed the pledge, have you?'

'Nay, lad,' replied Titus. 'There's nowt wrong wi' a drop of beer as long as tha knows when to quit. But no need to put thy hand in thy pocket, the barrels'll be flowin' freely this afternoon thanks to the candidates.'

They walked back towards the town centre, Hannah hardly able to believe that James Hindle had joined them, except that he was walking on ahead, chatting with Titus and she was left to walk behind with Jennet and the children. She was enjoying watching his back though. His shoulders were broad and his hair curled at the back around his ears, and his walk was graceful and long-legged as he strode along, glancing back every now and again.

'Tha's not heard a word I've said.' She turned to see Jennet's look of amusement.

'I have,' she protested.

'No tha hasn't. Tha's only got eyes for yon schoolmaster – calf eyes an' all!' said Jennet, laughing.

Chapter Twelve

As they approached the centre of town the shouting and raucous laughter grew louder and Jennet stared in disbelief at the men and women gathered around the barrels in the churchyard. Most were drunk and two more barrels were being rolled out from the pub across the road. She reached to grasp Bessie by the hand.

'Let's get off home,' she said to Titus. 'I don't want to stay here and have the childer watch this.'

'Aye, tha's right. We'd best get back,' he told James.

'Hannah?' Jennet touched her sister's arm. 'Tha'd best come back with us.'

'But I'll be late,' she said. 'I'm supposed to be back by four to help Cook.'

'Which way are you going? I'll walk with you,' James offered.

Jennet watched the look of amazement and gratitude that flitted across her sister's face. It was clear that she was quite enamoured of the schoolmaster, but Hannah was such a dreamer at times and she didn't want her to get hurt. She suspected that Mr Hindle was only offering out of courtesy, but from the look on Hannah's face anybody would think he was proposing to marry her.

'To the Feildens' town house on King Street.'

'Really? I was there the other night.'

'I know. I saw thee.'

'Well, you should have said something.'

'I don't think Mrs Feilden would have been right pleased to have her maid of all work chatting with Mr Feilden's guests,' Hannah told him.

'No, I suppose not.'

Jennet saw that his smile was warm as he held out his arm for her sister to take. Jennet watched them go. She was about to say to Titus that she wasn't sure about the propriety of it, but when she turned he'd gone.

'That went well,' remarked Titus when she caught up with him.

'I'm not so sure. Our Hannah's a clever lass, but he's a schoolmaster.'

'I meant thee and Dr Bowring!'

149

'Right. Aye, that went well. He seemed more open to the idea than Mrs Whittaker. But we're still a way off getting owt done. I'll just pop in next door and see how little Annie is,' she said when they reached their door. 'Put t' kettle on for tea.'

She tapped on Molly's door and pushed it open. 'Only me!' she called.

Molly and Harry were sitting on either side of the range. Neither of them spoke but they both looked up and she could see from their faces that something bad had happened.

'Not Annie?' she said as all the joy of the afternoon was snatched from her in a moment. They didn't need to nod sadly for her to know that Annie had gone. The house felt empty, as if a soul was missing from it. 'When?'

'Not an hour ago,' said Harry. His voice was little more than a whisper. 'It were peaceful though. She just faded away.'

'I'm right sorry. I thought she were gettin' better.' Jennet almost said that at least their other children were recovering, but she held back, knowing that it wouldn't help them with the loss of their daughter – their youngest, their baby, who Harry had doted on.

'Dost tha want to see her?' asked Molly.

'Aye,' said Jennet and followed her up the twisting steep stairs into the front bedroom where the slight figure was laid on the bed covered in blankets.

'Dost tha want me to fetch Ma Critchley to lay her out?' she asked.

'In a bit,' said Molly. She sat on the edge of the bed and took hold of her daughter's hand. 'She's gettin' cold,' she said, tucking the blanket more firmly around her.

Jennet laid her hand on the other woman's shoulder. It was a hard loss for her to bear and she worried that Molly might crumble under it.

'I did everything t' doctor told me to,' said Molly.

'I know. Tha did thy best.'

'I should have listened to thee when tha warned me about yon river water,' she said, sobs catching her breath.

'Don't blame thyself,' Jennet told her. 'There should be better provision than only one public pump in a town this size – and who knows how clean that is?' She wanted to tell Molly about Dr Bowring and the things he'd promised he would do for them, but she knew it wasn't the time. She'd tell her later and she'd ask her to join her fight for a washhouse. It would give her something to occupy her mind whilst she grieved for Annie.

Hannah tightened her fingers on James Hindle's arm and walked close to him as they skirted the churchyard where the worst of the drunks were lying across the graves, insulting the folks whose ancestors were buried there. It was a shocking sight, but she was finding it hard to be angry or affronted when all she could think about was him. She saw one or two people glance at them and she wondered what they were thinking. Would it be all around town tomorrow that the schoolmaster was walking out with a lass?

As they went down King Street, Dr Bowring's coach passed them.

'There goes Bowring,' said James with a frown. 'He makes a good speech and he's ardent in his beliefs but I'm not sure Blackburn is the place for him.'

'But he'll get the votes, won't he?' asked Hannah. 'Titus thinks he will.'

'I'm not so sure, especially now that Turner's thrown his hat into the ring. He's well known and well liked – for obvious reasons.' He nodded back towards the melee fading behind them. 'He thinks he can buy his way into Parliament.'

'And what about Mr Feilden?'

'He's a good man too, though not as radical as John Bowring. He has his supporters and the shopkeepers who supply his meat and groceries will vote for him because they don't want to lose his custom.'

'Mrs Feilden won't be pleased if he doesn't win,' said Hannah. 'I think she has a fancy to go to London.'

'And what about you? Would you go as well?'

'I don't know. I'm not sure I'd want to. It's a long way,' said Hannah.

'But it would be nice to see something of the world.'

'I wouldn't see much more than the kitchen sink!' She glanced up at him. 'Hast tha ever been? To London?'

'No. I'd go given the opportunity though.'

They'd reached the gates and Hannah reluctantly withdrew her arm. 'I'm grateful to thee for seein' me back safe,' she told him.

'It was a pleasure,' he replied. 'And if I ever get invited to supper again I'll be sure to look out for you.'

'And if I ever get to take our Peg to school again I'll be sure to look out for thee.'

The gate squeaked as she opened it. She would have liked to linger, but she didn't want to get into trouble. As she walked up the path she glanced back. He was striding up King Street. Such a handsome man.

'Tha looks like the cat that's had the cream,' said Cook when she went in. 'I'd no idea that politics were so excitin'. Anyroad, it's time to get tea on. Fetch an apron and slice that loaf. Time to get back to t' real world.'

Mary had watched the crowds heading up to Tacketts Field. She had no interest in politics. It made no difference to her life. Instead she set off in a different direction, hoping that she might find John at the stables.

The town centre was almost deserted and she could hear the cheering coming from the field as she walked up Thunder Alley. The schools on the far side were quiet and locked up today and she remembered the night she and Hannah had gone to a lecture there about the gas. Hannah had been brave enough to breathe some of it and she'd laughed and laughed all the way home, making Mary laugh along with her although she'd had no idea what was so funny. She'd had some good times with her friend and she felt disappointed that Hannah had let her down. She missed her but she doubted that they could ever make their friendship up now. She'd seen Hannah in the street once, but she hadn't wanted to speak to her so she'd hurried away and ducked into a shop.

Mary hesitated when she reached the gates of the stable yard. There were a couple of horses with their heads out over the half-doors and a man sweeping up some soiled straw and loading it into a wheelbarrow.

'I'm looking for John Sharples,' she said.

'In t' tack room,' said the man with a nod of his head.

The door was ajar and she saw John sitting on a stool cleaning some harness with a rag. He looked up when he heard her footsteps and his serious face broke into a wide smile.

'Mary! What's tha doin' here?'

'I wanted to see thee, to make sure tha were all right.' She saw that he still hadn't got any new clothes. His bony wrists protruded from the ends of his frayed sleeves as he reached to get her a stool to sit on.

'I don't need to be here this afternoon,' he said, 'but it's more peaceful than being at home and I like the work.'

'Tha were always fond of animals.'

'Aye. I like the horses well enough.'

'But it's not the job tha were hopin' for,' said Mary as she watched him dip the rag into the tin of leather polish and rub the noseband of the bridle. 'I've brought thee another shilling,' she said, taking two sixpences from her purse and holding them out to him. They were coins that Mr Starkie had given her that she'd kept from Mrs Hall. 'Go to the pawnbroker's shop on Shorrock Fold,' she said, 'and tell them as Mary sent thee. They'll find thee a jacket and trousers to fit, and when I've some more money I'll get a length of flannel off the market to sew thee a new shirt.'

'I don't want thy money, Mary.'

'But look at thee! Tha can't go around like that. Not when the winter comes.' He shrugged and continued to polish the bridle. 'Take it!' she insisted and put the coins down on the table. After a moment he reached for them and slipped them into his pocket.

'I'm grateful,' he said.

'And don't say a word to Mam and Dad. Don't let them have any of it.'

'But they're bound to comment when I go home in new things.'

'Tell 'em as tha were given 'em at work.'

'They'll not believe me.'

'That doesn't matter.'

'They'll say I've been thieving again. Dad said he'd put me out if I stole owt again.'

Mary shook her head. 'Don't let him bully thee,' she told him. 'Anyway, it would be better if tha could find somewhere else to live.'

'Is that why tha left?' he asked. 'Because he were bullyin' thee? I never saw it. He seemed to be more fond of thee than the rest of us.'

'Aye. It seemed that way,' she replied. 'But it wasn't a good sort of fondness. I had to get away and live my own life.'

He nodded and she knew that he had no inkling of what she was talking about and that she could never tell him. He wasn't much more than a child himself, even though he was on the verge of manhood. She hoped he'd turn out to be a better man than their father. It was her father that should have been locked up, she thought, not her little brother.

Mary looked up as the man with the wheelbarrow came in.

'I didn't know tha had a sweetheart, Johnnie!'

'I'm his sister.'

'Aye. That's what they all say.' He winked at her. 'I've seen thee at the Star,' he said.

'Aye, well, that doesn't stop me from being his sister,' she retorted, standing up to leave. 'Take care,' she told John. 'And think on what I said.'

She pushed past the man who deliberately blocked the doorway so she had to squeeze past him. He grinned down at her and she caught a faceful of his bad breath. He laughed as she crossed the yard and said something to John that she didn't catch. Tears were blurring her eyes as she hurried away down Thunder Alley. It seemed that she already had a reputation and she had no idea how she would ever shake it off.

She hurried back towards Shorrock Fold as the meeting on Tacketts Field was breaking up. She was afraid of getting caught in the crowds of excited people who were flooding on to the streets and she was glad when she reached the door of the Star and got inside safely, though she wasn't glad to see Mr Starkie sitting by the fire. He didn't usually come in on a Sunday and she hadn't prepared for him.

'What the dickens is going on out there?' asked Mrs Hall as the sound of excited voices grew nearer and louder and then faded away.

'They all seem to be heading for the Old Bull,' said Mary.

'Aye. Turner said he was going to roll out the barrels,' Mr Starkie told them.

'Then I'm surprised to see thee here if there's summat for nowt on offer elsewhere,' remarked Mary, daring to insult him in front of Mrs Hall but knowing that she'd probably pay for it later.

'There's better here than free beer,' he said. 'Let's go upstairs whilst it's quiet.'

Mary went up ahead of him. She often wondered what he used to laugh about with Alice because she'd found that he didn't have much of a sense of humour with her. She'd been afraid of him ever since the first time, and he often hurt her.

He closed the door and she began to take off her clothes. She knew what he expected now. She was to be compliant. He watched her as she folded her dress and her petticoat and her drawers. She reached for the sponge.

'No!' he said. 'I don't like it when tha puts that in. It doesn't feel right.'

'But Mrs Hall said I was to be sure to use it every time.'

Everything went dark. For a moment she wasn't sure what had happened. Then she realised that he'd slapped her face, and slapped it hard. Pain throbbed through her nose again and she gasped but knew better than to cry out. He'd slapped her before, but not like this, not on the face where it would show. She dropped the sponge back into the dish and put a hand to her nose to see if it was bleeding. There was a smear of blood on her hand and she was thankful it wasn't worse.

He was unfastening his trousers and she knew what to do. He got on top of her and she braced herself. He growled at her to part her legs and she did what he said, fearing more blows. He was like a different person when they were up here. Downstairs he was charm itself, calling her his

Mary and bringing her gifts. Anyone who saw the way he treated her in the parlour would think he loved her, but she knew he didn't. There was no love in this, just raw, animal lust.

'That were much better,' he said when he'd finished. 'Don't use that again.' He pointed at the sponge. She wanted to protest that she was frightened of getting with child, but she feared it would provoke another blow so she nodded, desperate to control her tears until he'd gone. 'Come down when tha's dressed,' he said when he'd fastened himself up. 'I'll treat thee to a drink.'

So there was to be no sixpence this time. She was disappointed because it meant John would have to wait longer for his new shirt and she resolved to try to please Mr Starkie better in future. She knew that he paid Mrs Hall, which meant she could live rent free and eat as much as she wanted in return for her waiting-on work, but if she could save some money she'd not only be able to help John, she might be able to get away. As it was she was totally dependent on him, and although it was nice to have dresses and bonnets and shawls and shoes, she was trapped here and she could see no way of ever getting free.

She gave herself a good wash and hoped that it would suffice. She'd seen her mother produce bairn after bairn, some living and some not, and she didn't want the same to happen to her, not when she wasn't wed and had no means of supporting a child.

There were a few customers in the parlour when she went down. Although beershops weren't permitted to open on a Sunday, Mrs Hall often opened her door to a few select friends who she trusted to say nothing. Mr Starkie was in his usual seat by the fire with his feet up on the fender and his pipe in the corner of his mouth. The others were sitting round a table talking about the elections. One of them was the young man who was always smiling at her, William Hart, whose family had a ropemaking business on Church Street.

'My father says it's a disgrace, that drunkenness in the churchyard,' he was saying as she brought their bowls of hotpot to them. He smiled as he thanked her and held her gaze for a moment longer than was comfortable. She wished he wouldn't. She didn't really like him and she wished he would stop coming on to her. She always found it awkward when she had to turn men down, but she'd promised Mr Starkie that she wouldn't go with anyone else and she could see him glowering at them across the parlour.

'All right, Mary?' asked William. 'Tha looks a bit flushed.'

'I'm fine,' she lied, her hand going to the cheek, which was still sore and burning.

'Bring another beer, will tha?' He held up his pot to be refilled. 'Anyone else?'

The others nodded enthusiastically at the offer and Mary wondered if they only befriended him because he had a bit of cash in his pocket. He wasn't the usual type of regular that they got in the Star. He'd just come for the Reform meetings at first, but now he seemed to be in most nights.

'Can I buy thee a drink, Mr Starkie?' he asked.

'Aye, all right,' he said moodily, draining his cup and giving it to Mary as she passed.

As she filled the cups Mary heard the raised voices and wondered if some new customers had arrived, but when she went back into the parlour she saw that both Mr Starkie and William Hart were on their feet.

'And I'm tellin' thee to stay away from her!' Starkie was shouting as he jabbed his forefinger at William Hart's chest.

'Tha doesn't own her! She can do as she likes!'

For a moment Mary wondered who they were arguing about; then as they both looked at her she felt a cold fear creep through her – a fear that Mr Starkie would accuse her of encouraging another man. She put down the beer with shaking hands, but knew better than to say anything.

162

'Tha can keep thy drink!' Starkie picked up his pint and threw it in William's face. It stunned the ropemaker for a moment. Then his temper rose as he wiped his face on his sleeve. William picked up his own pint, as if to retaliate, but thought better of the waste of good beer and set it down again with deliberation before balling his hand into a fist and taking his opponent by surprise as he swung a punch at him. It was more good luck than talent, thought Mary, that he caught Mr Starkie full on the jaw and sent him staggering back towards the unguarded fire. Starkie caught at the mantelpiece with his hand to save himself. He'd hung his jacket on the back of the chair and his shirt was well tucked in, but he was still lucky not to catch light and there was a moment of silence in the parlour as everyone watched.

'That's enough!' roared Mrs Hall as she strode out from the kitchen. But Starkie's temper was out of control and he growled as he flung himself at young William Hart, knocking him to the floor and kicking him again and again as he lay there feebly trying to protect himself with his hands. Mrs Hall grabbed at Starkie and cried out for help. The other men pulled him back and pinned his arms to his sides. Sweat was running from his temples and a trickle of blood from his nose. Mary watched as they helped William up and put him on a chair, asking him if he was all right, though he'd taken a battering and would be black and blue by morning.

'Tha'd best go,' Mrs Hall told William. Mary knew that she wouldn't put Mr Starkie out, even though he was to blame. He was too good a customer.

'Aye. And don't thee show thy face in here again!' added Starkie as William was helped to his feet. Then, when the door had swung shut, he walked across to the table, picked up William's pint and drank it down. 'And don't let me see thee anywhere near him!' he warned Mary.

Chapter Thirteen

Hannah put down the duster and eased the first volume of *Ivanhoe* off the shelf. She turned the pages until she found where she'd left off last time and began to read. Ivanhoe had disguised himself as a pilgrim and was determined to return to his father's castle to win the hand of his beloved Rowena. Hannah was so hoping that he would succeed. She wished that she could read more than a few pages at a time, although the fear of being caught added to the excitement.

As she came to the end of a chapter she reluctantly closed the book and put it back to continue the dusting. She wondered if anyone would miss it if she borrowed it. Perhaps next time the Feildens were at their country house she might risk it. She was sure that none of the other staff would notice because she was the only one who dusted in here.

When she went back down to get Mrs Feilden's breakfast tray ready, she was surprised to see Jane sitting at the kitchen table. Cook was sitting with her and there was an untouched cup of tea growing cold.

'Jane?'

Cook shook her head to warn her and Hannah felt the horror of realisation. Eddie must have died. Why else would Jane have come back?

'Eddie?' she whispered.

'Aye. Gone in the early hours,' said Cook. 'She's in shock.'

'I'm sorry.' Hannah couldn't think of any words that would be adequate.

Jane continued to stare at the floor. She was twisting a handkerchief around and around her fingers, but she wasn't crying. She just seemed stunned.

'I killed him,' she said after a moment. 'It were all my own fault.'

'What nonsense tha's talkin',' said Cook.

'No. It's true. I were on the market and there were a chap selling pills. Morison's Pills, he called them. He said they would cure the cholera even when the doctor's potions had failed. And I were that worried about Eddie, because he wasn't getting any better, so I bought them and I gave him a dozen, like the man said, and he brought

166

up such a quantity of bile that I was sure he'd be cured. He fell asleep straight after. He seemed peaceful for a while. But then he woke and he were that thirsty he pleaded and pleaded for a drink but the doctor had told me he hadn't to have nowt or he'd never get well. Pitiful it were, but eventually he fell asleep again. Then when I went to check on him in the night he were that cold and I could barely hear his voice but he were still pleading for a drink, and then he just faded away ...'

Mrs Feilden's bell rang, and Hannah jumped up to get her tray. 'Shall I say owt?' she asked Cook.

'I suppose she'll want to know,' she replied. 'But spare her the details.'

Hannah climbed the stairs, balancing the tray carefully. She hoped, selfishly, that Mrs Feilden wouldn't offer to take Jane back. She liked having the room upstairs to herself so that she could practise her writing. She didn't want to share it again.

She put the tray down on the dressing table and poured the hot chocolate that Mrs Feilden liked from the little jug with the handle. Mrs Feilden was still in her robe with her hair falling around her shoulders. She looked tired, as if she hadn't slept well.

'What is it, Hannah?' she asked. 'You look upset about something.'

'It's Jane. She's in the kitchen. Eddie's died.'

Mrs Feilden took a sip of chocolate and then replaced the china cup on its flowered saucer. 'I was afraid that would happen,' she said. 'He was a fine young man. Please tell Jane that she has my condolences.'

'I will. Do you want me to help you dress?'

'Not just yet. I'll ring for you when I'm ready.'

Hannah hesitated at the top of the stairs. She was reluctant to go down and face Jane and her grief. It made her feel so sad, but helpless too. She wished that there was something she could do to make things right, but she knew that there wasn't and she had no idea what she was supposed to say to her. It seemed so cruel, when Jane had been so happy only weeks before. Even on the day Hannah had gone with the food basket, Jane had seemed happy.

She went down and Jane was still sitting there, although Cook was getting on with preparing the dinner.

'Mrs Feilden says she's sorry.' Jane nodded slightly. 'What will tha do now?' Hannah asked her.

'I don't know. I can't afford the rent on th' house on my own. I suppose I could take in lodgers, but who'd want to live in a house where someone's just died of the cholera?'

'What will tha do about the funeral?' asked Cook.

'They've already taken him,' said Jane. 'They took him straight away. Said that he needed to be buried quickly to stop it spreading. I think Mr Whittaker said the prayers. I'm not sure.'

Cook took away the cold tea and poured a fresh cup, adding three or four spoonfuls of sugar. 'Drink that,' she said as if everything could be made better with a brew.

Jennet stood at the graveside as the earth was piled on top of Annie's little body. Molly and Harry had no money for a coffin and she'd been put in her grave wrapped in a pitch sheet. Molly was sobbing and Harry had his arm around her shoulders, not knowing how to comfort her and deal with his own grief as well. Jennet held Bessie closer to her and prayed that nothing bad would happen to her own daughters, although she had begun to wonder if God was even listening.

Mr Whittaker offered a few words of comfort but had to hurry away. There was another burial awaiting, and other graves were being dug. The whole town smelled of the burning pitch and limewash that was being used to combat the spread of the disease, and when Jennet arrived home, she saw that Molly's house had been cleaned and the cobbles on the street were white with the lime that trickled down towards the Blakewater.

'I wish we were back at Pleck Gate,' she told Titus when he came in for his dinner. 'I feel like we have a death sentence hanging over us in this town.'

'Aye, it's a mess,' conceded Titus. 'But they're sayin' as there's been less deaths the last few days. They think the worst of it might be over.'

'Aye, so I heard. Mrs Whittaker were supposed to be asking her ladies' committee if they'd hear what I had to say about a washhouse, but they keep puttin' me off. Last time I asked her she said that the cholera was coming to an end so there weren't much need for one now – as if folk only need to keep clean when there's illness about.'

'They've no idea,' agreed Titus. 'They just hands their dirty linen to a laundry maid and it comes back clean.'

They looked at one another as a knock came on the door. It sounded timid and no one pushed it open or called out.

'Who is it?' asked Jennet, thinking that it was probably yet another neighbour with an armful of wet sheets wanting to use her mangle. When there was no answer she sighed and got up. The little lass on the doorstep, only a year or two older than her daughters, looked up at her, wide-eyed.

'Peggy's been sick,' she announced. 'Miss Parkinson said I was to come and fetch thee.'

A shiver of terror ran through Jennet's body as she reached for her shawl. 'I'm coming. Ask Molly to mind our Bessie, will thee?' she said to Titus.

'I'll come with thee.'

'No. Tha'll be docked an afternoon's pay. Get back to t' mill. I'll get her and take her to the Dispensary.'

Neither of them said the word but *cholera* hung unspoken in the air between them and Jennet could see that Titus was as afraid as she was.

She wanted to run all the way to Thunder Alley, but set her pace by the child who trotted at her side whilst she quizzed her about Peggy.

'How many times was she sick? Is she gripin'? Has she got the runs?'

'She were sick all over the desk after dinner. Miss Parkinson had to fetch the mop and bucket. It were a funny colour,' the child told her.

Please don't let it be cholera. Please don't let it be cholera. Jennet chanted the words in her head as they turned on to Thunder Alley and had to wait whilst the fresh horses for the Preston coach were brought out of the stables. They crossed the road and the child led her into the girls' school. Jennet had never been inside before. The room was filled with rows of benches with desks in front of them. Miss Parkinson sat at the front with her back to the fire, which was banked up and smoking. The smell of vomit pervaded the room and she saw Peggy with her arms on a desk and her head resting on them. She looked as if she was asleep.

'Margaret Eastwood, your mother's here!'

Peggy roused herself. She was white and Jennet could see that she'd been crying.

'I'll take her home,' she said. She took off her shawl and wrapped it around Peggy, who was shivering. 'I'll keep her off until she's better,' she said to the schoolteacher.

'It may just be an upset,' said Miss Parkinson. 'I hope she'll be better soon. She's doing very well and it would be a shame if she fell behind.' She didn't mention cholera either, but Jennet saw the fear in her eyes just the same. 'Perhaps you should get some limewash,' she suggested. 'Just in case.'

Jennet took Peggy straight down King Street to the Dispensary. It wasn't open when they arrived, but Jennet thought Peggy would never make it to Water Street and back again, and she wanted Dr Scaife to see her, so they sat down on the step to wait. At least they were first in the queue.

'Don't think the worst,' the doctor told her when he'd examined Peggy. 'She's grown into a strong girl and many have recovered well. And it may be something else. Children are prone to sickness.' He got up and went to his drawers where he measured out a quantity of white powder into a small brown bottle. 'Give her a gram of this twice a day with no more than half a teaspoonful of water. Apart from that give no food or liquid at all. If the bowels continue to purge than give it every half an hour until the secretions stop. Keep her in bed. Keep her warm and away from draughts. If she's no better in forty-eight hours then bring her back and I'll take some blood which may help to relieve any cramps.'

'Thank you, doctor,' said Jennet. She put the bottle in her pocket and found a shilling to pay, wondering what she would use to buy food for the rest of the week.

Peggy was sick again when they got outside, and Jennet was only thankful that she hadn't thrown up over the doctor. There was nothing she could do about the mess, so she left it for the sun and air to dry and took Peggy home to Water Street where she undressed her and tucked her into bed before dosing her with the medicine.

'How is she?' asked Molly when she came round with Bessie.

'She's gone off to sleep for a bit. Doctor said it might just be an upset.' Jennet clung to the words like a talisman.

'Aye. That's what they always say,' replied Molly. 'Give us a shout if there's anything we can do.'

'Aye. Thanks,' she said.

Her neighbour went out and Jennet put the kettle on to boil to make a drink of tea. Strong and sweet for herself, with just a dash of milk, and milky for Bessie who stood and looked at her in silence, knowing something was very wrong but not being able to comprehend it.

As she sat drinking her tea, Jennet stared at the pile of laundered clothes that were waiting to be pressed, at the clothes on the rack above the range, the sheets flapping on the line in the yard, and the bedding that was soaking in the tub waiting to be boiled and then mangled and hung up to dry. She put her cup down and sank her face into her hands, trying to cry in silence so that Bessie wouldn't be alarmed. It was too much, and she had no idea how she was going to get it all done and nurse Peggy too – and Titus would be back later, expecting his tea on the table so he could go out to his Reform meeting.

'Mam?' She felt the little hand on her knee and looked to see Bessie's bewildered face staring up at her.

'It's all right,' she said, lifting her daughter on to her knee and kissing the top of her head. 'It's all right.' It was far from all right though. She didn't know how she would go on if anything happened to either of her children. She pushed the thought aside. It was too painful to even think about.

Peggy woke later, whimpering and pleading for a drink.

'Not yet,' Jennet told her, stroking her hair back from her damp forehead. 'Doctor says tha's to have nowt until tha's better.'

'But I'm thirsty!' complained Peggy.

'It'll only make thee sick again. Try to sleep for a bit,' she soothed her. But Peggy wouldn't settle and every time Jennet went down to try to get on with her work she kept calling out and crying and crying and Jennet kept having to break off to go up to comfort her.

When she came down for the umpteenth time she smelled the burning. She ran to lift the hot iron, burning her hand on the handle because she forgot to use a rag. She'd left it face down on the back of the blouse and the cotton was brown and singed and the smell pervaded the parlour.

'No!' Jennet stared at the ruined garment in horror, unable to believe that she'd been so careless. She tried to recall who it belonged to and for a moment or two, as she stood there, she couldn't bring to mind the names of any of her customers. Then it came to her. Mrs Pickering from Richmond Terrace. *Oh God. Why did it have to be her?* She was amongst the fussiest of the women Jennet did washing for. She was always complaining and picking fault when there was nothing wrong. *What was she going to say about this?* She was a gossip too, and nasty with it. As soon as Jennet confessed what had happened it would be all over town and she'd be telling everyone not to trust Mrs Eastwood with their laundry. The blouse would have to be replaced too. Jennet fingered the cotton. It was good quality. It would be expensive. And the hems were neater than she could manage; she wondered if she could persuade Hannah to make a new one for her.

'Mam!' Peggy began to wail again upstairs.

'Shut up! Just shut up!' shouted Jennet from the bottom of the stairs. 'This is all thy fault!' As soon as the words were out she regretted them and felt guilty. Of course it wasn't Peggy's fault. The child couldn't help being ill – dying maybe, and if she died the last thing she might remember was her mother shouting at her. She went up the stairs.

'I want a drink,' moaned Peggy. 'I'm thirsty.'

'In a bit,' Jennet told her. 'In a bit. Here, have some more of the medicine. It'll help thee feel better.'

Peggy was still crying for a drink when Titus came home. Jennet had folded the spoiled blouse and put it at the bottom of her basket. She'd deal with it tomorrow, she thought. His tea was on the table and Bessie was sitting silently on a cushion, stirring her potato pie with a spoon.

'Can tha not just give her summat?' Titus asked.

'Dr Scaife said she was to have nowt. He were very insistent.'

'My mother used to give us a bit o' ginger in sweet milk for a tummy upset,' he said.

'This is more than a tummy upset!' Jennet felt rage and fear pulse through her. How could he not see? How could he be so calm when Peggy was so ill?

'Has she been sick again?'

'No.'

'And is she havin' the runs?'

'No. But—'

'Jennet,' he reasoned. 'They has the runs when it's cholera – uncontrollable, like. I don't think she has it. I think it's just an upset.'

'Tha's just tryin' to convince thyself she's not that poorly!'

'I don't think she is. Tha's taken good care of her. She's had nowt but water from the pump and we've kept her clear of yon river.'

'But we have to do as t' doctor says,' argued Jennet.

'No we don't. They're like a lot of folk with a bit of power. They're not so clever as they thinks they are half the time. How can we ignore her when she's pleadin' like that?' They listened to Peggy calling from upstairs. 'Give her a bit o' summat to drink and see if it stays down.'

'And then I suppose tha'll be off to thy meeting.'

'I'll not go tonight,' he said as he poured milk into a cup and set it to warm. 'Have we any ginger?'

'Dost tha think we can afford ginger?' she asked.

'We'll stir in some treacle then. She'll be all right. Tha'll see.'

'Aye,' said Jennet, although she was sure that Titus was deluding himself because he was too afraid to face the truth.

When the milk was warmed through he took a spoonful of treacle from the jar, twisting it around and around until the sticky strand broke. Then he plunged it into the milk and stirred it through. Jennet watched, hoping that it wouldn't be the death of her daughter. It was against everything the doctor had told her.

'I'll take it up,' he said and Jennet followed him up the stairs with Bessie. It was time she was in bed anyway.

She'd put Peggy in their big bed so that Bessie didn't have to share with her. She couldn't risk them both being ill. She tucked the little one under the covers and then went into the front bedroom where Peggy had the cup clutched in both her hands and was eagerly gulping down the sweetened milk.

'Go steady now,' she said. 'Drink it slowly.'

Titus was sitting on the edge of the bed and he took the cup when she was finished and reached out to stroke her hair. 'Better now?' he asked and she nodded, regarding him with affection. But she glared at Jennet, who she seemed to blame for her thirst.

'I hope tha's done the right thing,' she whispered to Titus, wondering how she would ever forgive him this time if he'd hastened Peggy's death with his stubbornness.

'She'll be right as rain by morning,' he predicted as he tucked the blankets around her and kissed her. 'Sleep now,' he told her. 'We'll be up in a bit.'

He picked up the cup and went downstairs without so much as glancing at her other daughter. Heaven help Bessie if she lived and they lost Peggy, thought Jennet.

Chapter Fourteen

Mary stared at the rags in her drawer and tried to count how many weeks it had been since she'd last needed them. It was definitely more than four, probably nearer six. Or even longer. She closed the drawer again, not wanting to think about it. She didn't feel much different. Her stomach was still as flat as it had always been, she thought as she patted it, trying not to imagine that a child might be growing inside her.

She picked up the boned corset that Mr Starkie had given her. He'd told her that all the ladies wore them under the new-style dresses to give some emphasis to the figure. She'd been hesitant at first. The thing made it so difficult to bend down and she refused to wear it when she was working, but now she thought that she would put it on. It was a fiddly thing. It really needed another person to do it up at the back. Which is why all the ladies had maids, she thought as she struggled to pull the laces through the eyelets so they would lie smoothly. She imagined that Hannah laced Mrs Feilden into something similar, but the thought of her friend made her feel resentful all over again. She would have loved that job.

She sat down on the chair and began to arrange her hair. She'd been experimenting with some of the modern styles where hair was piled up in a fancy knot on the top of the head. Mr Starkie had brought her some little yellow feathers and she wanted to wear them, but she was struggling to make it all stay in place no matter how many clips and grips she pushed into it. Still, she thought, it was good practice for when she managed to get back into service in a decent place.

Mr Starkie was taking her to the theatre on Market Street Lane. It had been closed during the worst of the cholera outbreak, but now that the infection seemed to be passing, it was reopening again. Mary was looking forward to it. There were compensations, she admitted to herself, to being Mr Starkie's friend.

He gave a low whistle of appreciation when she came down the stairs.

'Tha looks a real treat tonight,' he told her as he offered her his arm. She wished that he could always be such a gentleman.

They set off walking and Mary pulled her shawl tighter around herself with her free hand. It was chilly now that the heat wave had passed. Mr Starkie greeted people as they walked along, raising his hat and bestowing his best smile on them. Some returned his greeting; others simply looked anxious and hurried by – the ones who hated to be indebted to him and who had no idea how they would ever afford to get their belongings back. Mary hoped that none of them would recognise the clothes she was wearing as their own. Although it was nice to receive gifts, she knew that Mr Starkie picked the garments out from his shop and everything she was given had once belonged to someone else in the town who had pawned it when they'd fallen on hard times.

As they walked, Mary caught sight of a familiar figure with a cloth-covered basket on her arm. It was Hannah. Mary recalled that the last time she'd been to the theatre, she'd gone with Hannah, back before they went to work for Mr Sudell. She wished that she was going with Hannah tonight and that they'd never fallen out. How they would have enjoyed themselves and they would have gone for a drink later and then walked home by different routes so that their families wouldn't know they'd been together. She missed Hannah's friendship, but still couldn't find it in herself to forgive her. She watched as the other girl disappeared down Clayton Street.

'Someone tha knows?' asked Mr Starkie, following her gaze.

'I used to work with her at Woodfold,' Mary told him.

The theatre smelled of new paint and limewash, but there was also an underlying hint of dampness, rising from the river, after its closure. They found their seats; Mr Starkie had paid for the front row although Mary was disappointed he hadn't taken a box. That would have really made her feel like a lady. As they waited for the curtains to open and the play to commence, Mary glanced around to see if she recognised anyone. Unlike her previous visit, she noticed that the audience tonight was scant and wondered if it was because people were still afraid of the cholera, or if they simply didn't have the money for such diversions.

The play itself was entertaining and well acted, and Mary found that she was able to relax for a while and forget the worries that were tormenting her. Afterwards, they walked back to the beerhouse and Mr Starkie took her upstairs. He was in a good mood and for once was gentle with her. She wanted to tell him that she wished he was like that every time, but she said nothing. His temper could flare at any moment. He could be smiling and lovely one minute and then angry and landing blows on her the next. She'd learned that it was better to keep him sweet for as long as she could. And she dreaded to think what kind of a rage he would fly into if she hinted that she thought she was expecting a child. Although she was doing her best to put the thought aside, it was preying on her mind. She hadn't dared use the sponge again, although she was beginning to wonder it it had ever worked. Perhaps she ought to go to the Dispensary, or maybe the chemist's shop. But it wasn't something that she could talk about with a man. Perhaps she'd better ask Mrs Hall. She didn't want to. She knew she'd be angry with her for not using the sponge as she'd instructed.

Hannah was on her way to see Jane when she caught sight of Mary walking down Church Street on the arm of Mr Starkie, the pawnbroker. She was wearing a different dress from the one she'd seen her in last time. It was the latest fashion with a low bodice and a full skirt – and Hannah could have sworn that Mary was wearing a corset under-neath it. With a warm shawl wrapped around her shoulders, feathers in her hair, and a reticule swinging from her wrist, she looked quite the lady.

Hannah guessed that they were on their way to the theatre. She felt a mixture of relief and jealousy. Relief that Mary had done all right for herself after all and jealousy at the clothes she was wearing. Hannah loved nice clothes and she wished that she could be so well dressed, walking on the arm of James Hindle. She hadn't seen him since the afternoon the political candidates were announced. The Feildens had gone to their country house at Feniscowles to get a few days' respite from the electioneering and she'd been kept busy by Cook, first scrubbing the kitchen from top to bottom and now bringing food to Jane when it should have been her night off.

'Tha can go on to thy meeting afterwards,' Cook had told her, but Hannah knew that she wouldn't have the heart to leave Jane on her own, and Jane wouldn't want to go to the meeting so soon after Eddie's death.

She was going to stay in the same house on Clayton Street for the time being. As soon as he'd heard about Eddie's death, Mr Feilden had paid her rent for the next couple of months so that she wouldn't be turned out, although what she would do after that Hannah was unsure and she was sorry that Jane had the worry of insecurity on top of her grief.

She knocked on the door and called out before pushing it open. The parlour smelled of fresh lime-wash and there were splats of it across the flagged floors that Jane hadn't manage to scrub away.

'I wish I had a bigger rug to hide the stains,' she said when Hannah had taken her up on the offer of a cup of tea. Hannah was sitting in the chair opposite Jane. She knew it had been Eddie's and it made her feel uncomfortable. It was as if his ghost still haunted the place. 'It looks such a mess,' Jane went on. 'I've been asking about lodgers, but no one wants to live here.'

'What will tha do then?' asked Hannah. She felt guilty that she'd taken Jane's job, but she'd never thought that Jane would need it back. Now, with this and the trouble that it had caused between her and Mary, she wished that Titus had never insisted that she went to ask about it. She'd got it under false pretences anyway and she lived in constant fear that her bogus letter of character would be found out.

'I'm going to take in sewing, like I'd planned, but it's not enough to live on,' said Jane. 'If I can't find lodgers before I have to pay the rent again I'll be forced to move out.'

'Where will tha go?'

'I don't know.' She shrugged. 'I suppose I'll have to find lodgings myself, but that'll mean finding work outside the house and I know nowt about mills.'

'There's nobody takin' on anyway.'

'I suppose I could try getting back into service. I heard that Woodfold Hall has been sold to Mr Fowden. He might be wanting staff. But I were really looking forward to having a home of my own and it's all spoiled now that Eddie's gone. I keep expecting him to come in. I woke up this morning and just for a moment I thought he was there and everything was all right. Then I remembered and it was the shock of losing him all over again.' She stared down at the tea growing cold in her lap. 'I sometimes wish it had taken me as well,' she whispered.

'Don't talk like that,' Hannah told her. 'Things'll get easier.'

They sat in silence, listening to some footsteps coming up the street. Hannah expected them to pass on by, but they stopped at the door and there was a knock.

'Who on earth can that be at this time of night?' asked Jane, looking bewildered. She went to the window and pulled back the curtain to peep out; then she went to open the door.

'Come in,' she said and Hannah watched as James Hindle stepped over the threshold. Their eyes met, both of them surprised to see the other.

'I thought I'd call to see how you were doing,' James said to Jane.

'Muddlin' through,' she replied. 'Will tha have a cup o' tea?'

'Aye. Thanks.' She waved him to the empty chair and he sat down facing Hannah. 'How do,' he greeted her.

Hannah nodded a reply. She didn't know what to think. It was far too soon after Eddie's death for other men to be coming round and she was consumed with jealousy that the schoolmaster might be showing an interest in Jane. She watched as Jane poured his tea, seeming to know that he liked three spoons of sugar, and stirred it before she handed it to him.

'I went to the Reform meeting at the Star,' he told them, 'but it was called off. Titus didn't turn up,' he said to Hannah. 'I hope he isn't poorly.'

'I don't know. I haven't seen him,' she said, a sudden fear growing for her brother-in-law and sister. 'Did he not send word?'

'No. And they're short-handed because the lass who works there's gone out to the theatre. Some went on to the Old Bull, but I haven't got a thirst for beer tonight so I thought I'd call for five minutes before I went home.'

'I need to go,' said Hannah, putting her cup on the table. She was afraid that something bad had happened at her sister's house.

'I'll walk with thee,' said James, quickly drinking his tea as she fastened her bonnet.

'Will tha be all right?' Hannah asked Jane.

'Aye. Go and check on thy family,' she said.

James followed her out and they said goodnight to Jane. She walked with him to the end of the street where he offered his arm to cross the road.

'I feel so sorry for Jane,' he said as they made their way towards the river.

'Dost tha know her well then?' asked Hannah, dreading to hear his answer.

'I knew Eddie better. He was always keen on Reform, and then I got to know her when she started coming to the meetings. It's a shame what's happened to her so soon after their marriage.'

'Well, happen she'll not be on her own for long.'

'I wouldn't count on that,' he said. 'She thought the world of Eddie. I can't see her being interested in anyone else for a long time.'

The words brought Hannah joy. It seemed he didn't have designs on Jane after all, but was genuinely concerned about her welfare. He was a good man. And he cared about Titus too, or why else would he have offered to walk with her to

Water Street? She hardly dared hope that it was because he enjoyed her company.

Titus and Jennet were sitting by the fire when they went in. Jennet was mending and Titus was reading and smoking his pipe. At first glance everything seemed all right, but when they looked at her she saw that their strained expressions were at odds with the appearance of calm and neither commented on why she had appeared in the company of James Hindle – or maybe they thought she'd come from the Reform meeting as well.

'What's wrong?' Hannah asked her sister.

'Our Peggy's poorly.'

'Not ...' Hannah found she was unable to say *cholera*.

'It's just a tummy upset,' said Titus. 'But Jennet were concerned so I decided to stay home tonight. Were it a good meeting?' he asked James.

'It was cancelled,' he said.

James settled on the chair opposite Titus to talk politics and Hannah followed Jennet into the back kitchen.

'Is she very poorly?' asked Hannah.

'I don't know. I took her to Dr Scaife and he said she were to eat and drink nowt, but she were cryin' and moiderin' that bad that Titus give her some warm milk and treacle and I'm beside myself that it were the wrong thing to do and that it's made her worse.'

'She's quiet now though.'

'Aye. She's sleepin'. She were exhausted.'

'It might not be ... tha knows.'

'No. But I can't help thinkin' it might be. There's so many as have had it. Why should we be spared?'

'Because tha keeps the place clean, for one thing.'

'Aye. And it's not just that. Look here.' Hannah watched her sister pull out a blouse from a pile of laundry waiting to be pressed. 'She were carrying on so much that I left the iron on this. Belongs to Mrs Pickering an' all, and tha knows what she's like. She's bound to make a right to-do about it.'

Hannah stared at the brown mark on the back of the blouse. 'What will tha do?' she asked.

'I'll have to be honest and tell her I'm right sorry and I'll replace it, though I'm not even sure that will satisfy her. She'll not let me touch her washing again and she'll be spreading it all round town that I'm not to be trusted.'

'It's good quality,' said Hannah, fingering the fine cotton. 'And it's got lovely embroidery. It only needs the back panel replacing if tha could get material that would match.'

'I doubt that'll satisfy Mrs Pickering. She'll insist on a new one. If I get the cloth will tha stitch it for me? And do some fancy work? Tha's so much neater with a needle and thread than I am.'

'Aye. I'll do my best,' agreed Hannah, hoping that she could find the time.

'I'll try to get enough material so tha can make a new back for this one and keep it for thyself as payment,' Jennet told her.

Hannah nodded. It would have to be done late at night in her room and that would mean trying to get extra candles because the nights were drawing in and it was dark by the time she went upstairs now. And it would mean that she wouldn't be able to get on with her writing, but she couldn't refuse her sister.

They crept upstairs to check on Peggy and Bessie. Peggy was asleep in the big bed in the front room. She lay on her back with one arm flung out, breathing deeply. Jennet felt her forehead and she muttered in her sleep.

'She doesn't look too bad,' said Hannah. 'Maybe Titus was right.'

'Maybe.' Jennet didn't look convinced. 'At least she hasn't been sick again.'

Back downstairs they all drank tea and talked quietly about the coming elections. Then James walked her back to King Street.

'This is becoming quite a habit,' he said as they walked along.

'I hope it's not too much of an imposition.'

'No! I don't mind at all,' he reassured her. 'I only have an empty house to go back to.'

'It must be strange to live alone. Not many people do.'

'People tell me I should find myself a good woman.' Their eyes met for a moment. 'It would be nice to have someone to share my home with,' he said.

'And do the chores for you!' She hoped he wasn't offended by her teasing, but he laughed.

'That's very true,' he agreed. 'Although I can manage to sew on a button. I've had to learn to keep myself decent. Here we are,' he said as they approached the Feildens' house.

'I'm grateful,' she told him. She wished that he would lean in and kiss her on the cheek. That's what he would have done in her story, but he only opened the squeaking gate for her to go through, nodded his head and then retraced his steps as Hannah went inside.

'Where's tha been until this time?' asked Cook. 'I were thinking of sending out a search party for thee.'

Hannah told her that the meeting had been cancelled and she'd gone to see her sister. She didn't mention cholera. And she didn't mention James Hindle either. She didn't want Cook thinking that there was something between them because it felt like tempting fate when she so wanted it to be true.

Chapter Fifteen

'Can I ask thee about summat?' said Mary to Mrs Hall when she went down the next morning. It was early and Mrs Hall was sitting by the fire drinking tea as was her custom at the start of the day.

'What is it?' she asked. Mary saw that she already knew it wasn't going to be anything good.

She walked slowly across the flagged floor and sat down on a stool, feeling sick. 'I think I might be expecting.' Mrs Hall stared at her, tea half raised to her mouth and forgotten. 'I haven't had my monthlies.'

'How long since?'

'A couple of months. I'm not certain. And I felt a bit faint at the theatre yesterday, and I've been feeling a bit sickly first thing in the morning,' she admitted.

Mrs Hall frowned. 'Hast tha been using that sponge I give thee?'

'I don't think it worked,' said Mary. 'Please don't tell Mr Starkie. He'll only be angry and blame me,' she pleaded.

'Aye. Tha might have a point. We'd best deal with it quietly.'

'How?' asked Mary.

'Tha really is a little innocent, isn't tha?' sighed Mrs Hall. 'I sometimes forgets how little tha knows. Tha needs to go and see Ma Critchley. She'll give thee some of her female pills to bring on thy monthlies. Don't look so worried,' she told her as she counted half a crown into her hand. 'Lots of women use her pills. It's nowt to fret about. Go round this morning. Back Mary Anne Street. Last on the row.'

As Mary climbed the hill to Back Mary Anne Street the smell of brewing beer made her feel sicker than ever. Maybe she'd be better after she got the pills, she thought. She might be able to face something to eat when she got back. She'd had no idea that the solution would be so simple. She should have asked Mrs Hall sooner, she thought, then she would have been spared all these weeks of worry.

She walked down the narrow row to the last house and knocked on the door. A middle-aged woman wearing an apron and a cap with a frill opened it and gave her a reassuring smile, guessing why she was there.

'Come on in,' she told her. Mary stepped into a tiny parlour and was met by the aroma of drying greenery. The rack above the fire held no washing but was filled from end to end with bunches of grasses and herbs. 'Take a seat,' said Ma Critchley.

Mary sat down on the chair by the range and the woman lifted her big brown teapot from the hearth and poured a strong brew into a cup, added plenty of sugar and handed it to her. 'Now,' she said. 'How can I help thee?'

'Mrs Hall, from the Star, sent me. She said to ask for female pills.'

'For thyself?' Mary nodded. 'Aye. I can give thee some. How long is it since tha bled?' she asked.

'I don't know. A couple of months maybe.'

'Aye, well, don't tha fret. My pills'll see thee right.'

She went to a chest of drawers that stood to the side of the fireplace. It was similar to the one at the Dispensary but smaller. She opened it up with a key that hung from her waist and counted out some small brown pills into a little bottle. 'That'll be two and six,' she said, holding out her hand. Mary took the money from her pocket and handed the coins to Ma Critchley, who tipped them into a little leather bag and then locked the drawers. 'Take two now,' she said, tipping them into Mary's palm. 'Then one three times a day until thy flow comes on again.'

Mary popped the pills into her mouth one by one and swallowed them down. The sweet tea barely disguised their bitter taste.

'Tha may get a bit of tummy ache, but don't let it bother thee. It'll soon pass,' Ma Critchley told her.

'I'm that grateful. I've been worried sick.'

'Don't tha fret. Tha's not the first to need 'em,' she said.

Mary drained the tea and stepped back into the street with the little bottle safe in her pocket. Her steps felt light as she walked back and she held her head high in the sunshine. Everything would be all right now. She'd been silly to worry. It was easily solved.

Mary was at the sink peeling potatoes when the vague ache in her lower back intensified and she gasped and reached out to feel for a stool to sit on.

'What's to do with thee?' grumbled Mrs Hall when she came in and saw her sitting down.

'I don't feel so good.'

It sounded like Mrs Hall was speaking to her from a way off. Her voice was faint and Mary could feel the blood thumping past her ears as she struggled to hear. She felt the knife being taken from her hand and her senses steadied now that she wasn't standing.

'Did tha take them pills?'

'Aye. I took two at Ma Critchley's house and more about an hour ago,' she admitted.

'Well, best go and have a lie-down for a bit,' suggested Mrs Hall. 'I'll finish off in here.'

Mary put her hands on the table to steady herself as she stood up. She felt wet and when she moved away from the stool she saw the trail of vivid red blood that followed her steps. 'I'm bleeding!'

'Aye. The pills have done their work and brought on thy flow. Go and put thy cloths on and have a rest. Tha'll be right as rain later on,' said Mrs Hall.

Mary's legs felt weak as she crawled up to the attic bedroom on her hands and knees. At least she had reason to put Mr Starkie off tonight, she thought. She closed the door and went to get her rags. When she lifted her skirts to tuck them between her legs she saw that she was soaked through. She'd never had so much blood before, but she supposed it was the build-up of all the times she'd missed. That would account for why it was three or four times as much as normal.

She fetched clean drawers and put the soiled ones in the basin with some water to soak. She'd scrub them later, but hopefully a good soaking would stop them being stained. A fierce pain convulsed through her. It was like the times she'd seen her mother giving birth, but this wasn't birth. It was just a late monthly. She took off her skirt. It was an old one that she used to work in the kitchen but she still didn't want it spoiled. When she hung it over the chair she saw the huge wet patch at the back. She must have bled through it whilst she was sitting on the stool. She'd put it to soak in the tub later, she thought, as she eased herself down on to the bed. The faintness was coming over her again and she needed to rest if she was going to feel well enough to serve customers later on.

Mary opened her eyes and couldn't make any sense of where she was. Nothing looked familiar and she could hear a noise like someone rattling a door. Perhaps it was the wind, she thought as she closed her eyes again and sank back into the darkness.

'Mary? Mary?' Someone was saying her name over and over. She didn't know who it was although the woman looked familiar. She thought she should know her. 'Tha needs to get up now. There's work to be done,' the woman told her.

Mary tried to wake up and remember what it was she was supposed to do.

'Mary? Canst hear me?'

She tried to nod her head, but she wasn't sure how and she heard a little moan escape through her lips. She thought she must be ill. Cholera. That was it. People had the cholera, and now she must have caught it too.

The woman pulled back her bedclothes and Mary heard her sharp intake of breath.

'Stop there,' she instructed. 'I'll send someone to fetch Dr Scaife.'

So it was cholera, thought Mary as the door closed. She'd try to get up in a minute and clean herself.

'Off to another Reform meeting?' asked Cook. She'd made herself comfortable by the fire with her feet up on a stool. The Feildens were still at their country house and now that everything that could be scrubbed had been scrubbed, Cook was content to allow her a little time off.

'Aye,' said Hannah as she fastened the ribbons on her best bonnet.

'I think tha must be sweet on one o' them radicals,' remarked Cook. 'I don't know why else tha would be so keen on politics.'

Hannah blushed. It was true, although she'd never admit it. The trouble was that tonight she was torn. She wanted to go to the meeting in the hope that she might see James Hindle again, but it was at the Star and she wasn't sure that she wanted to see Mary.

'Or I may just walk round to see my sister,' she lied.

'Aye, well, mind tha's not late back.'

Hannah slipped out of the side entrance and unlatched the gate. She wondered if she should call round at Jane's and try to persuade her to come, but if James was at the meeting she didn't want to risk him spending all evening talking to her friend. So she hurried to the Star alone, keeping her head down as she passed a crowd of drunks on the corner, ignoring their cries and whistles as she went by. It was much darker when she turned into Shorrock Fold. There were no gas lamps down the narrow street where the uneven cobbles threatened to turn an ankle in the gloom. Only the oil lamp hanging over the door to the beerhouse guided her way.

She pushed open the door and the fug of the parlour hit her. The smoke inside was thicker than the smoke outside on a foggy day and her eyes burned and watered as she looked around for Titus. He was sitting at the far side of the room and she shoved her way through the crowd to ask him if Peggy was any better.

'Aye. She's improving,' he told her. 'She wants to go back to school so that's a good sign.'

'So it wasn't cholera.'

'No. I told Jennet it weren't but tha knows how she worries about the childer.'

'What's tha havin'?' asked Mrs Hall.

'She'll have half. My treat,' said Titus, pulling out a stool for Hannah to sit down. 'And I'll have another pint.'

Hannah glanced around for Mary but she was nowhere to be seen and Hannah was relieved. She would have hated to see Mary ignoring her, or giving her black looks all night. She missed her, though. She wanted to make things right between them, but she had no idea how if Mary refused to speak to her. She just hoped that her friend was happy here at the Star. Even though she knew that it wasn't what she would have chosen, Mary always looked well dressed when she saw her on the street and Mr Starkie wasn't ashamed to have her on his arm. Hannah hoped that he genuinely liked her. Perhaps he would marry her, she thought. That would give her a happy ending.

Every time the door opened Hannah tried to glance round to see who had come in without it being too obvious, and every time it was someone other than James Hindle she felt her spirits plummet. She wondered about asking Titus if the schoolmaster was coming, but she was afraid that he would laugh at her.

The parlour was full now and Mrs Hall was struggling to get everyone served so that the meeting could begin.

'Where's Mary tonight?' asked a man who had joined them at their table. Titus had introduced him as William Hart. He was an anxious-looking man who seemed out of place. He was a cut above the ordinary working men, but not quite gentry. He wasn't well dressed or well spoken enough to be mistaken for the likes of the Feildens, but he stood out like a sore thumb in the Star with his silk cravat and polished boots. James Hindle negotiated the two spheres with more ease, thought Hannah. He hadn't looked at all out of place at the Feildens' supper party, but he was accepted by the men in the Star, who sometimes asked him to read something for them or help with a letter they were struggling to write.

'Mary's a bit poorly,' said Mrs Hall as she put his beer down in front of him.

'Not the cholera?'

'No!' Mrs Hall's face darkened with anger at his unthinking remark. Hannah knew that even a rumour of cholera on the premises would be enough to close her down. 'Of course not! I keep a clean place here and there's no illness!'

'Sorry. I was just worried.'

'What's it to thee anyroad?' she demanded. 'I can do without thee pickin' another fight with Mr Starkie. She's steppin' out with him serious now, so keep away from her!'

'Aye, I know,' he mumbled, half hiding his face in his beer.

'What's to do with her then?' asked Titus, trying to defuse the situation.

'Women's troubles,' Mrs Hall told him. 'She's havin' the night off.'

Hannah watched as she went back into the kitchen for more beer and wondered what was really wrong with Mary. *Women's troubles* was enough to stop any man enquiring further but she knew that Mary would never take to her bed unless she was really ill. She was worried about her and wondered if Mrs Hall would let her go upstairs to check on her friend. It would have to wait until later though. Titus was rapping on the table for attention and beside her, James Hindle squeezed on to the stool that she'd been keeping hidden under the table. He grinned at her and his knee brushed hers as he handed Mrs Hall a coin when she put beer down next to him.

'Just in time!' he said as Titus called the meeting to order.

'A washhouse!' Titus told them. 'What this town needs is a washhouse. And who's going to build one? That's what I'd like to know. Feilden and Turner haven't shown any interest. They just want the support of the ten-pound voters so's they can go off to some fancy house in London and forget all about us working folk here in Blackburn. Dr Bowring, though – he's different. He cares about what happens to us. He's already promised that when he's our member of Parliament then we'll get a washhouse. There's just one problem. We're not allowed to vote for him. And until we all get the vote and not just them who's well off, then nothing will change.'

He paused and there were cries of *'Hear! Hear!'* around the parlour, and 'What we want is a vote for every man!' The cries increased and the men banged their cups on the tables in agreement. 'One man, one vote!' they shouted. And Hannah joined in, banging her cup in time with James Hindle, who turned and smiled at her.

Later, as the crowd drifted off home, Hannah remembered Mary. She wondered whether to ask Mrs Hall if she could visit her. The trouble was she could see James hanging around and she hoped that he might be waiting to walk her back to King Street. But he seemed deep in conversation at the moment and she needn't stay long. Mary might refuse to see her anyway.

She tapped on the kitchen door.

'What is it?' asked Mrs Hall. 'I'm up to my eyes in it here.'

'I'm a friend of Mary's,' said Hannah. 'It sounded as if she's proper poorly. What's wrong with her?'

Mrs Hall looked at her suspiciously for a moment and then beckoned her to come in. 'Shut the door,' she said. 'She's not so good. Dr Scaife's been but he's not much use – not when it comes to women's troubles. I sent a message to Ma Critchley, but it seems she can't be found. Probably in the gin palace.'

'It isn't cholera then?'

Mrs Hall gave her a sharp look. 'Were tha born yesterday?' she asked. 'She's taken the female pills to bring on her monthlies. Trouble is she's bleedin' too much.'

'Female pills?'

'Did tha not know? I thought tha said tha were her friend?'

'I haven't seen her for a bit. Not since I started at the Feildens' house.'

'So tha didn't know she were expectin' a child?'

'A child? No!' Hannah was shocked.

'Aye. Well, she was.'

'And she isn't now?'

Mrs Hall shook her head at Hannah's innocence. 'Is it any wonder lasses get themselves in a fix,' she muttered.

'Can I see her?' asked Hannah.

'Aye. Up the stairs, right to the top.'

'I know. I've been afore.'

Hannah hurried up the steep steps and tapped on Mary's door. When there was no answer she pushed it open and looked in. There was a rushlight flickering on the washstand and Mary was lying in bed. She was very still and Hannah bent over to check that she was breathing. She was. But her breaths were very shallow.

'Mary?' she whispered. Her friend's eyelids flickered and she seemed to struggle to open them, as if she didn't have the strength. 'Mary? It's me, Hannah.'

'Hannah,' she whispered. 'Is tha really here?'

'Aye. I'm here. Mrs Hall said I could come up to see thee. What happened?' she asked.

'I'm dying,' whispered Mary.

'Don't talk daft,' Hannah told her, but she was afraid that it might be true. The only people she'd ever seen who looked this bad hadn't lasted the night.

She heard Mrs Hall come up and turned to her as she stood in the doorway. 'What's wrong with her?' she asked.

'The bleedin' won't stop. It's drainin' all the life from her.'

'But there must be something to be done!'

'Dr Scaife says to watch and wait. He's coming back in the morning. But I don't think ...' Her voice trailed off.

'Dr Barlow!' said Hannah. 'Send for Dr Barlow.'

'The fancy surgeon up at Spring Mount?'

'He helped my sister when she was giving birth to our Bessie. We thought she were a goner, but he got the baby out and sewed her up and she were fine. I'm sure he can help Mary.'

Mrs Hall looked doubtful. 'Would he come?'

'I'm sure he would. He's good with women's illnesses and such. Will tha send for him?'

'He'll want payin',' said Mrs Hall. 'Mary's got no money and I can't afford it.'

'What about Mr Starkie?' asked Hannah. 'I'm right in thinking he's the one responsible, aren't I?'

'Aye. He is.'

'Tha could ask him. Tha could go to his door. It's only across the way.'

'He'll not be in at this time.'

Hannah looked down at Mary. She'd drifted off again and she doubted that her friend would wake if she didn't get help for her.

Titus's voice called up the stairs. 'Mrs Hall? Hast tha seen our Hannah? She's disappeared.'

'I'm up here,' she called back from the top of the stairs. 'It's Mary. She's in a real bad way.' Titus came up and looked from one woman to the other. 'She's bleedin' to death,' said Hannah. 'We need to send someone for Dr Barlow. He saved Jennet. I'm sure he can save Mary.'

'What's wrong?' James Hindle was halfway up the stairs. 'Are you all right, Hannah?' He sounded concerned.

'It's Mary,' she repeated. 'Someone needs to go up to Spring Mount and fetch Dr Barlow.'

'I'll go,' said William Hart, who had followed them up. 'I'll get a horse. It'll be quicker than walking. What shall I tell him?'

'Tell him she's miscarryin' a child. Tell him that Dr Scaife has seen her, but nowt'll stop the bleeding,' instructed Mrs Hall. 'And tell him he'd best be quick.' She turned to Titus. 'Put the sneck on the door behind him, will tha? Unless tha wants to get off home.'

'Well, Jennet'll be worried about me if I'm out much longer. And there's nowt I can do here,' he said, glancing towards Mary's bed.

'Would you like me to walk you back to King Street?' James Hindle asked Hannah. It was what she'd been hoping he would ask all evening. She wanted to accept and feel her hand in the crook of his arm, his body close to hers, but her concern for Mary was stronger. She didn't want to leave her, knowing that she might never see her alive again.

She shook her head. 'Thanks, but I think I'm going to stay here,' she said. She knew she'd be in trouble with Cook, but she didn't care. She wasn't going to let Mary down a second time.

When the men had gone, Hannah helped Mrs Hall to change Mary's bedding. It was soaked through with blood and Hannah carried it down to the kitchen, the ironlike smell haunting her nostrils as she put it to soak in a dolly tub in the scullery.

'It's worse than ever,' whispered Mrs Hall when she'd climbed the stairs again. The landlady shook her head. 'She'll not survive this,' she said.

Hannah said nothing. She knelt by the bed and took her friend's cold hand in hers and prayed. *Don't die, Mary. Please don't die. I'm so sorry. I don't want to lose thee.*

It seemed an age before she heard hooves in the narrow ginnel and a banging came on the door. Mrs Hall took one of the candles that they'd brought up so that the doctor would have a good light and hurried down to let him in.

Hannah got up from her knees as she heard Dr Barlow climbing the stairs. He was a man well past middle age with cropped iron-grey hair, but he was nimble enough on the steep steps. If he'd been roused from his bed, it didn't show. His shirt was clean, she noted, as he took off his jacket and handed it to her.

'What did she take?' he asked, rolling up his sleeves. Mrs Hall showed him a small bottle with some brown pills in it. He tipped one on to his hand and sniffed it. 'How many?'

'Three at least,' she said. 'Happen more.'

Dr Barlow handed the bottle back. 'Ma Critchley?' he asked.

'Aye.'

He folded back the bedding and asked Hannah to bring a candle closer. She could see that blood was seeping out from the fresh cloths between Mary's legs already. Gently the doctor moved them aside and felt her stomach with the flat of his hand.

'How many months?' he asked.

'She said two.' He nodded. 'Is there owt tha can do?' asked Mrs Hall, looking dubious.

'Yes,' he said. 'I need to pack her tight to stop the bleeding.'

'What? Up her Mrs Fubbs?'

'Right into the opening of the womb if possible,' he said, taking out some lengths of lint from his pack. 'I need some clean cold water and some vinegar please – and a basin – with all haste.'

Hannah held the candle as the doctor worked. She could tell by the juddering shadow on the wall that her hands were shaking, but the doctor exuded an air of calm authority, just as he had when he'd saved Jennet's life. She trusted him. If Mary could be saved then he was the one to save her.

He worked quietly, only speaking to ask her to pass him something or bring the light closer. Mary moaned and Hannah spoke reassuringly to her, telling her that everything would be all right, but she wasn't sure that what Dr Barlow was doing would be enough. It seemed hopeless.

At last he seemed satisfied and told her to tuck the blankets in around her friend to keep her as warm as she could.

'Get her to drink too,' he told them as he packed his bag. 'Not beer,' he warned Mrs Hall. 'Lukewarm tea with plenty of sugar is what she needs. Then let her rest. I'll call again tomorrow to change the dressings,' he said as he put on his coat.

Chapter Sixteen

Hannah had to bang repeatedly on the door when she got back to King Street. No one came and she was just thinking that she was locked out for the night and would have to go to Water Street, and risk being dismissed from her job, when she saw a flickering candle approaching through the kitchen and Cook called out, 'Who is it?' in an uncertain voice.

'It's me! Hannah!'

She heard the scrape of the bolts being drawn back and then the door opened a crack and she saw Cook's face in the candlelight. She looked both worried and furious.

'Where hast tha been until this time?' she demanded, making no move to open the door wide enough for Hannah to go in.

'I've been helping the doctor care for a friend.'

Cook sniffed as if she didn't believe her. 'Hast tha been drinking?' she asked.

'I had a half-pint earlier, at the Reform meeting. That's all. Let me in!'

Cook stood back and opened the door a few more inches to allow Hannah to squeeze through. Then she closed it and shot the bolts again. 'I don't know what Mrs Feilden will have to say.'

'Tha'll not tell her?' Hannah could see no reason why she should, other than to be perverse. 'I really was with a friend. She's very ill.'

'Tha's takin' advantage cause tha knows t' family's away,' said Cook. 'I'll not be made a fool of,' she warned. 'I were asleep in my bed and I don't like being knocked up in the middle of the night. Tha's lucky I opened t' door to thee at all. It could have been anybody, and Mr Feilden would never have forgiven me for letting in burglars.'

Hannah thought that Cook was being fanciful but held her tongue.

'I'm sorry,' she said. 'But Dr Barlow were tending to Mary and I couldn't just leave her.'

'Giving birth, was she?' asked Cook, putting on the kettle. 'She were lucky as Dr Barlow came out.'

'She lost the baby,' said Hannah. It was true in a way and she didn't want to go into the full details.

'Poor lass. That's always hard.' Cook set the tea on the table to brew. 'I suppose tha won't say no to a slice o' bread and jam?' Hannah knew then that she was forgiven. Bread and jam was a rare treat and she was hungry. 'Then tha'd best get to bed. We've to be up early to make ready for the family coming.'

'Are they coming back tomorrow? I thought they were staying at Feniscowles until next week.'

'Don't sound so disappointed. Tha can't be on easy street all the time,' Cook told her. But it wasn't the work that was on Hannah's mind. Whilst the family had been away she'd borrowed the first volume of *Ivanhoe* and smuggled it upstairs to read. She would have to make sure it was back on its shelf before they arrived.

It was late morning when the carriage came and Cook sent Hannah hurrying up the back stairs with a tray of hot chocolate for Mrs Feilden and her daughters. They were in the morning room, looking relaxed after their time in the country.

'Good morning, Hannah,' said Mrs Feilden. 'Will you go up to my room and unpack my bag please? Everything's clean. It can be put straight away.'

Hannah left them to pour their own chocolate and dashed up the main stairs, hoping that Mr Horrocks wouldn't see her.

In Mrs Feilden's room she began to unpack the clothes. She put the petticoats in one drawer and then picked up the two white blouses. She knew that Mrs Feilden had several and that she kept more at her country house as well as the ones that were here. There was one already in the drawer. Mrs Feilden always rejected it – saying that it felt too tight around the neck. Hannah fingered the fine cotton. It was almost identical to the one that Jennet had burned, probably stitched by the same seamstress. For a moment, she wondered if Mrs Feilden would miss it if she took it as a replacement, and whether Mrs Pickering would even realise it wasn't hers. It would cost Jennet more than a week of her earnings just to buy the material for a new one. But she knew that Jennet would be furious if she ever found out that she'd stolen from her employer – even if Mrs Feilden did have more blouses than she could possibly wear – but it was so tempting. Reluctantly she put the blouses away and closed the drawer. She wouldn't do anything now. She would think about it.

She went and collected the empty chocolate pot from the morning room and carried the tray back down to the kitchen. Sometimes, if Cook wasn't looking and there was a little left at the bottom of the pot, she would pour it into a cup and taste it. Although it would be cold, she loved the texture of the thick drink as it coated her tongue and the sweetness would linger for hours afterwards. But today the pot was drained and she frowned in disappointment as she rinsed it out. She was tired. After all the trauma of yesterday and then getting back so late and having to be up early she felt as though she'd hardly slept. She wondered how Mary was this morning and when she would be able to slip out and see her. She hoped that Mrs Hall was taking proper care of her. After Dr Barlow had gone, Mrs Hall had shaken her head and said it was a mess. But she'd seemed genuinely worried, as if she'd grown fond of Mary, and that consoled Hannah, because she had to trust the woman to care for her friend when she really wished that she could go and nurse her herself.

She was helping to prepare vegetables for the dinner when Mr Horrocks came down to the kitchen with a stern face. 'Mrs Feilden wants everyone upstairs in the morning room,' he told them.

'What for?' asked Cook. 'I'm just getting this meat on.'

'She's talking about something being missing,' he said. His gaze lighted on Hannah. 'She wants to know if the staff know anything about it.'

'What's missing?' asked Cook as she closed the oven door on the leg of lamb and wiped her hands on her apron.

'She seemed to be referring to a book.'

Hannah felt herself blushing bright red although she knew it couldn't possibly be *Ivanhoe* because she'd carefully replaced it first thing that morning.

She followed Cook and Mr Horrocks up the back stairs and into the morning room. Mrs Feilden was pacing the room. She'd sent her daughters out and Mr Feilden had gone down to the mill. She paused when they came in and stood in a line in front of her.

'I've been looking for a very valuable book, and it isn't here,' she told them. 'Do any of you know anything about it?'

'What book is it, Mrs Feilden?' asked Cook.

'*The Life of Samuel Johnson.* My brother was asking me about it and I promised him that he could borrow it. It should be on the shelf, there.' She pointed. 'But it's missing.'

'I can't see neither me nor Hannah being interested in summat like that,' said Cook.

Mrs Feilden froze her with a glance. 'It isn't a matter of the content. It's a matter of the value,' she told her. 'Have you had anyone in whilst we were away?'

'No. Of course not.' Cook bristled.

'I'm sure there must be an explanation, Mrs Feilden,' said Mr Horrocks. 'I'm sure that Cook is perfectly trustworthy. She's been with us for a long time.' His gaze paused on Hannah and she realised what they were all thinking. She was new. She hadn't proved her trustworthiness. And she was the one who dusted the rooms and set the fires. But surely they didn't suspect her of stealing the book?

'It must be found,' insisted Mrs Feilden.

'And I'm sure it will be.' Mr Horrocks's attempts to placate her weren't meeting with much success, thought Hannah as she watched Mrs Feilden begin to pace the room again.

'We will search for it,' she announced. 'Everywhere! Until it is found!'

'It may well be in Mr Feilden's study,' reasoned Mr Horrocks.

'No. I've looked. It isn't there.'

'Then perhaps the drawing room. Will you permit me to take a look?'

'It isn't there. Cook, you must search the kitchens. And Mr Horrocks, you must search the bedrooms.'

Their faces turned towards Hannah and she knew now that she really was under suspicion.

'I haven't taken it,' she said, knowing that she looked guilty even though she wasn't.

'Then you won't have any objection to us looking in your room,' said Mrs Feilden. 'Come!' she instructed as she went out of the morning room towards the back stairs. 'I won't rest until every inch of this house has been searched.'

Hannah hurried after her. Her astonishment at being suspected was turning to anger. Mrs Feilden had no business in her room. She had things in there that were private to her, that she didn't want anyone else to see – and none of them were stolen books.

The door was unlocked. Hannah had never been given a key. She watched Mrs Feilden turn the handle and go in. She wanted to run in and pull her out, to tell her that she couldn't go looking through her belongings, but the house was hers and Hannah was only a servant. She could only comfort herself with the thought that the woman would find nothing.

Mrs Feilden glanced along the shelves where Hannah kept her hairbrush and hairpins and her best bonnet. She pulled at the skirt and dress that were hanging up and she took down Hannah's little coat and felt inside the pockets, though heaven knows how she thought a book could be hidden in there. If Mr Horrocks hadn't been standing half in front of her to prevent her running forward Hannah would have grabbed Mrs Feilden by the hands and shouted in her face to get out and leave her belongings alone.

Mrs Feilden turned back the covers on the bed, bent to look under it, finding nothing but the clean chamber pot, then ran her hands under the mattress. She paused.

'What's this?' She pulled out the chopping board. 'Cook? Is this from the kitchen?'

'It looks very much like it, Mrs Feilden. I wondered where it had got to.'

Hannah stared at the floor. She was going to be in trouble after all.

'What's this doing in here, Hannah?' demanded Mrs Feilden. 'Were you hoping to sell this as well?' She paused as a thought struck her. 'You're friendly with that girl from the Star, aren't you? She was a maid at Woodfold Hall with you. She's walking out with Mr Starkie, the pawnbroker.' She stared at Hannah and then spoke to the butler. 'Horrocks, you had better go down to Mr Starkie's shop and enquire about the missing book.'

'I've taken nothing!' protested Hannah, shocked at the unfairness of the accusations.

'You've taken this!' Mrs Feilden shook the chopping board and for a moment Hannah feared she was going to strike her with it.

'I only borrowed it.'

'Borrowed it? Why on earth would you borrow a chopping board and hide it in your room? It's not as if you're going to be preparing vegetables up here, is it?'

'I ... I ...' Hannah hesitated to tell the truth but she knew that it was the only thing that might save her. 'I borrowed it to do my writing.'

They all stared at her as if they thought she was mad.

'Writing?' repeated Mrs Feilden.

'It makes a hard surface, like a desk, to rest my paper on. I put it on the bed.'

'And what do you write?' asked Mrs Feilden, seemingly torn between incredulity and a wish to know what fanciful tale Hannah would come up with next to cover her crimes.

'I'm writing a story.'

Mrs Feilden snorted. 'You're certainly very good at telling one. I wonder what other items you have concealed in your room.' She tipped the flock mattress aside and the blankets and sheets pooled on to the floor. On the criss-cross of ropes beneath it lay a stack of papers covered with close writing. She picked up the top page and began to read. Hannah thought that her face could not get any redder and her heart was pounding in her chest and her ears. She moved to snatch the page back but Mr Horrocks caught her by the arm.

'What nonsense is this?' asked Mrs Feilden. 'It sounds like one of the penny novels that they sell on the market. The kind of badly written tripe that I try to steer my daughters clear of. I will not have this in my house.' She gathered up the papers and thrust them at Mr Horrocks. 'Burn them!' she told him.

'No!' Hannah grabbed at her precious pages. She caught hold of one but it ripped in two. 'No,' she moaned again as tears flowed freely. 'They're mine! I've worked hard on them. They're *mine*. You can't take them!'

'And what is this?' demanded Mrs Feilden. Hannah glanced round from where she was desperately clinging to her pages as Mr Horrocks tried to wrestle them from her grasp and saw that Mrs Feilden was holding up the blouse that belonged to Mrs Pickering. 'You've stolen this as well!' She turned it over and saw the brown burn on the back.

'That's not one of yours!'

'It looks very much like it. Although you've ruined it with your carelessness. Is that why you've hidden it? So that you won't have to admit your fault? The cost will be taken from your wages.'

'It isn't yours!' Hannah was sobbing now but she was determined to clear her name. She'd done nothing wrong. 'It was our Jennet that spoiled it. It belongs to Mrs Pickering from Richmond Terrace.'

'So your sister's a thief as well? Mr Feilden will be disappointed. He assured me that he trusted Titus Eastwood and that you would make a good employee. But you've let me down badly, Hannah. You and your family.'

'I've done nothing wrong. I promised Jennet I would make a new one. She's getting the material and then I was going to mend that for myself.'

'And what does Mrs Pickering have to say about it?'

'I don't know,' admitted Hannah as she watched Mr Horrocks go out with the pages of writing she'd laboured over. Her story about the maid and the schoolmaster.

'Well. I'll have to speak to Mr Feilden about this,' said Mrs Feilden.

She walked out, followed by Cook, and Hannah gazed around the room. She thought about running down after Mr Horrocks, but her story would be on the fire by now. And she was probably going to be dismissed. And when James Hindle heard about it he would want nothing more to do with her. She was sure of that. And Titus would be furious. He might not even let her back into Water Street. Then what would she do? End up like Mary, who might well be lying dead at the Star by now, despite the best efforts of Dr Barlow.

Chapter Seventeen

Jennet fingered the various materials that were laid out for sale on the market stall, assessing their quality.

'Is tha buyin' or just determined to rub a hole in it afore I can sell it?' demanded the stall-holder. 'That's the best quality cotton tha'll get anywhere.'

Jennet tended to agree. She'd been to every stall and there was nothing better, but she was reluctant to ask the price in case it was more than she had in her purse.

'Tha'll not get better,' the stall-holder told her. 'It's local made with best quality thread.'

'I'll take two yards,' said Jennet and watched as the man measured the cloth twice with his long stick and then cut it, allowing it to rip in a straight line before folding it up and handing it to her.

'Twelve shillings.'

Jennet handed over most of the contents of her purse, glad that she had a penny or two left to buy a couple of sticks of toffee from Old Jem at the top of Church Street. She exchanged a few words with him about the weather and the cholera, both agreeing that it was cooler and the worst was over. Then she walked home with Peggy and Bessie sucking on their treats. Peggy was still pale and although she'd asked to go back to school, Jennet had kept her off for another day. She wanted to be sure that all risk of illness had gone before she allowed her to mix with the other girls again, but as she watched her walking ahead with her little sister, playing a counting game as the laden wagons rolled past, she was thankful that it hadn't been cholera after all. Titus had been right and the milk had settled Peggy's stomach. By the time she woke the next morning she'd been demanding porridge.

'I've just seen Horrocks, that chap who's butler to the Feildens, comin' out of Starkie's pawn shop,' Titus told her when he came in for his dinner.

'Dost tha think he were pawnin' summat?' asked Jennet, putting the plates on the table.

'I don't know. It seemed odd. I wouldn't have thought the Feildens are so badly off that they've been reduced to sellin' the silver.'

'Happen he were sellin' summat of his own.'

'Happen so. He's not the usual sort tha sees comin' out of there though. I could scarce believe my eyes.'

'What were tha doin' down Shorrock Fold anyway?' asked Jennet. 'I though tha were late in for thy dinner.'

'I went to ask about Mary.'

'What? Our Hannah's friend? Why?'

'She were in a bad way last night. They went to fetch Dr Barlow.'

'Dr Barlow? She's not had a child, has she?' asked Jennet, trying to picture Mary the last time she'd seen her. She hadn't looked like she'd been expecting.

'I think she'd tried to do away with one,' said Titus.

'And is she all right now?'

'Aye. Mrs Hall said she's not too bad.'

Jennet wondered if it was Titus's conscience that had prompted his concern. She'd worried about Mary ever since Titus had said she couldn't lodge with them, and more so when he'd told her she was working at the Star. She hadn't argued with him about it. That would have done no good, but the unfairness of it had stayed with her. It was true that Mary's parents had treated them badly – her more than Titus. When she'd lost her job at the mill she'd been left with no income to feed herself and Peggy. But that wasn't Mary's fault. She and Hannah had been such firm friends throughout it all and she thought, not for the first time, what a tragedy it was they hadn't been able to stay on at Woodfold Hall.

'Does our Hannah know?' she asked.

'Aye. She were there. She stayed whilst they waited for t' doctor to come.'

'He's a good man is Dr Barlow. He saved me. And Bessie.'

'Aye.' Titus glanced at the child and Jennet wondered if he sometimes wished her daughter hadn't been saved. The thought made her angry and she poured his tea in silence.

'Perhaps I'll go down later,' she said. 'To see if there's owt she needs. I've to call at the Feildens' house anyway with this material for our Hannah.'

After she'd washed up, Jennet left Bessie with Molly next door and walked down to King Street. The gate on the Feildens' house squeaked when she opened it and she cringed, hating to draw attention to herself. The main path led up to the front door but there was another and she followed it around to the kitchen door, hoping that she could have a quick word with Hannah. She knocked and waited. After a moment a thin man with oversized ears opened it slightly and looked at her as though she was something he'd just trodden in.

'Can I help you?' he asked with a clear undertone of contempt.

'I'm Jennet Eastwood, Hannah's sister. Is she about?'

'She isn't allowed to receive visitors. I'm sure you know that.'

'Aye, I do. But I brought this parcel for her and was hoping for a quick word.'

The man stared at the parcel. 'I'll ask Mrs Feilden if she may receive it,' he said, taking it from her and holding it as if he were suspicious about its contents.

'It's only a length of cotton for a new blouse,' Jennet told him. 'And can tha tell Hannah as I'm goin' to see her friend Mary and I'll let her know how she is.'

'I'll pass the message on,' he said and without another word closed the door in her face, leaving Jennet standing on the step wondering what it was she'd done to offend him or if he treated everyone like that.

Shaking her head she went back to the gate and tried to close it quietly. She failed. It seemed to squeak more than ever and she thought the butler would have been better employed putting some oil on the hinges rather than treating folk as though they were worthless. She must ask Hannah about him next time she saw her. She hated the thought of her sister being at the beck and call of such an old misery guts.

Mary opened her eyes and wondered if she was still dreaming. She felt as if she was floating. She blinked and then tried to turn over, but the pain in her stomach stopped her and she called out. There was a strange feeling of fullness down below that she couldn't explain. In fact she was finding it hard to explain anything to herself. She was in bed at the Star, she thought, after a few moments of struggling to clear her fuzzy mind. Everything seemed to hurt. A vision of a man bending over her formed and for a moment she thought it had been Mr Starkie and that he must have hurt her badly this time. But it hadn't been Mr Starkie. The man had been a stranger and she didn't think he'd been the one who had hurt her. He'd seemed kind and spoken to her gently – but then you never could tell with men.

She heard a tap on the door and Mrs Hall came in. She expected the landlady to shout at her for still being in bed, but she spoke kindly.

'Tha's awake. How dost tha feel?'

'I don't know. Sore. What happened?'

'Dost tha not recall? Tha took too many of Ma Critchley's little pills,' Mrs Hall told her. 'Tha very nearly bled to death and it were only Dr Barlow that saved thee.' So the man she remembered had been Dr Barlow. 'Tha's got thyself in a right mess and now I'm expected to nurse thee an' all.'

'I'm sorry,' said Mary. She hated to be a burden to anyone, especially this woman, even if she didn't sound quite as cross about it as her words implied.

'Aye. Well. I've brought thee a bit of broth. Tha needs to build up thy strength.'

She helped Mary ease herself up on the pillows and then brought the little bentwood chair to the side of the bed so she could sit on it and spoon a little of the warm meal into Mary's mouth.

'I'm going to have to get another lass to help in t' kitchen for a bit,' she said. 'Tha'll not be fit for owt for a week or two yet.'

The warmth of the broth spread through Mary and made her feel a little better. As her mind cleared she began to try to separate what had happened from her dreams. Had Hannah been here? Or had she only imagined her? She wasn't sure. And she didn't dare to ask in case it had only been a dream.

*

232

Jennet wasn't one for frequenting the beerhouses. She didn't like Titus going into them either, although she would never have said so, and at least he only went when there was a Reform meeting. Not like some of the husbands of her neighbours, who were in them every night. She sometimes heard them coming home, shouting and laughing in the street as they made their way to their doors, and she worried that they'd spent all their wages and had nothing left to give their wives to feed the children. Mr Whittaker often spoke out about the scourge of drunkenness in the town when he was preaching on a Sunday. Not that it made any difference. Those who'd been drunk on a Saturday night were too busy nursing their sore heads on a Sunday morning to be in church to hear what he had to say.

She hesitated outside the Star, not really wanting to go in. The door was locked anyway so she knocked gently, then again more forcefully when no one came.

'We're shut!'

'I've come about Mary!' she called.

The door opened and a woman peered out at her. She was of ample proportions with a bosom hiked up above a corset and a double chin that quivered as she eyed Jennet with her small bright eyes.

'I'm Jennet. Titus Eastwood's wife. He said Mary were poorly.'

'Aye. Come in,' said the woman.

'How is she?' asked Jennet, stepping inside and glancing around the neat parlour, trying to imagine what it would be like when Titus and his friends were here. It seemed clean, at least, she noted, and the smell of cooking from the back kitchen was appetising.

'Dr Barlow says he thinks she'll pull through. But she's lost a lot of blood,' confided the woman. 'Dost tha want to see her?'

'Just for a minute.'

Mrs Hall led the way up the steep stairs to the attic and tapped on a door. 'Visitor for thee.'

She stepped aside and Jennet went in. Mary was lying in bed. She was white and barely seemed aware.

'Mary? It's Jennet. Hannah's sister.'

There was a chair and she moved it to the side of the bed and sat down. She reached out for Mary's hand. It was icy cold.

'What did she do?' she asked Mrs Hall, who had stayed in the doorway.

'She took too many of Ma Critchley's pills. They should have been safe. Lots of women use 'em.'

Jennet didn't comment. She glanced around the little room and saw the sponge on a ribbon on the washstand. She didn't ask about that either, but she wished with all her heart that she'd tried harder to persuade Titus to let Mary stay with them.

'Is there owt she needs?' Jennet asked Mrs Hall. 'Has she got money to pay for the doctor?'

'It's been paid,' she told her. 'And money for her to be nursed until she's better.'

Jennet nodded. 'I'll come again,' she said to Mary, although she wasn't sure if she could hear her. 'Tha'll take good care of her?' she asked Mrs Hall when they got back downstairs.

'Aye. I'll look after her,' she assured her. 'She's a good lass. Did tha say Hannah were thy sister?'

'Aye. Does she come in often?' Jennet didn't like to think of her younger sister in the beerhouse even if she was only visiting her friend.

'She sometimes comes when it's Reform night. Not always though. She's not a mill lass, is she?'

'No. She's in service. With the Feildens on King Street.'

'Aye. She were lucky. Mary were a bit put out about it,' Mrs Hall told her. 'She'd have liked to get back into service.'

Jennet reached out for the door as it was pushed open from the outside and a tall, lanky man ducked in.

'I'm not open,' Mrs Hall told him.

'I've only called to ask about Mary.'

Jennet looked at him again as she went out, wondering if he was one of Mary's admirers. She really ought to find a way to get the lass out of there once she was better.

Chapter Eighteen

Cook hadn't spoken to Hannah since her room had been searched except to give her curt instructions about what needed to be done. Hannah was glad. She didn't want to talk about it and the sight of the browned and curled edges of her work on the kitchen fire had reduced her to a state of such sobbing that she'd thought it would never stop.

She'd taken the dishes up for dinner and placed them on the table in a glum silence, escaping quickly when she heard the voices of the family coming through for their meal. She didn't want to see them and could hardly bear to hear their merry voices when they'd caused her so much misery.

Back in the kitchen she toyed with her own food. She wasn't hungry. Everything had gone horribly wrong. She'd lost Mary. She was about to lose her job. Her family would be furious, and even if she went back to her mother and father, she would be nothing but a burden to them.

'Hannah!' She looked up when Horrocks said her name for the second time. 'Mrs Feilden wants to see you. Upstairs in the drawing room.' So this was it, she thought. She'd be out on the street before suppertime.

She went slowly up the back stairs, one step at a time. She would be sad to leave the comfort of this house where everything was new and clean and go back to sharing a bed with her nieces. Peggy wouldn't be impressed either. And now that she was walking to school by herself Hannah wouldn't even have an excuse to see James Hindle. Though maybe that was a good thing, because he wouldn't want to associate himself with a lass who'd disgraced herself so much that she'd been dismissed – especially when he was friendly with the Feildens. And the worst part was that she'd done nothing wrong.

She knocked on the door of the drawing room and listened. Mrs Feilden called her in.

'Hannah. Thank you for coming up so promptly.'

Mrs Feilden was smoothing invisible creases from her skirt and didn't look Hannah in the eye straight away, and when she did glance up she soon looked away again. She reached out and touched a book that lay on the table next to her chair. Hannah didn't recognise it.

'The book has been found,' she said.

'Was it at the pawnbroker's?' asked Hannah, unable to stop herself.

'No.' Mrs Feilden looked embarrassed. And so she should, thought Hannah. 'No. My husband had lent it to Mr Hindle, the schoolmaster. He hadn't told me.'

'So it weren't stolen after all?' Hannah was surprised by her own insolence.

'No. I'm sorry if you thought that you were being accused.'

'Well, it did seem that way.'

'But you have to understand, Hannah, that it is very valuable. It had to be found.'

Hannah didn't reply. She was in fact quite enjoying Mrs Feilden being so unnerved at being forced to give some sort of apology, although she would have liked a better one. The accusation of theft she could have dealt with, but the loss of her writing she would never forgive.

'I've checked the blouses in my drawers too,' she admitted. 'And everything is in order. In fact, Horrocks says that your sister called earlier with this parcel for you. It's cloth for the new one you're to make for Mrs Pickering.' She held out the package and Hannah made her wait a moment before stepping forward to take it. 'As for the other matter ...' Mrs Feilden paused. 'I was disappointed by that, Hannah. You did take a chopping board from the kitchen without Cook's permission and you hid it in your room. And as for the writing – well, writing is a good skill to have if it's used properly, but I can't condone the writing of the fanciful drivel that I found in your room. It's not the sort of thing that I would expect to find in my house and it has no place here. I don't know whether you have been wasting your money on penny novels as well as on paper and pencils, but such reading matter is to be abhorred. A fanciful and over-active imagination is a dangerous thing, Hannah, and I must counsel you to guard against it. Turn your mind to better things as you go about your work, and if you must read and write in your spare time then stick to the scriptures and don't allow yourself to be led astray by things that will corrupt your mind. I will overlook it this time,' she went on as if she were doing Hannah a great favour, which Hannah supposed she was if she'd decided not to dismiss her after all. 'You are a diligent worker and I would like to give you another chance, but you must promise me that there will be no more story-writing. Will you promise me that?'

Hannah looked up and met her eyes, but didn't reply immediately. It was a promise that she was unwilling to make. Those stories meant so much to her that the loss of them was like losing her friends. But if she defied Mrs Feilden and continued to write and was found out then it would mean dismissal without a doubt.

Mrs Feilden pursed her lips in the way she did when she was annoyed. 'If you cannot promise then I don't think you will be able to continue with us,' she warned Hannah. 'Come now. It is something so trivial that I'm not sure why you are being stubborn about it.'

Hannah knew that Mrs Feilden would never understand. But she needed this job. How would she ever explain to Jennet and Titus if she was dismissed over this?

'I promise,' she whispered, although she kept her fingers crossed behind her back.

Hannah knew that there was another Reform meeting that evening. The radicals were meeting every night now, in the run-up to the election. She wanted to go to the Star to check on Mary, but Cook shook her head.

'There's too much to do,' she told her.

Hannah accepted her words with the best grace she could muster. She knew that she was lucky to still have a job, and if she didn't go out she might have the opportunity to begin work on the blouse.

'What was all that writing tha'd done?' asked Cook as they scrubbed the copper pans and dried them carefully before putting them away on the shelves. 'I've never seen a body so upset about some words before.'

'It were nowt important,' Hannah told her.

'Really? It made Mrs Feilden cross though.'

'She thinks I should stick to the scriptures, that's all.'

'Well, happen she's right. What's in the parcel?'

Hannah, relieved that Cook was speaking to her again now that she'd been cleared of stealing the book, explained about the blouse. Cook admired the cotton and said that she could use the kitchen table if she liked. Hannah was grateful because the light was better in here and she would have Cook's company, even if she did keep asking awkward questions.

She began to quiz her about Mary as Hannah cut out the pieces of the blouse, using the original one as a pattern. She seemed frustrated when Hannah wasn't forthcoming with the details of that either. She muttered about Jane being better company and how she missed her and Hannah said nothing and tried to imagine what James

Hindle was doing. Had he gone to the meeting hoping that she'd be there?

'I think I'll come with thee to the meeting,' said Jennet to Titus as she cleared away the tea things. 'Molly'll look in on the girls and we won't be late. It'll give me chance to visit Mary again.'

'All right,' he said as he settled his cap on to his head. 'Get a move on though, if tha wants to walk down with me.'

Jennet pulled her shawl around her head and shouted upstairs to Peggy and Bessie that she wouldn't be long and to knock on the wall for Molly if they needed anything.

They made their way down Shorrock Fold and as they approached the Star, Jennet saw Mr Starkie come out of his shop with a woman. She was dressed up to the nines and giggling as if she'd been at the gin.

'That's Alice as used to work here,' Titus told her. 'Looks like Starkie's taken up with her again now that Mary's poorly.'

Mr Starkie nodded a greeting to them as he passed and the woman stared insolently at Jennet, obviously sneering at her working dress and clogs. Jennet ignored her, but it sowed a doubt in her mind. Earlier she'd thought that it was Mr Starkie who had paid for Dr Barlow, but now she wasn't so sure. She wondered who the man was who'd come in to enquire about Mary earlier. If she saw him here tonight, she'd ask Titus if he knew him.

They stepped into the noise and smoke of the parlour. Titus found them stools to sit down and ordered some beer. There was a strange mix of men and women waiting for the meeting to begin. Some were just ordinary working folk like themselves, but there were other men who looked more well-to-do. Titus said that they were the ones whose rent wasn't much short of the ten pounds that would have got them the vote and they thought they were entitled to have their say as well and wanted the threshold to be lowered.

Jennet kept trying to catch the eye of Mrs Hall to ask her if she could go up and see Mary, but the woman was run off her feet serving all her customers and soon Titus stood up to bang on the table to bring the meeting to order.

He spoke again about Dr Bowring and how he would work for them and try to ensure that they all got a vote, regardless of the rent they paid. *All the men, that is,* thought Jennet as she listened. But she felt proud to hear Titus speak. He was articulate and people listened to what he had to say.

'This election is only the beginning,' he told them. 'We will not rest until every man has a vote regardless of property. We work hard and we pay our way and we should have a say in the way this country is run. The power has been in the hands of the rich and the privileged for far too long, and they have abused that power. The time of the working man is coming! We will have our vote – and it will be a secret ballot so no pressure can be brought to bear. We will vote freely and with our consciences for what we know is right!'

A few other men stood up to speak, but Jennet thought none of them were as good as Titus, and she was proud of him. When they were first married he'd been nothing more than a humble handloom weaver and she'd never dreamed that he would take an interest in politics. He'd always been happy to let others take the lead until he ended up in the House of Correction at Preston. It had changed him, and she didn't think the changes were the ones that those in authority had intended. He was fervent in his pursuit of Reform now. He'd found his purpose in life and she knew that he would never be satisfied until he himself could cast a vote in the elections.

Jennet was about to go up to see Mary when she saw James Hindle threading his way across the parlour to speak to them.

'No Hannah?' he asked as he perched on a spare stool. He sounded disappointed and it reaffirmed

Jennet's suspicion that he genuinely liked her. It would be a real step up in the world for her sister if she could marry a schoolmaster, she thought.

'Not tonight. I think the Feildens are back in town,' she said.

'Aye. They are. That's why I wanted to see her – to see if she was all right.'

'All right?' asked Jennet. 'Why wouldn't she be?'

'Apparently there was a bit of trouble about a book,' he told her. 'It was one that Mr Feilden had lent to me, but he'd neglected to mention it to his wife and she thought it had gone missing.'

'What's that got to do with our Hannah?' asked Titus.

'Well, Mr Feilden said that his wife had got alarmed and the house had been searched for it and that although the book wasn't there, she'd uncovered some papers in the maid's room that upset her. I wondered what it was all about.'

Jennet stared at him and then turned to Titus. 'Is this owt to do with thee teaching her to read and write?' she asked.

'How should I know?' he replied. 'What sort of papers?' he asked James. 'Pamphlets and such like?'

'I don't know,' he said. 'That's why I was hoping Hannah would be here, so I could ask her about it.'

'She'd better not have done owt silly,' Jennet told him. 'She did well to get that job and she'd be a fool to lose it.'

'Mr Feilden has no call to object to pamphlets,' Titus told her.

'Tha doesn't know it were pamphlets,' Jennet replied, wishing that she could see Hannah herself and find out what had gone on.

'Well, she's not been dismissed so it can't have been anything of importance,' said Titus. 'Storm in a teacup, that's all.'

'Let's hope so,' said Jennet. 'She's a good lass,' she told the schoolmaster, feeling the need to defend her sister. 'She wouldn't have done owt wrong.'

'I'm sure she hasn't,' he replied. 'I was concerned, that's all.'

'Is tha talkin' about that maid at the Feildens?' said a man who was sitting at the next table. He must have been listening all the time he had his back turned to them, thought Jennet, and now that he'd turned round she recognised him as the tall man who'd been enquiring about Mary.

'What's it to thee?' she asked. She wanted to add that she didn't like folk who listened in on other people's conversations, but he sounded as if he knew something more and she needed to know what it was. If people were talking about her sister then she needed to set them straight.

The man shrugged his shoulders. 'I heard she stole a valuable book and pawned it.'

'Who told thee that?' Jennet felt indignant anger rising like a flood inside her. How dare this man accuse her sister of stealing?

'My brother was in Starkie's shop when the Feildens' butler came in and asked to have it back.'

Jennet was furious now, but worried too. She knew that Hannah hadn't stolen anything but she also knew that when rumours began they could take on a life of their own and there were plenty of folk who would believe them and pass them on as if they were the gospel truth.

'The book was never missing,' James told the man. 'Mr Feilden lent it to me.'

'Oh aye,' he replied. 'Well, tha knows what they say. There's no smoke without fire.' He drained his pint and stood up to leave.

'Who was that?' demanded Jennet as she watched him bid goodnight to Mrs Hall.

'That's William Hart. One of the ropemakers.'

'How dare he say stuff like that about our Hannah?'

'Take no notice,' said Titus. 'James has explained it to him now.'

'Well, he didn't sound convinced. And I'm not happy about him going round saying things like that. He needs to be stopped.'

'There's nowt tha can do about it,' Titus told her. 'It's just a story. No one's going to believe it. Go up and see Mary. That's what tha came for.'

She picked up her shawl and stood up. 'Our Hannah's a good girl,' she told James again. She'd never forgive that man if he'd sown any doubts in the schoolmaster's mind about her sister. She would like nothing more than to see Hannah well married and provided for so that she would never have to set foot in a mill or be in service to the gentry ever again.

'How is she?' she asked Mrs Hall about Mary before she went up.

'Stronger,' said the woman. 'She's eaten a bit and the bleeding's much less now. She's young and resilient. I think she'll come through.'

Jennet went up the steps and tapped on Mary's door. She was still lying in bed, but she was awake and didn't look so deathly as she had earlier. Jennet pulled up the little chair and sat down.

'Was Hannah here?' asked Mary. 'I'm not sure if I dreamt it.'

'Aye, she was here,' said Jennet. 'It was Hannah as made them go for Dr Barlow.'

'She's not come again.'

'She's busy at the Feildens. They're back from the country house. I'm sure she'll come to see thee again when she can get away.'

'Aye. I'd like that,' said Mary. 'I didn't want to fall out with her.'

'I'm glad,' Jennet told her. 'Thee and Hannah were always such good friends. It would be a shame if summat spoiled that.'

'Aye. I were just upset, that's all.'

'About our Titus not lettin' thee stay?' asked Jennet.

'No. About her gettin' that job and me being stuck here. It didn't seem fair. She never told me about it and I had no chance to enquire until it were too late. Not that it would have done me any good, I suppose, because I only had Mrs Hall to write me a character.'

'What dost tha mean?' asked Jennet.

'A character letter to say that I'm honest and hard-working. No one'll take a maid on now without one. I should have had one from Mr Sudell, but he never give us one.'

Jennet tried to make sense of what Mary was telling her. 'So Mr Sudell never wrote one for Hannah either?'

'No. If tha'd not been so friendly with Mrs Whittaker and got her to speak for her then Hannah would never have got that position. But

I had no one to speak for me. That's why I ended up like this.'

'I never asked Mrs Whittaker,' said Jennet, puzzled by what Mary was telling her. 'But I'm right sorry tha didn't get chance of a proper job. I wish that I'd tried harder to persuade Titus to let thee stay on with us.'

'I don't suppose it would have made much difference. I couldn't have imposed on thee when I couldn't find work,' Mary said. 'And I suppose it could be worse. I have a roof over my head and Mrs Hall is kindly, in her way, and Mr Starkie has paid for the doctor and suchlike.'

'I'm glad of that,' said Jennet. She didn't say that she'd seen Starkie with Alice and that she had her doubts about him.

Chapter Nineteen

Mary washed herself carefully in the warm water that Mrs Hall had carried up the stairs from the kitchen. She'd had enough of being stuck in her room and was determined to get dressed and go downstairs. For one thing, the weather had taken a turn for the worse and it was chilly up in the attic unless she stopped in bed with her blankets pulled up under her chin.

She clung on to the bannister rail as she eased herself down the steps. The bleeding had just about stopped, but she still felt very sore where the bandaging had rubbed her delicate skin, and she was glad that there'd been no visit from Mr Starkie. She hoped that he would wait until she was fully recovered before he resumed his attentions. Still, she was grateful that everything was being paid for. She doubted that Mrs Hall would have nursed her otherwise, and she might even have packed her off to the workhouse if she'd thought she was too much of a burden.

She heard voices as she approached the parlour door and wondered who was there at this time of the day. She went in to find William Hart and Mrs Hall sitting by the fire, each with a drink in their hand. There'd be hell to pay if Mr Starkie found her with him, she thought to herself. She was surprised that Mrs Hall was still letting him in after what had happened, but she supposed that Mrs Hall wasn't one to ever turn away a paying customer.

'Mary!' he said. 'Is tha feeling better? Come and sit down.' He fetched a chair and placed it near to the blaze, even plumping up a cushion and sliding it in behind her back as she lowered herself gingerly to the seat. She wished he wouldn't. It wasn't just that she was afraid of Mr Starkie accusing her of encouraging him; she really didn't like the man. It was hard to explain why she found him so irritating, but she disliked the way he allowed his gaze to linger on her for far too long, the way he hung around like a damp miasma even when she tried to hint that he should go away, and his tall lanky body that seemed to make him stoop all the time. He certainly didn't have the charm of Mr Starkie and although she supposed he was nice enough in his way, he just wasn't her idea of how a man should be.

'Here.' Mrs Hall put a half-pint of beer down next to her. 'Dost tha want owt to eat? There's a hotpot about ready?'

'Aye. Thanks.'

'What about thee?' Mrs Hall asked William Hart.

He shook his thin face. 'I'd best get back before I'm missed,' he said, his eyes hardly leaving Mary. She would be glad when he was gone, she thought, although he still lingered for a while watching her eat, until he eventually made it to the door and let himself out.

'He's an odd one. He gives me the creeps,' said Mary as she scraped her dish.

'His heart's in t' right place,' Mrs Hall told her.

'More than can be said for the rest of him,' replied Mary, pulling a face. 'I thought I might get a bit of air. I'm that sick of being cooped up.'

'Aye. Well, mind tha doesn't go far. I don't want to have to be sending a search party after thee,' Mrs Hall told her.

Mary wore her clogs and put her shawl over her head. She was in no mood to draw attention to herself and just wanted to be warm and comfortable. She'd walk up to the top of King

Street and back, she thought. That would be far enough for her first time out.

When she reached the top of Shorrock Fold she had to lean against the wall for a moment to steady herself. Although she'd felt much better whilst she was inside, the shock of the cold air seemed to have robbed her of what strength she'd built up and her legs were dithering like a jelly. Behind her she heard a door slam and turned to see Mr Starkie coming out of his shop. He must have seen her and come to check if she was all right. She stood upright, so's not to appear ill, and pushed the shawl back from her head on to her shoulders, ready to greet him with a smile.

She saw him hesitate when their eyes met. He looked surprised.

'Mary.' He glanced behind him. 'It's good to see thee up and about.'

'Aye. I'm feelin' better.' She was about to thank him for making the arrangements for her care but he interrupted her.

'I'm in a bit of a hurry,' he said. 'I'll see thee later.' And he was gone. Striding off down King Street as if he had a very important rendezvous.

Mary heard the shop door again and recognised Alice, who purposely averted her gaze as she walked past. She must have been embarrassed to be seen coming out of the pawnbroker's, thought

Mary as she made her way back to the Star. She'd looked well dressed though, not like she was living in poverty.

Mary was glad to get back inside and sit down in the kitchen where she could warm her hands at the fire.

'Tha looks like tha's seen a ghost, tha's that pale,' remarked Mrs Hall. 'I'll make a pot o' tea.'

'I saw Mr Starkie.'

'Oh, aye.' Mrs Hall paused from counting the spoonfuls of tea into the pot.

'He said he were rushing off. I didn't get chance to thank him.'

'Thank him? What for?'

'For payin' for t' doctor and for my keep.'

'Aye.' Mrs Hall grasped a cloth to pick up the hot kettle and poured boiling water on to the tea leaves. 'Best say nowt to him about that,' she advised.

'Why not?'

Mrs Hall didn't answer for a moment. 'I'm not at liberty to say. Sworn secret, tha knows,' she said, touching the side of her nose with a fore-finger.

'But it was him as paid?'

Mrs Hall shook her head. 'I can't say,' she repeated.

'Then who?' Mary couldn't think of anyone else. Her father certainly wouldn't have sent money. John would, of course, but he had no money other than what she'd given him, unless … She really hoped that he hadn't gone back to stealing to pay for her care. There was Titus and Jennet. She knew they felt a bit to blame for her ending up here and Jennet had been kind to her, but she doubted they had the cash to spare.

'Don't fret about it,' said Mrs Hall. 'Everything's paid for a while and then tha can get back to work as usual.'

'I'm not sure I want to get back to that kind of work,' she told Mrs Hall.

'Well, if tha wants to go back to t' mill or into service again, tha's got time to look for summat,' she said. 'But when t' money's done I'll expect thee to pay thy way if tha stays here.'

Mary stayed downstairs for the rest of the afternoon, keeping warm by the fire and watching as Mrs Hall went about her jobs.

'I could be helping,' she offered. 'I could be shelling peas or summat whilst I'm sitting here.'

'Rest up whilst tha can,' Mrs Hall told her. 'It's a rare thing to have chance to be idle.'

It was true. Mary couldn't remember ever having been able to sit about like a lady and do nothing, and to tell the truth she thought it was a bit boring. She would have welcomed some honest work to help pass the time, but Mrs Hall would have none of it.

As it approached knocking-off time in the mills, she went to open the front door and Mary heard her talking to William Hart in the parlour. She sighed. He didn't seem able to stay away.

'Take him his tea, will tha?' asked Mrs Hall when she'd spooned a generous portion of potato pie into a dish.

'Has he no home to go to?' grumbled Mary, wincing as she stood up.

'He's not wed, if that's what tha's asking. And he's not short of a bob or two either.'

'Aye, well, some lass'll be lucky then,' she said as she pushed open the kitchen door.

'Mary!' He appeared to have taken over Mr Starkie's seat by the fire. She put the meal down on the table and fetched him a spoon. He smiled up at her and she hoped that he didn't think he was in with a chance now that Mr Starkie had made himself scarce. The thought made her shudder. Tomorrow she would begin to go round the mills again. Hopefully she'd find a proper job before the money ran out and she could say goodbye to this place for ever.

Next morning Mary got up early and washed and dressed herself. She didn't feel too bad and after breakfast she put on her shawl and went out to look for work. But rather than going to the mills she found herself drawn towards King Street. She'd thought about Hannah more and more whilst she'd been ill and she wanted to thank her for what she'd done that night. She knew that if Hannah hadn't sent someone to fetch Dr Barlow she probably wouldn't be alive now. She ought to go and thank her. Besides, she missed her friend and maybe it was time for them to make up.

Mary had passed the Feildens' house many times and she walked past it now before pausing and then walking back to the gate. She'd seen Mrs Feilden going out in the carriage so she knew the family weren't home at the moment. Would it do any harm to knock on the back door and ask if Hannah would see her for a moment?

She pushed open the gate and made her way around the side path. She knocked and it was opened by a man with a sour expression.

'Is Hannah here?' she asked.

'Who's asking?'

'I'm Mary Sharples. I'm her friend.'

'Hannah is working. She has no time to be chatting with the likes of thee. Tha can see her when it's her afternoon off.'

The man closed the door in her face. Mary wondered whether she should knock again, but she knew she'd only get the same answer. She trailed back to the gate, glancing up at the windows where she thought she saw someone twitching at a blind. Maybe it was Hannah and she'd seen her coming up the path and told the man to send her away. Mary closed the gate behind her with a click of the latch. She had no idea when it was Hannah's afternoon off. She'd just have to wait and hope that she came down to the Star again. And if she didn't want to be friends then Mary could hardly blame her. What she'd said was cruel and unnecessary. She'd been angry and disappointed, but she could understand why Hannah had wanted the job for herself, and she had to admit that in her place she would probably have done the same.

Chapter Twenty

There was to be yet another supper party and Hannah was kept busy running up and down the stairs preparing the table. Every time she went up, she peeped out of the dining room into the hallway to see if she could catch sight of any visitors so she could go back down to tell Cook who had arrived. It was satisfying to see the disbelief on her face every time she related a name.

'Mr Swarbrick, the shopkeeper? Mr Pilkington, the joiner?' gasped Cook in disbelief when Hannah told her who Mr Horrocks had answered the door to. 'Tradesmen!' she muttered as she stirred her sauce. 'I never thought I'd be cooking for tradesmen. They'll be getting above themselves, mark my words. They'll be thinking they can come and ring the front doorbell every time they arrive instead of coming round to the back door.'

Hannah laughed to herself at the image of Mr Horrocks having to welcome Mr Duckworth, the butcher, at the front door when he'd been more used to making him stand at the back entrance whilst Cook sniffed at the meat he'd brought to check that it was as fresh as he claimed. But these were the people Mr Feilden had to impress if he wanted to take his seat in Parliament.

On her next foray upstairs, Hannah recognised the lanky frame of William Hart, handing his hat and coat to Mr Horrocks. She was pretty sure he wasn't a property owner, but his father was, so perhaps he'd come in his stead.

'The ropemaker?' asked Cook when Hannah reported it to her. She shook her head as if it was an affront too many.

'He was talking to Mr Feilden in the hall,' related Hannah. 'They were deep in conversation – like old friends!'

'Tha's having me on now,' declared Cook. 'I'm sure of it.'

'Go up and look for thyself!'

'I've too much to do here,' she complained. 'Even though them as are going to eat it don't know duck from goose. It'll be wasted on 'em,' she declared as she added the finishing touches of garnish to the roast bird.

The last thing to be carried up for the table was the soup tureen. It was heavy and hot. Hannah was afraid of it slipping from her grasp as she climbed the stairs with it clutched in a thick cloth. She pushed the door open with her hip and placed the tureen carefully, wiping away a slight spill as she heard Mr Horrocks announce supper. She slipped into the shadows of the stairwell to watch. The men were well dressed. Most had made an effort even if their clothes were not as fashionable as the usual guests. They looked satisfied, she thought, as their glances darted here and there as they took in the finery of the grand house.

Her stomach lurched as she caught sight of James Hindle. He was talking with William Hart. She stepped back, not wanting him to see her. She knew she would be in trouble with Mrs Feilden again if she was seen speaking to one of the guests.

'No meeting tonight?' Jennet asked as she folded laundry on the table ready to return it to her customers the next morning.

'Not worth it,' said Titus, settling at the fireside and packing his small pipe with a twist of tobacco. 'Feilden's got most of the voters I know at his house for a fancy supper. And as for the rest of 'em, Turner'll be plying 'em with drinks down at the Old Bull until they're so fuddled they'd agree to vote for t' cat if it were puttin' up.'

'And what about Dr Bowring?'

'No sign of him yet. They say he's coming tomorrow, but he's above that sort of common bribery. I just hope there's enough upstanding folk to see what's right and fair and vote for the chap.'

'Aye,' said Jennet. 'Mrs Whittaker says there's little chance of a washhouse if he doesn't get in.'

'Well, it would only take thy trade,' said Titus as he watched her parcel the laundry.

'That's not the point though, is it? They say as cleanliness is next to Godliness, but whilst Mr Whittaker's keen to preach his Godliness he doesn't seem to care about how folks are keeping clean.'

'Aye, well, that's not a man's concern,' agreed Titus.

'It's a pity then as women don't have more of a say.'

'Tha sounds like that Mrs Kitchen now.'

'But she's right, isn't she?'

'I suppose so,' conceded Titus. 'But politics is men's work.' He lit his pipe and the smoke drifted up to the ceiling and gradually filled the parlour as he puffed. Jennet took the laundry into the back so it wouldn't be returned smelling worse than when it had come.

'Well, we'll soon know,' she said, sitting down and picking up a stocking from the overflowing pile of her own mending. 'Though I bet it won't make a difference.' She sewed in silence for a few minutes. 'Dost tha think our Hannah will go to London with the Feildens?' she asked. 'I can't imagine her going all that way.'

'James Hindle would be put out about it,' he replied.

'So tha's noticed then? I thought he were taken with her, but I didn't like to say owt. It would be a step up for her if she wed him.'

'Aye, it would. And he's a good man.'

'It'd be nice to see her settled with a school-master for a husband.'

'So tha thinks a weaver like me wouldn't be good enough for her?' he asked.

Jennet paused and studied him for a moment. 'I thought tha were good enough to wait for thee,' she reminded him.

He said nothing. They never discussed George Anderton and rarely alluded to him, although Jennet knew that he was always there, between them. There had been an unspoken agreement that nothing would ever be said to Bessie either. The child would always believe that Titus was her real father. It was better that way.

'Aye,' he said at last. 'And I'm grateful.'

They sat in silence for a while, Titus smoking and Jennet sewing as a brisk wind got up and rattled at the ill-fitting windows and blew under the front door, making the rug rise up from the floor. There was a sound of shouting in the distance and Jennet thought Titus was right about Mr Turner rolling out the barrels again.

'Mary said a funny thing,' said Jennet after a while. 'She said that she couldn't get a job as a maid without a character reference and that Mr Sudell had never written one for her or Hannah.'

'That right?'

'But Hannah got a job.'

'Aye.' He seemed engrossed in the pamphlet he'd picked up, but she knew that he wasn't reading because his eyes never moved across the page.

'Mary seemed to think that I'd asked Mrs Whittaker to speak for her.'

'Did she now?'

'Titus!' Jennet waited until he looked up at her. 'Tha knows summat, doesn't thee? It were thee that told our Hannah about the job.'

'Mr Feilden mentioned they were looking for a new maid and I said I knew someone. That must have been good enough.'

'Aye.' Jennet still wasn't convinced, but Titus had gone back to his reading and she needed to make sure the girls' clothes were mended ready for church in the morning.

The vicar's sermon seemed to go on and on for an eternity as he preached about the responsibilities weighing down on the shoulders of the new voters. The atmosphere was sombre and Peggy kept asking when they were going to sing again. Jennet had every sympathy with her and began to think that Titus had a point when he said he'd rather spend his Sunday morning at leisure than stuck on the uncomfortable pews of the parish church. Still, it was over at last and she exchanged a brief greeting with Mrs Whittaker before they walked home.

An air of excitement pervaded the town and people seemed to be hurrying here and there with a purpose, unlike the usual quiet of a Sunday. After a quick dinner they walked up to Tacketts Field to listen to the candidates give their final speeches. Apart from the hustings it was like a fair. There were stalls selling gingerbread, toffee and hot black puddings. Beer was flowing freely, and even those with no vote were taking advantage of the generosity and filling up their cups. Meanwhile, at the far end of the field, the Temperance Band was playing a selection of hymns suitable for the Sabbath day and Mr Livesey was preaching a warning about the demon drink, though few appeared to be listening to him.

Titus elbowed through the melee and managed to get two cups of beer, though much of it spilled on to the churning mud beneath their feet before he managed to get back to where Jennet was waiting on the edge of the crush with Peggy and Bessie. She took her drink and Titus pulled two pieces of toffee from his pocket, giving the larger one to Peggy.

'Bowring's here,' he said. 'I've just seen his carriage pull up. They should be starting soon. Shall we try to get to the front?'

'I don't know. I'm worried about the childer getting trodden on,' she said, hoping that he wasn't going to leave her alone with them.

'Aye. We'll probably be able to hear from where we are,' he conceded. 'Look, there's our Hannah. She must have got the afternoon off.'

'Where?' Jennet stood on tiptoe and searched the crowd for the familiar figure of her sister, waving a hand in the air when she saw her to try to attract her attention.

Hannah waved back and squeezed through until she reached them.

'I never thought to find thee in this,' she gasped. 'I've never seen so many folk all in one place. But I wanted to give thee this.' She thrust a brown paper parcel into Jennet's hand. 'It's the new blouse for Mrs Pickering. I've sat up late every night to get it finished.'

'I'm that grateful!' Jennet kissed her then grasped her by the arm and pulled her close. 'But what were that trouble about? James Hindle said tha'd been accused of stealin' a book.'

'I never did!' she protested. 'Did he not say that it'd been lent to him?' She hadn't had the opportunity to speak to James since the trouble about the writing and she was worried about what his reaction would be. She was afraid that if he agreed with the Feildens that she'd done something wrong, she could never think of him in the same way again.

'Aye. But William Hart seemed to think there were more to it,' Jennet told her.

'Aye, there was. It were the spoiled blouse. It's that similar to one that Mrs Feilden has in her drawer that she thought it were hers at first.'

'But tha set her right?'

'Aye. She knew I were being truthful when tha called with the cloth for a new one. I didn't know tha'd been.'

'I came round t' back,' Jennet told her. 'But that chap who's the butler took it from me and then just closed the door on me like I were a beggar or summat.'

'Aye. That doesn't surprise me. He always acts as if he has a stick up his arse.'

'Hannah!' Her sister giggled.

'Well, it's true. Though he had his nose put out of joint last night when Mr Feilden invited all and sundry to a supper party. He seems to think they'll all vote for him now and not for Dr Bowring. Dost tha think they will?' she asked Titus. 'Surely they know Dr Bowring should get one of their votes?'

Titus frowned. 'Who knows?' he asked. 'The trouble with Bowring is that he's not local and folk tend to side with them as they knows – and them as buys 'em a pint.'

'Tha's drinkin' their free beer.'

'Aye, but I've no vote to cast. If I had, it'd go to Bowring and many are of the same opinion, but we get no say and Reform or no, it doesn't go far enough,' he grumbled.

'Look, there's James Hindle now,' said Jennet, nudging her sister's arm as she saw the schoolmaster weaving a path towards them.

Hannah watched as James threaded through the surging crowd. She could feel the fluttering in her stomach and wasn't sure whether she really wanted to see him or not. She was afraid that he would be disappointed in her, but a wide smile lit his face when his eyes met hers.

'I've never seen anything like it!' he exclaimed. 'I think the whole town's come out!'

'Aye, and so they should,' said Titus. 'It's just a pity they can't all come out for the voting rather than being at their jobs whilst just the privileged few get their say.'

Hannah wanted to ask James what he knew about the missing book, but before she had chance the band finished with a flourish and the candidates climbed up on to the stage. People began to shush one another and at first they couldn't hear the speeches, although a few of the words were caught on the breeze and carried towards them.

Dr Bowring spoke first and his words were earnest as he repeated what he intended to do for the working man. He was met with cheers amongst those who cared to listen, although others were more intent on getting their cups refilled than paying heed to what any of the speakers had to say. Mr Feilden's speech was aimed at the tradesmen and mill owners. He spoke about making the town prosperous, but neglected to comment that it would come at the expense of the working men and women who toiled in the mills for their employers. Mr Turner said nothing much, but received the loudest cheers, mostly from those with drinks in their hands. The temperance folk had given up, Hannah saw. They'd furled their banner and dismantled their small stage. They were fighting a losing battle this afternoon and were probably tired of the insults and manky cabbages being hurled in their direction.

Once the speeches were over, the crowd began to disperse back towards the centre of the town, heading for the pubs.

James touched Hannah's arm. 'I'm right sorry about that trouble with the book,' he told her.

'Tha weren't to blame.'

'No, but it still made me feel bad. And I was that vexed when I heard that they'd put the blame on you.' She glanced up and saw the anger flash in his eyes. Anger on her behalf – and it warmed her through. 'I hope they told you they were sorry.'

'Aye, I got an apology of sorts from Mrs Feilden.'

'Only of sorts?'

'There were more to it,' she said, knowing that she needed to be truthful with him. 'When she were searchin' for the book she found some stuff I'd been writing, hidden under my mattress.'

Hannah felt a hot blush rise to her cheeks. She never talked to anyone about her writing, and she knew that she would never feel quite the same way about him if he disapproved of it as much as Mrs Feilden had. She was taking a risk by telling him, but he was a schoolmaster, so surely he wouldn't think there was anything wrong in reading and writing – and if he asked what she'd written about she needn't tell him. There was no evidence now that it had all been set fire to.

'I didn't know you could read and write!'

'Our Titus taught me.'

'And did Mrs Feilden not approve? I thought she was more forward-thinking than that.'

'I think it were the content,' mumbled Hannah, realising that she would have to tell him more.

'Why? Was it political?'

Hannah shook her head. 'It were a story,' she admitted.

'A story? You write stories?' He sounded impressed. 'What sort of stories?'

'Oh, nowt much.' She thought he must be able to see how red her face was and she half turned away from him. 'But Mrs Feilden said I should stick to the scriptures.'

'There's nothing wrong with stories,' he told her. 'I've had a go myself, but I prefer poetry.'

'What? To write? Tha writes poetry?'

'Aye.' It was his turn to look slightly shame-faced. 'It's not good poetry, but I like to have a go.' They looked at one another for a moment and then he grinned and Hannah laughed too. 'I don't know why we both feel so guilty about it,' he said.

'There are worse vices.' He hesitated. 'Would you let me read some of them? Your stories?' he asked. 'I'll let you see my poetry too, if you'd like.'

'I can't.'

'Well, no matter.' He sounded disappointed. 'I know it can be hard to let someone else see.'

'It's not that,' she told him. 'Mrs Feilden had them burned.'

'What? She burned your work?'

Hannah nodded. She could feel her eyes brimming again at the thought of it.

'She'd no right to do that!' he said. 'I'd be furious if someone did that to me.' He looked at her and saw her tears. 'Aw, Hannah.' He reached out and put his hands on her upper arms. 'I'm that sorry,' he said. 'You must be upset. You've every right to be.'

His sympathy made her cry even more and she felt him pull her towards him, put an arm around her shoulder and hold her against him. He was warm and strong and he smelled of starch and tobacco and ink.

'What's to do with her?' she heard Titus ask.

'Don't tell him,' said Hannah, pulling away and wiping her eyes. 'It's nowt to do with him.'

She saw her sister take Titus by the arm and pull him away. 'Come on,' she said. 'Give 'em a moment.'

James pulled Hannah's arm through his. 'Thing is,' he told her as they walked towards the town centre, 'stories are never lost. The words written down on paper might be gone, but never the story. That's still there, in the imagination. All you have to do is write it down again – and it might even be a better story the next time.'

'I would,' she told him, 'but Mrs Feilden made me promise I wouldn't, and I don't want to lose that job.' She didn't admit to the secret stash of paper and pencils under the floorboard.

'It seems a high price to pay. Do you want me to have a word with Mr Feilden?'

'No.' She shook her head. 'He always listens to his wife.'

'I wonder what it is she's so afeared of.'

'She were afraid I might be writing a penny novel. She's scared to death her daughters might read one.'

He laughed. 'And was it a penny novel?' he teased.

Hannah blushed again. 'No. Not really.' They walked on through the crowds.

'What time do you have to be back?' he asked her.

'Cook said no later than four.'

He took his watch from his waistcoat pocket and glanced at the time. 'That's well over an hour,' he said. 'Would you like to come back to Thunder Alley and read a bit of poetry?'

Hannah paused, but only for a moment. She wasn't sure whether she should go with him, but it wasn't as if he was a stranger and she didn't think Jennet would mind.

'Aye,' she said. 'I'd like that.'

They turned through the market square, away from the worst of the crush, and walked up to Thunder Alley. It was quiet on there, it not being a school day, but one of the stable lads was bringing out a couple of horses. They looked like the ones from Dr Bowring's carriage. As the boy approached he glanced at Hannah and she recognised him.

'Hello, John!'

He nodded in reply to her greeting, but didn't stop as the prancing horses clattered down the street on either side of him, snorting and tossing their heads.

'Someone tha knows?' asked James as Hannah watched him go.

'He used to be a neighbour, when we lived on Paradise Lane.' She didn't elaborate, but she was secretly pleased to see that John looked as if he was doing all right for himself. Seeing John reminded her that she really ought to go to see Mary again when she had her next afternoon off.

She hoped that Mary would find it in her heart to forgive her and that they could be friends again. She missed her company more than she ever expected.

James delved into his trouser pocket for his key and unlocked the door. He glanced around before he opened it for her to go inside and she realised that he was taking a risk too. He might be dismissed from his job if anybody saw him taking a woman into the schoolhouse.

The inside of the house was as neat as a new pin. There was a scrubbed table with two chairs and a wooden rocking chair by the hearth with a well-used cushion lying on it. In front of the fire there was a rag rug crafted from a variety of coloured cottons and she wondered who'd made it for him. He poked at the fire and added another couple of big cobs. It smoked and then the coal caught alight with a blue flame and the room began to warm.

'Sit down,' he said, pointing at the rocking chair and she settled into its curves, thinking that his was the last body to sit there. She plumped the cushion and put it behind her back; then she unfastened her bonnet and slipped it off. The room lacked a woman's touch, she thought as she looked around curiously. The walls were bare except for one picture of a place she didn't recognise and there seemed to be hardly any personal items at all.

He opened a drawer and took out some sheets of paper. She saw that his handwriting was neat, as she would have expected, and not too small. He handed them to her.

'I'll make some tea,' he said, going into the back kitchen for water. She knew exactly how he felt. She would never have been able to stay in the same room with him if he was reading her work. The verses were very good though, and clever too. There were some words that she didn't know and she wasn't sure of their pronunciation, although the rhymes gave her a clue. She wondered if she dared ask him what they meant, but she didn't want to sound stupid.

He was ages coming back and when he did he looked worried. She smiled at him. 'I like them!'

'Do you? I've never shown them to anyone before,' he admitted. 'There's a poets' corner that meets in the beershop on Nab Lane. I keep thinking I should go along and read some out, but I worry that they're not good enough.'

'Tha should go,' she told him as he filled the kettle and put it on to boil.

'Aye. Maybe I will. It would be nice to hear what others are writing too.'

'What sort of folk are they?' asked Hannah, wondering if any of them were women.

'All sorts, I think. Working men. Not gentry.'

'Gentry don't seem to hold with it,' she reminded him.

'It's a pity you can't come with me. If you'd been a mill girl you'd have finished work by then, but the Feildens seem to keep you working all hours.'

'Aye. But it's all right at the Feildens' really, though it's best when they're at the country house. It's a bit of a holiday then and Cook might let me slip out for an hour or two.'

'Sugar?' he asked as he poured her tea.

'Aye, put two in – if tha can spare it,' she added, suddenly feeling guilty at her greed.

He spooned in two generous helpings and handed it to her for her to stir it herself. 'Would you have let me read your stories?' he asked. 'If they hadn't been lost?'

'Aye, of course I would,' she replied, knowing that she would have done no such thing.

They talked for a while about the poems until Hannah had finished her tea. She put the cup of dregs carefully on its saucer and got up to put it on the table. 'What time is it?' she asked, hoping that he wouldn't say it was time to go just yet.

He looked at his watch. 'Twenty to four. I'd best walk you back.'

She put on her bonnet and tied the ribbons into a bow and he refastened his cravat, which had come loose. He banked up the fire so that no sparks would fly on to the rug whilst he was out and then went to the door. He cast an eye up and down the street. There was no one about so he opened it wider for her to go out and briefly she brushed against him as she passed.

She took his arm and they walked towards King Street. The town was still busy, especially outside the pubs, where there seemed to be nothing but shouting and swearing. She saw him frown.

'There's not much respect for the Sabbath,' he muttered as they passed a group who were singing a rude song about the Parliament.

He opened the gate of the King Street house and walked her right up to the back door and knocked. Hannah wished that he would kiss her, but he only smiled and looked her in the eye and said that he hoped he would see her again soon. She wished she knew what he really thought of her. Did he have feelings for her too? It was hard to tell, but she hoped that he did.

Chapter Twenty-One

Jennet had tugged Titus away when she saw the schoolmaster with an arm around her sister.

'I were hopin' to have a word with him,' he grumbled.

'Not now. Let 'em have a while on their own. They don't often get the chance,' she told him. 'There's other things besides elections that're just as important – if not more so!' He didn't look convinced but he followed her across the field and even took Bessie's hand when he saw that she was struggling to keep her feet on the slippery mud.

As they walked, Jennet caught sight of Mary and saw that she was making her way towards them.

'I'm right glad to see thee up and about,' she told her. 'How's tha feelin'?'

'Much better, thanks,' she said. 'Is Hannah not with thee?'

'No. She was, but she got talkin' with somebody. Did tha want to see her?'

'Aye. I were hopin' to have a word with her to thank her properly for what she did.'

'Mary!' The tall figure of William Hart was unmistakeable as he came through the thinning crowd.

'Damn,' she swore softly when she saw him coming. 'I thought I'd managed to give him the slip.'

'Mary,' he repeated, coming up. 'I thought it were thee. I wondered if tha'd like to take my arm, in case tha were feeling tired.'

'I'm all right,' she told him, her irritation clear. 'I'm talkin' with my friends.'

William looked at Titus and Jennet but his face held no trace of a smile. 'She needs someone to look out for her,' he told them. The unspoken accusation was clear. 'Lass like her should never have ended up in a place like the Star.'

'I am here!' Mary told him. 'Tha doesn't need to talk about me like I'm simple or summat. It were my choice to stay at the Star. It were nowt to do with anyone else, least of all thee.'

'Lass like thee deserves a better life,' he persisted. 'Tha should have been able to get a proper job.'

'Aye, well, Mr Sudell never wrote me a character,' she replied. 'So that weren't going to happen.'

'But some managed it all right,' William said, glaring at Titus from under his thick eyebrows.

'I'll tell our Hannah tha were askin' after her,' Titus told Mary and began to walk away.

'Will tha be all right?' asked Jennet, not sure about leaving her.

'Aye,' she said as she slipped her hand through William's arm. 'Don't fret about me.'

'I will tell Hannah,' added Jennet. 'Happen she'll come to see thee if she has some time off.'

She took Peggy's hand and they hurried after Titus who was striding away with Bessie hurrying beside him. She could tell that he was annoyed.

'He's a rum beggar,' she said when she caught up with him. 'He seems to be sweet on Mary though.'

'She could do worse.'

'She doesn't seem to like him very much.'

'Can't blame her for that,' he replied.

'Why dost tha not like him? I thought he were one of the Reformers?'

'Aye. He's started coming to meetings, but only because he fancies his chances with Mary. Anyroad, why should I like somebody as speaks to me like that?'

'He were a bit ill-mannered,' admitted Jennet. 'He seems to think that what happened to Mary were our fault. Perhaps it was in a way.'

'She has family of her own,' said Titus. 'Just because she were Hannah's friend doesn't make her our responsibility. We've our own to think about,' he said.

Mary tried to hold William's arm without really touching him, but he pulled her closer. 'Hold tight. Tha doesn't want to slip and fall down in this mud,' he said.

'I'll be all right. Tha doesn't need to walk all the way with me.'

'I was going that way anyway. I'll see thee safe back,' he said.

They walked in silence until they reached the marketplace when William suddenly said, 'I hated seeing thee with that Starkie.'

'Aye, but I've reason to be grateful to him,' she told him. 'I'd have been on the street or in the workhouse if it weren't for him.'

'Not necessarily,' he replied.

'No. But if it hadn't been him it would have been someone else.' She almost said *even thee* but she held her tongue. She didn't want to give him any ideas.

'But tha's not the sort of lass that does that.'

'I am – if it's a choice between that and starvin'.'

'But look how it ended.'

'I'm all right now. Anyway, it's nowt to do with thee.'

They turned down Shorrock Fold to find it was filled with drunks who'd been moved on from the town centre and who'd begun to stagger down the smaller alleyways looking for trouble. A couple of men were knocking seven bells out of one another outside the pawnshop whilst a third was throwing up on the doorstep.

'Tha can't stop on here,' said William as they waited for Mrs Hall to answer the door. 'Is there really nowhere else tha could go?'

'It's nowt to do with thee,' she told him again.

'Tha looks tired. I'm worried about thee.'

'Tha needn't be. I can take care of myself.'

She would have liked to linger by the fire and have a drink and a bowl of hotpot, but she was keener to shake him off and Mrs Hall seemed in no rush to turn him out, even though the beerhouse was officially closed. So she climbed the stairs to sit alone in her room, listening to the rumpus outside. He was a nuisance, she thought. And if he thought that she was going to take up with him now that Mr Starkie had gone, he could think again. She picked up the sponge with its ribbon attached and after heaving open the sash window she threw it out into the street to be trampled underfoot. She had no clear idea of what she was going to do, but she was finished being made a fool of by men.

Next morning, Jennet brushed her hair and put on her best bonnet to take the new blouse to Mrs Pickering. It was an errand she would have liked to postpone, but she reasoned that the sooner she did it, the sooner she could put it behind her.

The sun was trying to break through an overcast sky and although it kept brightening a little, it never really shone and the gloom added to Jennet's mood as she walked down Richmond Terrace. Peggy was in school and she'd left Bessie with Molly for half an hour.

She climbed the steps to the black-painted door of the Pickerings' house and rang the bell. Footsteps sounded in the hall and a young maid opened the door.

'I've brought this for Mrs Pickering,' she said. 'It's her laundry.' She half hoped the maid would just thank her and take it, meaning she wouldn't have to face the owner of the garment she'd ruined, but she knew that she needed to apologise and explain about the new blouse.

'Please, step inside a moment. I'll tell Mrs Pickering that you're here.'

Jennet wiped her feet on the doormat and stood in the hall. The black and white tiled floor was identical to that in Mrs Whittaker's house and she wondered if the same workman had laid it.

'Mrs Eastwood,' said a voice. Mrs Pickering was a middle-aged lady whose husband ran a carting business. Jennet knew that she was no better than herself and had begun her life in one of the back streets, but since the Pickerings had come into money she considered herself to be a cut above her former acquaintances. 'You're very late returning my laundry.'

'I know. I'm sorry, Mrs Pickering. I had an accident with thy blouse,' confessed Jennet. 'I've had to replace it with a new one. But I'm sure tha'll find it's even better than the first.'

Mrs Pickering sniffed; then she took the parcel and tore off the wrapping. She shook out the blouse and held it up to the light to examine it carefully.

'The embroidery is different,' she complained.

'It's better,' Jennet told her. 'No one can match our Hannah's workmanship when it comes to stitching. Look how neat the seams are. The old one wasn't anywhere near as well made.'

Mrs Pickering sniffed again. 'I'm not sure my seamstress would be very pleased to hear you say that.'

'I didn't mean any disrespect,' said Jennet, realising that the woman was determined to find fault with her.

. 'I suppose it will have to do,' said Mrs Pickering as she folded it up and handed it to the maid. 'Hannah's your sister, isn't she?'

'That's right.'

'Works at the Feildens' house on King Street?'

'Aye, she does.'

'I heard she worked for the Sudells before?'

'Aye. Yes. She's very experienced,' said Jennet, wondering what Mrs Pickering was leading up to. Her tone didn't strike her as being that associated with polite conversation.

'Sally here worked for the Sudells, didn't you?' she said to the maid.

'That's right, Mrs Pickering.'

'Did you know a Hannah who worked there?'

'Hannah Chadwick? Yes. She was one of the parlour maids.'

'Sally came to us on the recommendation of a friend,' said Mrs Pickering. 'She was struggling to find another post because Mr Sudell neglected to write characters for the staff he left behind. Isn't that so, Sally?'

'That's right, Mrs Pickering.' The girl's gaze flicked from her employer to Jennet and back again.

'So your sister did well to get a position at the Feildens' house. I know Mrs Feilden is very particular about her staff.'

Jennet didn't reply. She knew that the woman had a point. Mary had said the same thing. And if Mrs Feilden had insisted on a character, which was what the woman was implying, then where had Hannah's come from?

'She did do well,' Jennet told Mrs Pickering, hoping that her anxiety didn't show. 'She's very competent.'

'Pity the same can't be said for you,' remarked Mrs Pickering, seeing her chance to be even more obnoxious. 'I think it goes without saying that I will employ another laundress in the future and I won't be giving you any recommendations.'

'Well, I'm sorry for that,' she replied, determined to remain polite under the woman's provocation. It would be her loss anyway. She'd soon realise that when her petticoats came back greyed and creased.

'Show her out,' Mrs Pickering told the maid and turned her back on Jennet to return to her parlour.

Jennet was tempted to make a face and stick out her tongue at the retreating figure but she resisted.

'So tha's Hannah's sister?' whispered the maid as she pulled open the door.

'Aye, that's right.'

'Hannah were good to me when I were at Woodfold,' said Sally. 'And if that new blouse were made by her it's bound to be better than the old one. She's lucky to have summat stitched by Hannah.'

'I'll tell her tha said so next time I see her,' said Jennet as she stepped out.

She walked home feeling worried. The interview with Mrs Pickering had gone much as she'd expected and even if the woman did try to ruin her business for her, she doubted she'd succeed. She had a lot of loyal customers and this was the one and only time that she'd spoiled an item she was laundering. And even though she'd cursed herself time and again for her moment of inattention, she hoped that most folk would see reason and know that accidents occasionally happened.

What worried her more was the talk of Hannah and how she'd got her job. There was something odd about it and she knew that she'd have to have it out with her sister the next time she saw her. She just hoped to goodness that there was an explanation and that Hannah hadn't done something dishonest.

Chapter Twenty-Two

Election Day greeted the candidates and voters with a fine drizzle that was barely visible in the air, but soon soaked through the clothing of anyone who stood out in it for more than a few minutes. The hustings stood empty and abandoned. The few flags and colours that hadn't been cleared away hung limp and still, and puddles formed in the hollows where so many feet had trodden the Sunday before.

The sound of the engines in the mills filled the air with a steady beat and Mary thought that there would be plenty whose heads were thumping along in unison after the amount of free beer that had been drunk in the past few days.

Mrs Hall was morose. Beershops had been told that they must close by eight and as she sat drinking her morning tea, Mary could see her mentally calculating how much the restriction would cost her.

'Dost tha need anything doing?' she asked her, noticing that she hadn't made a start on the potatoes.

'Leave 'em,' replied Mrs Hall. 'Nobody'll come in tonight. It's not worth it.'

'Is it all right if I go out for a bit then?' she asked.

'Aye. Do what tha pleases.'

Mary went upstairs for her bonnet and the little jacket that Mr Starkie had given her. She'd earned them, she thought – more than earned them.

She let herself out into the drizzle and began to walk briskly. She followed the gathering crowd towards the theatre, where the election was being held.

She was surprised by the number of people who thronged the outside of the building – men, women and children. They looked thin and their clothes were either patched or hung in tatters where there was no longer enough cloth to mend. They cheered when they saw Dr Bowring.

Mary watched, the drizzle soaking dark patches on the shoulders of her jacket, as the other candidates arrived. As well as Dr Bowring there was Mr Feilden and Mr Turner. And she recognised Mr Hargreaves from the Dandy Mill. Like many of the overlookers he'd been sworn in as a special constable for the day to help keep the peace.

The magistrates had forbidden the bands and the flag-waving, but even so there was a palpable excitement as the crowd watched the electors come, sometimes alone, or sometimes in a group, to say who they were voting for. Some came wearing their best clothes, others, like Mr Duckworth the butcher, whose striped apron was besmirched with blood where he'd wiped his hands, came straight from their shops or businesses.

Mary eased her way in through the open doorway to stand out of the rain and try to hear the votes that were being given to Mr Fleming, the returning officer, who sat at a table carried down from the furniture shop, with pens and ink in front of him to record the votes of each elector in his book.

As the votes were cast, the crowds of supporters cheered, trying to outdo one another as if those who made the most noise would garner the most votes for their candidate. The three potential members of parliament sat on the stage behind Mr Fleming and acknowledged their gratitude for each vote they were given – and gave black looks to those who had made them a promise they didn't keep. Some of the men in the crowd were trying to keep a tally, but they soon lost count and began arguing amongst themselves about who was winning.

Mary sat down on one of the red plush seats. She thought that if she kept still and quiet no one would notice her and it was better than being out in the rain or going back to the Star.

'Mary, isn't it?' A shudder ran through her as she recognised his voice. 'Tha remembers me from t'Dandy Mill, doesn't tha?'

'Aye. I remember thee,' she said, glancing up at Hargreaves's leering face as he leaned over the back of her seat.

'I thought tha'd gone off to work in one of them big country houses.'

'Aye. It were for Sudell.'

'Right. So tha's back now. Is tha lookin' for work?'

'Is there owt going?' she asked. It was the only mill where she hadn't enquired so she doubted it.

'I could always find summat for thee.' Hargreaves winked at her and she knew that he would never take her back on at the Dandy without expecting her to do him a 'favour', as he referred to it. That's why she'd never been to ask him. But had she ended up any better off? Mr Starkie, for all his charm and promises, had been no different.

He put his hand on her shoulder and patted it. 'Come and see me if tha wants a job,' he told her.

She made an excuse that she had to be somewhere. She just wanted to get away from him, so she went back out into the rain and wandered about for a while. She bought a hot potato from a cart for her dinner and sat in the wet to eat it. Then she walked down to the marketplace where the stalls were packed away and the cobbles were slick. She was cold and miserable and she knew that she ought to go back to the Star, but she couldn't face it in case William Hart was there. He wouldn't let her alone.

In the end she went back to the theatre and pushed her way in again, hoping that Hargreaves wouldn't see her. She was soaked through to her petticoat and one of her fancy boots had let in water. She guessed that the little feather on her bonnet would be a sorry sight too and she was glad that she hadn't caught a reflection of herself in a window.

It was busier now that the time for voting was approaching its four o'clock deadline. Men who'd been busy all day came rushing in and approached Mr Fleming at his table. They gave their names and told him who they voted for: *Mr Turner, Dr Bowring, Mr Feilden*. The votes seemed evenly spread and as Mary sat in her damp skirts she listened to the whispers around her as people predicted the winners.

Soon Mr Fleming stood up and banged his gavel several times in rapid succession. 'It is now four o'clock and the voting is closed!' he announced. 'I will total the votes and shortly there will be an announcement of the new members of Parliament for the town and surrounding district of Blackburn!'

He reseated himself and took up his pen with an air of quiet concentration. The candidates looked tense and the crowd fell silent so as not to disturb the calculating.

Mary decided that she would wait for the announcement and then go back to the Star to tell them. She knew they were all hoping that Dr Bowring would get a seat.

Hannah was helping Cook prepare what was expected to be a victory supper, although she couldn't help but wonder if their certainty was a little misplaced. Although Mr Feilden was well known and well respected in the town, she knew that men could be fickle and, like not counting chickens until they were hatched, she wondered whether the Feildens weren't being too optimistic. Besides, she was secretly hoping that Mr Feilden would lose. There had been talk of her and Cook as well as Mr Horrocks accompanying the family to London. The Blackburn townhouse would be closed up or even sold, and when they did return next summer, when Parliament took its recess, they would go to their country house and Hannah feared that she would be required to stay in London. The thought of it made her want to cry because it would mean that she would never see James Hindle, and just when he had begun to make it plain that he actually liked her. It was too cruel.

'Baste that leg of lamb, will thee,' said Cook and Hannah took a thick cloth to pull the meat-laden tray towards her whilst she spooned its own juices over it. It smelled so good that she felt her mouth begin to water and she hoped that there would be enough left for it to come back down to the servants' table after the family had eaten.

Mr Horrocks came down to the kitchen. 'I hear that the voting is over,' he told them.

'Did Mr Feilden win then?' asked Cook as she put the lid back on the simmering soup pot.

'They're still counting,' he said. 'I've promised a lad sixpence to run back with the result as soon as it's announced.'

He sat down at the table and Cook poured tea. Mrs Feilden and her daughters had gone to the theatre to be with Mr Feilden for the result and the house was quiet.

Then they were disturbed by a frantic knocking at the back door. Mr Horrocks went to open it and Hannah caught sight of a scrawny little boy with a dirty face and a missing front tooth, hopping from one leg to the other.

'Tha promised me sixpence,' he said.

Mr Horrocks felt in his pocket and took out the silver coin, which the lad eyed greedily.

'Well?'

'Turner,' he said.

'What? No. Tell me who won the seats!'

'Turner,' repeated the boy, holding out his hand.

'I don't believe it,' said Mr Horrocks. 'Tha's never been to get the real result. On thy way!'

The boy let out a howl after he tried to grab the coin and Mr Horrocks dealt him a slap around the head. 'It were true!' he protested. 'They're all saying as the winner is Turner!'

Mr Horrocks shut the door on him and turned to Cook. He looked shaken. 'That can't be right,' he said as the lad continued to protest outside.

Moments later they heard the carriage stop at the front of the house and the grim-faced butler hurried up the stairs to open the door. Cook sighed. 'I hope they still want their supper, even if Mr Feilden has lost,' she said.

*

When it was announced that the seats had gone to Mr Feilden and Mr Turner there was a deafening roar of *'No!'* that nearly raised the roof right off the theatre. Men jumped to their feet and stared at one another in disbelief, asking if what they'd heard was true. Others were demanding that Mr Fleming count the votes again. There was only one vote in it between Dr Bowring and Mr Turner and surely he'd made a mistake. But Mr Fleming shook his head and told them that he'd checked the numbers twice. Mr Turner had won one of the seats and there was nothing more he could do.

On the stage, Mr Turner was grinning and shaking hands with his supporters as they offered their congratulations. Dr Bowring sat very still and never spoke, even though several men were trying to offer him condolences.

She could hear the shouts of disbelief and anger as the news spread outside to the waiting crowd. Mr Fleming banged his gavel and appealed for calm, and Hargreaves and the other special constables rolled up their sleeves, prepared for trouble.

Mary thought that she'd best get back to the Star. The situation was on the brink of turning nasty and she realised that she should have left sooner. The doorways were all blocked by milling bodies and their faces were dark and thunderous. Then, above the noise of shouting, came the sudden sound of breaking glass and a stone thumped to the floor inside the theatre, followed by another and then another. Mary ducked down between the seats and covered her head with her hands. One man nearby had been hit by flying glass and blood flowed copiously from a gash on his head.

The crowd began to panic under the assault. Some rushed for the doors whilst others climbed up on to the stage away from the windows. She saw Mr Feilden put his arms around his wife and daughters and usher them away, calling for someone to bring his carriage around to the back.

Mary crept between the rows of seats to follow them. There was more chance of her getting out that way than at the front. She squeezed past people one by one as they swore at her and tried to push her to the back of the heaving mass of bodies, but she slipped through and out into the late afternoon. The engines were still thumping, but men were spilling out of the mills, seemingly having abandoned their work to hear the result. And although it wasn't yet dark, fires were being lit and there was a thick smell of burning in the streets. The sound of breaking glass came again and again as more windows were smashed and fighting broke out between the mob and the special constables.

'Tha's not safe here, lass.' Mary turned at the sound of Hargreaves's voice. He must have seen her and followed her out.

'I'm all right,' she told him. 'I think tha's probably needed elsewhere.'

'Nay,' he said, shaking his head. 'They can manage.'

She tried to move away as he reached to take her arm but she was hemmed in by the crowd.

'Come with me,' he said. 'I'll make sure tha stays safe.'

Mary tried to shake him off. 'Let me go. It's not far to the Star. I don't need any help from thee.'

As more of the men from inside the theatre began to surge out she was caught in the flood of bodies and swept along. Hargreaves lost his grasp on her, for which she was thankful, but she soon realised that she had no choice but to run in the same direction as the men and women who were heading up the street towards the Old Bull or be trampled underfoot. She thought she'd never been so afraid.

The mob slowed as it reached the pub where most of Mr Turner's friends were gathered. It seemed that every person bent to pick up a rock or other missile from the floor and hurl it towards the windows. The sound of shattering glass filled the air and it hardly paused as the bugles of the dragoons sounded as they rode up from their barracks on King Street.

Mary turned and tried to push her way back through the crowds, who were chanting, *'Bowring! Bowring!'* But for every step she took she seemed to be pushed two backwards. She tried to stay calm, but the urge to weep was strong. Her legs began to feel weak again and she wanted to sit down but she knew it would mean certain death if she didn't stay on her feet.

The bugles sounded again, just around the corner, and the crowd split as the first of the horsemen galloped through, slashing right and left with his sword. Mary saw a man lose part of his ear and the blood streamed down his face as he clutched at his head in surprise. She turned a full circle, searching for a way to escape, and found none. Her face felt wet and she wiped it with her fingers and glanced at them, expecting to see blood, but realising that she was sobbing.

'Mary!' She looked desperately around to see who was calling her name. 'Mary! This way!'

The unmistakeable figure of William Hart forced his way towards her and she allowed him to put an arm around her shoulders and pull her into the protection of his body.

'What's tha doing out here? Tha shouldn't be out in this lot,' he said.

'I were trying to get back.'

'Aye. It's all right now. Tha's safe with me.'

He forced a way through the mob, holding her close to him, until they reached Shorrock Fold.

'I'll be all right now,' she told him.

'No. I'll see thee safely inside,' he said.

Mrs Hall had barred the door and although William kept on banging it with his fist, it was some time before an upper window was thrust up and her voice shouted at them to go away.

'It's William Hart,' he shouted back. 'I've got Mary, and she's in a bad way!'

The window slammed and moments later the bolts were drawn and the door opened a crack.

'Get in,' said Mrs Hall, glancing at the melee behind them. 'And be quick about it.'

Mary stumbled over the doorstep and collapsed on to the nearest chair. She could feel her whole body trembling from her chattering teeth to her useless legs and she could hear her own sharp intakes of breath as the uncontrolled sobs shook her.

'Mary! Mary!' Mrs Hall was pushing a cup against her lips. 'Drink this.' She swallowed and the liquid hit the back of her throat, hot and fierce, making her gasp and cough before the warmth spread from her gullet to her extremities, but still she couldn't control the shaking.

'Fetch her through to t' kitchen,' she said and Mary felt herself lifted and carried to the chair in front of the range. Mrs Hall added more coal. 'She looks like she's been wet through an' all,' she said as she unfastened the spoiled bonnet. 'What was she thinking of? Especially when she's been so poorly. It's like she has no care for herself.'

Mary could hear them talking about her but hadn't the strength to form any words herself. She felt Mrs Hall rubbing her cold hands between her own work-roughened ones and William Hart was kneeling on the hearthrug unfastening her wet boots and taking them off. It felt too intimate. She didn't want him touching her feet and she tried to pull them away but he fetched a towel and rubbed them vigorously.

'Should I carry her up to bed?' he asked.

'No. She's better here by the fire. Help me get this jacket off her.'

She was gently pulled forward and they tugged at the sleeves. Then a blanket was wrapped around her and she was given more of the spirit to drink. She began to rally a little, and tried to hear what William and Mrs Hall were saying about her as they talked in low voices, but she couldn't make out the words for the noise of the riot roaring outside.

She must have dozed a little because she woke with a jump, not sure where she was. It had gone quiet outside and Mrs Hall was snoring in the chair opposite. William Hart had gone and she was glad of that. She was thirsty and she eased herself up and went to pour some water. She wondered what time it was. It was dark outside and the only light was from the embers of the dying fire. She wondered about going up to bed but it was warmer down here so she threw another shovelful of coal on to the fire and settled on the chair again with the blanket pulled around her and slept until morning.

'It sounds like they've called out the dragoons,' said Cook. She went to open the back door to look out and Hannah followed her to see the uniformed horsemen pouring out of the barracks on the other side of the street, bugles sounding and sabres drawn. 'They must be rioting.'

Hannah watched as the horsemen pounded up King Street. She hoped that James was all right and that Peggy was safely back from school. She didn't dare to think what might happen to the child if she was left to walk home alone in this. She hoped that Titus had stayed in the mill too. It would be just like him to get involved and she didn't want him to be arrested again. He'd got off lightly last time but no judge would be so lenient for a second conviction and the best they could hope for this time would be transportation.

'I knew no good would come of it,' announced Cook. 'Thank goodness the family got home before the worst began. Carry up the roast,' she told Hannah.

She carried the platter up and set it in the middle of the table. The dishes of vegetables were already there, along with one of Cook's chicken and ham pies. It all looked and smelled so good, thought Hannah. Mr Horrocks opened the door and the family came in before she could leave. She saw that they were still wearing their day dresses and it shocked her more than the result of the election or the rioting. She'd never known Mrs Feilden not to dress for supper before.

'Thank you, Hannah. Please tell Cook that it all looks delicious.'

'Yes, Mrs Feilden.' Hannah curbed the instinct to curtsey and went back downstairs.

'Well tha can kiss goodbye to thy washhouse,' said Titus as he hung his cap and jacket behind the door.

'Tha's late. I were worried,' said Jennet. 'What happened? It sounds like there's trouble.'

'Aye, there is that. Bowring were beaten and folks have no more sense than to chuck rocks through the windows of all the pubs and beerhouses.'

'At least tha stayed out of it,' said Jennet. She'd been twitching at the curtains for the last hour, watching for him and wishing that he'd come home. The night he'd been arrested was still fresh in her mind, even now, and she'd been terrified that he'd got caught up in the rioting again. 'Sit down,' she told him. 'I've kept thy tea warm.' She fetched the dish of potato pie from the little oven at the side of the range, holding it in a towel, and put it down on the table. It looked a bit dried up, but it was his own fault for not coming straight back.

'I never thought Turner'd get in,' he told her. 'It goes to show how easily men can be swayed.'

'If they were swayed by owt it were the amount of free drink he handed out,' said Jennet, thinking that Titus was right: Mr Turner would have no interest in her demands for washing facilities for the poor.

'That were a part of it,' said Titus as he blew on his food to cool it before putting it into his mouth. 'But Turner has influence over too many tradespeople and they weren't going to vote openly for Bowring in case he took his custom elsewhere. There'll never be a fair ballot until it's done in secret so men can vote with their consciences without risking their livelihoods.'

'Dost tha think that'll ever come about?' she asked. 'Folk are doin' themselves no favours by rioting. Gentry'll use it against 'em when they ask for a vote. They'll tell 'em they're not fit to have it.'

'Aye. But gentry need to understand that folk are unhappy and they won't just sit back and say nowt like they used to. We have to keep fighting,' he said.

Jennet didn't reply. She'd been hoping that once this election was over Titus would lose interest in politics, but it seemed that he wasn't prepared to let it drop. He was like a dog with an old bone. Not that he didn't have a point, she admitted, but she just wished he'd leave it to others now and pay more heed to her and the children.

'This result's a travesty,' he told her. 'Bowring should have got in. He would have made sure things were different around here.'

Jennet took the pots into the back kitchen to wash them up. She was bitterly disappointed about the washhouse. It would have made such a difference to so many families, but laundry wasn't a man's business and promises of boilers and mangles would never have influenced their votes. It was a pity no one was campaigning to give a vote to women as well. Now there was an idea, she thought as she scrubbed the last stubborn bits of baked potato from her earthenware dish. And why not? Plenty of women were working in the mills now, so why shouldn't they have their say as well?

Chapter Twenty-Three

Next time Mary woke it was daylight and Mrs Hall was making breakfast. She cut two thick slices of bread and stabbed the prongs of a toasting fork through one before handing it to Mary to hold in front of the fire.

'We might as well eat this up,' she said. 'It's too stale to give to customers now.'

Mary looked down at her skirts. They were filthy and needed to be put to soak. She'd do it later, she thought as Mrs Hall spread butter on the toast and handed it back to her on a plate. She bit into it hungrily. It was a rare treat and she savoured it.

'Tha were lucky to get home in one piece,' Mrs Hall told her. 'William Hart had come here lookin' for thee and when he heard tha were out in town he went straight back out to search for thee, but he were gone that long I didn't think he were coming back so I locked up to be safe.'

'They were smashing windows all over town,' Mary told her. 'The military had to come out.'

'Aye, so he said. It sounds quiet enough now though. Happen I'll open for a bit later on.'

'I hope he doesn't come in again,' said Mary.

'Who? William Hart? Why not?'

'I can't stand him,' she said. 'And I've decided not to have owt to do wi' men any more. If I can't find work here I might try Preston way.'

'I doubt tha'd be any better off. At least here tha has a roof over thy head.'

'Aye, but only until the money runs out.'

Mrs Hall hesitated before she answered. 'It were William Hart as paid me that money,' she told her. 'He's very fond of thee.'

'If he thinks he can pick up where Starkie left off then he's got another think coming,' Mary told her. 'I'm sworn off men.'

'Tha should be grateful!' said Mrs Hall. 'It's allowed thee to be a lady of leisure this past while. And by all accounts owt could have happened to thee last night if he hadn't fetched thee back when he did.'

'But tha wouldn't turn me out, would tha?' asked Mary. She'd begun to think that the land-lady was her friend.

Mrs Hall shrugged. 'I've a business to run. I can't afford charity,' she told her. 'So tha's going to have to make a decision before very long. He'll not keep paying thy bed and board without owt in return. So if tha's really sworn off men and there's no jobs to be had, it looks like tha's going to be knockin' on the workhouse door.'

Mary watched in silence as Mrs Hall slammed a bowl down on the scrubbed table and began to chop onions for the hotpot. It was a stark choice.

She filled a jug with hot water and went upstairs to her room where she stripped off her clothes. She washed herself all over, enjoying the warmth on her body and wondering what it would be like to slip into a bathtub as the Sudells had done. She shivered as she stood naked, deep in thought, then opened a drawer to take out a clean petticoat. She looked through the dresses that were hanging on her rail. They were all things that Mr Starkie had given her and she didn't want to wear any of them. Not now. Instead she put on a dark skirt and white blouse that were her own. She brushed out her hair and fixed it into a simple bun. She pinned her paisley shawl around her shoulders and carried the used water back down to throw it out of the door. The air was thick with the smell of smoke and gunpowder and somewhere she could hear people brushing up the broken glass.

She heard footsteps and William Hart turned the corner. He smiled when he saw her.

'Come in,' she said and he ducked his head under the lintel, pulling off his cap and tucking it under his arm.

'How's tha feeling?' he asked.

'I'm all right.'

'It's a mess out there,' he said. 'We've had some windows put through at t' shop and my father's furious. I told him it were his own fault for voting Turner rather than Dr Bowring. He weren't best pleased.' He grinned. 'I've slipped out for a bit until he calms down.'

'I'll just go and stir the hotpot,' said Mrs Hall and she gave Mary a look as she passed her.

'Dost tha want a drink?' asked Mary.

'Aye. Pour me a half and get one for thyself.'

Mary carried the drinks over to where he was sitting by the freshly lit fire.

'Thank you,' he said as he took his from her. 'Sit down, Mary. I've summat to say to thee.'

'I have work to do in the kitchen.'

'No. Sit down.' He was firm and insistent and although her heart had plummeted to her damp boots she perched on the edge of the chair with the untasted beer clasped in her hands. No matter what she thought, or what she felt, she had reason to be grateful to him and she'd do him the courtesy of hearing what he had to say even if it meant she would be forced to disappoint him.

'Tha must know that I'm fond of thee,' he began, turning his cup around and around in his hands as he spoke. 'I know tha's fallen on hard times and that being here isn't entirely what tha wants. I'd like to help thee.'

'I think tha's helped me enough already,' she told him. 'It's not that I'm ungrateful. I'd have been in the workhouse otherwise. But this isn't the life for me. I'm sworn off men from now on. I've got to get myself out of here and get a proper job.'

'Just hear me out,' he said. 'I really want to help thee do just that.'

'How?' she asked, hoping that perhaps he could offer her work.

'I'm not short of money,' he told her. 'I wouldn't say as I were rich, but I've enough to get by and be comfortable.' He looked up from under his dark brows to see if she was listening. 'I'm living at home at the moment, but there's a house on Penny Street coming vacant and I've been to ask about it.' Mary stared at him as he spoke. Was he going to offer her a house? He would want plenty in return for that. 'It's a nice street and I can afford the rent. It'd even give me the vote,' he added.

'Pity tha didn't have it yesterday,' she told him. 'It might have made all the difference.'

'Aye, it might,' he agreed. 'But the thing is, Mary, would tha like to live there?'

'What would tha want in return?' she asked. 'I've already told thee I'm sworn off men. I'd rather go to the workhouse than do that again.'

'No!' He looked shocked. 'I wasn't meaning that,' he told her. 'I was thinking that we'd be married.'

Mary was speechless for a moment. 'Married?' she repeated eventually. It wasn't what she'd expected. 'Why would tha want to marry a lass like me?'

'Because I love thee, Mary.' His face turned crimson to the roots of his hair but he held her gaze. 'I love thee, Mary,' he repeated.

'No.' She shook her head. 'No. It would never do. What would thy father say?' she asked. 'He'd never agree.' It was one thing for him to have a lass on the side in a beerhouse, but she knew that his family would never approve of her as a wife.

'Then I'd marry thee without their agreement,' he said. 'I can get other work. It doesn't have to be for my father.' He reached out and grasped her hand. 'Just tell me tha'll be my wife, Mary, and I'll make it all right, I promise I will!'

She stood with her hand trapped in his. He gazed at her imploringly and still she felt nothing. But she was tempted. It would be better than the workhouse and it couldn't be any worse than it had been before – with her own father and then Mr Starkie. She knew that William would be kind to her. Surely that was better than the alternatives, better than waiting in some forlorn hope that someone that she actually liked might come along to rescue her. And it would mean that she could do more for John. William might even agree to letting him come and lodge with them and that way he'd be able to keep his wages and she'd see to it that he was well fed and clothed. It would be the making of him because he was never going to amount to much whilst he was stuck at home on Paradise Lane.

'I know tha doesn't love me – not yet anyroad. But it'll come, Mary. It will. I promise. I'll be good to thee. Tha'll never have to worry about where thy next meal's coming from ever again.'

Still she hesitated. Even though she could see Mrs Hall behind the kitchen door and knew that she was listening to every word.

'I'll think on it,' she said at last and pulled her hand free. 'Tha's taken me a bit by surprise and I need time to think.'

'Then tha might say aye?' He sounded hopeful.

'I might,' she agreed, wanting to buy herself some time. 'But I need to think.'

He nodded; then he stood up and fixed his cap on his head. 'I'll come again tomorrow,' he said, and with a nod towards Mrs Hall he left, leaving a cold draught from the door behind him.

'Tha's a ruddy fool!' burst out Mrs Hall as soon as he'd gone. 'What's tha thinkin' of? Tha should have told him aye straight away!'

'But tha knows I don't like him.'

'What's likin' him got to do with it?' she demanded, her ample bosom heaving with indignation. 'He's just offered thee marriage, a nice home, food on the table, respectability ...' She counted off the reasons that Mary should agree on her fingers. 'Tha'll not find anyone else who'll do the same. And it'll be too late to consider whether tha might have grown to like him when tha's toilin' fourteen hours a day in the workhouse for a bowl of gruel! I could slap thee for being so stupid and stubborn!'

She gave a huff and wobbled off into the kitchen, muttering about lasses who had their heads filled with too many romantic notions and asking why they couldn't recognise the chance of a lifetime when it was thrust underneath their noses. Mary was about to follow her and protest again that she didn't like him, but instead she sat down by the fire and began to wonder whether it really was reason enough not to accept him.

Chapter Twenty-Four

The morning after the election, Mr Horrocks came to the kitchen to tell Hannah that Mrs Feilden wanted to see her in the morning room.

'Tha must have missed a bit when tha were dustin',' Cook teased as Hannah fiddled with her hair to make sure it was tidy. 'There's a mark on that apron. Put on a clean one. Tha can change back after.'

Hannah tugged off the offending pinny and put it over the back of a chair before pulling a fresh one over her head and fastening it into a neat bow at the back – all the time wondering what might make Mrs Feilden summon her upstairs in the middle of the morning. She hoped she wasn't going to be told that she must pack her bags to go with them to London.

When Hannah got to the door her employer was sitting at her desk with some papers spread in front of her.

'Come in, Hannah,' she said. She didn't sound pleased. 'I've been looking at this letter,' she said. 'It's the one you brought when you came about the job. You told me it was a character reference written by your former employer, Mr Sudell. That's right, isn't it?'

'Yes, Mrs Feilden,' Hannah said as a cold horror began to gnaw away at her. Had her employer somehow discovered that it wasn't the real thing after all this time? It had been so long that Hannah had stopped worrying about it.

'It's come to my attention that when Mr Sudell left he neglected to provide characters for any of his maids.' Hannah didn't answer. What could she say? How had Mrs Feilden found out? 'So I'm wondering how you came by this?' she said, holding it out towards her.

The pattern on the Turkish rug seemed to be swirling as Hannah stared down at it, not knowing how to reply.

'It isn't Mr Sudell's signature,' went on Mrs Feilden. 'When Mr Feilden repeated to me what he'd been told, I asked him to show me a document that did have Mr Sudell's signature attached. He'd done business with him in the past so it was easily compared – and this one bears no resemblance.'

'I'm sorry,' whispered Hannah. She knew that she was sure to be dismissed this time.

'Did you write it?'

'No!' Hannah was taken by surprise at the question.

'Then who?' She looked at Mrs Feilden's face and then back at the carpet she'd brushed earlier that morning. 'Who wrote it for you?'

Hannah couldn't bring herself to tell the truth. She didn't want to get Titus into trouble. She knew that the Feildens thought well of him.

'I thought it was from Mr Sudell,' she lied.

'Did he give it to you?'

'Not personally, no. But I was led to believe that he'd left it for me.'

'And did you not think it was strange that there was a character for you but not one for the other staff?'

'I don't know anything about that, Mrs Feilden.' With every word Hannah knew that she was digging herself in deeper, but having begun with a lie it was too late to backtrack now.

'Were you given it at Mr Sudell's house?'

'No. It was given to me later.'

'Who gave it to you?'

'I don't quite remember ...' She floundered in her attempt to cover up the truth. She wondered whether to admit that Titus had written it. But what purpose would it serve? She was bound to be dismissed anyway.

320

'This is so disappointing, Hannah,' said Mrs Feilden, 'especially after the other trouble – and it's because of that I'm not entirely convinced that this letter isn't just another example of your fiction. Are you sure you didn't write it yourself?'

Hannah looked her in the eye and told the truth. 'I didn't write it. I'll write summat now and you can compare my hand,' she offered.

'There wouldn't be any point,' said Mrs Feilden. 'We both know it isn't from Mr Sudell and that means that you came to us without a genuine character reference.' She folded the letter and pushed it away from her before looking at Hannah again. 'It is a pity because your work is good and I might have been able to overlook you not having a character if I thought you were being entirely honest with me, but I don't think you are, Hannah. If you didn't write it then someone else must have written it for you, and whilst I admire your loyalty in not naming them, the fact remains that it is a forgery and you are party to that forgery. And that's a serious offence.' Hannah's heart began to beat faster. Surely the woman wasn't thinking of sending her up before the magistrate? 'Added to that other matter, I really don't think I can keep you in our employment,' she finished.

'I were guilty of nothing!' protested Hannah. 'The book had been lent to the schoolmaster.'

'Yes, I know. But the writing I found in your room was not something I wanted in my house.'

'But it weren't against the law!'

'True. But I have certain standards and I expect them to be upheld in my house by those who are in my employment.'

'There were no need to have it burned!' fumed Hannah. She hadn't forgiven the woman and she never would, so she might as well speak her mind. 'I'm sure it must be wrong to burn other folk's stuff, if not in the eyes of the magistrate then in the eyes of God!'

'That's enough!' Mrs Feilden stood up and Hannah could see that she was furious. 'Pack your belongings and go – immediately! Horrocks!' she called and Hannah watched as the butler came to the door and looked from one to the other of them as they stood, both red-faced, glaring at one another. 'Hannah is dismissed,' she told him. 'Go with her to her room and wait whilst she packs her things and then accompany her to the back door.'

She sat down at her desk again and made a pretence of being busy with her papers. Hannah looked at Horrocks. His expression remained unchanged, so she had no idea what he was thinking.

'I'm supposed to be helping Cook with the dinner,' she said.

'She'll manage. Go and get your things,' he said, and Hannah was left with no choice other than to precede him up the back stairs where he stood in her doorway and watched as she packed her belongings haphazardly into her bag.

'And Horrocks!' called Mrs Feilden from the lower landing. 'Make sure she leaves her uniform.'

He raised an eyebrow.

'At least turn thy back!' she hissed at him before she pulled off the dress, balled it up and flung it on to the floor. She pulled one of her own back out of the bag and stepped into it, fastened it quickly and put on her little jacket and bonnet. For a moment she stared at the floorboard where her paper and pencils were hidden. She didn't want to leave them, but decided that she wouldn't demean herself by scrabbling under the floor for them and proving that she had been dishonest after all. So, bag in hand, and with her head held high, she followed Horrocks back down to the kitchen.

'Whatever's happened?' asked Cook.

'I've to go,' she said as Horrocks opened the door and waited for her to step through.

'Why? What's she done?' she heard Cook ask just before the door closed behind her for the last time.

The gate squeaked on her way out. Hannah didn't bother to close it behind her, but left it swinging. She stood for a moment on King Street until the worst of the tears of anger, frustration and disappointment passed; then, with no other option, she began to walk towards Water Street.

Jennet was turning some sheets through the mangle in the back yard when she heard the front door open and close.

'Who is it?' she called. 'I'm out here.' She glanced up from her work and saw her sister standing in the back doorway, clutching her bag in her hand. 'Hannah! What's happened?'

'I've been sacked.'

'What's tha done?'

'I've done nowt!' she shouted. 'It's all Titus's fault!'

'Titus? What's it to do with Titus?' asked Jennet. 'Let's go inside,' she said, abandoning her work. 'I'll put the kettle on.' She could sense Molly listening in on the other side of the wall and it was none of her business.

Hannah slumped in the chair by the fire still wearing her jacket and bonnet. She looked stunned, thought Jennet as she spooned tea into the pot, and it was obvious that she'd been crying.

'What's it to do with Titus?' she asked again.

'He forged Mr Sudell's name on my character,' said Hannah. 'Unfortunately not very well.'

Jennet shook her head, not knowing what to say. She was too angry to speak.

'I think he just wanted me out of the house,' Hannah went on, 'but I'm back now and probably for good.'

'Tha knows tha's always welcome here.'

'Am I?' asked Hannah.

'Of course!'

Hannah unfastened her bonnet and took it off. 'Well, I'll not get another job now. And I doubt that James Hindle will ever speak to me again.' Fresh tears flowed freely down her face and she wiped her nose on the back of her hand. 'A schoolmaster can't be seen with a disgraced maid who's narrowly missed the magistrates' court. Mrs Feilden said as forgery was a crime.'

'Did tha tell her that Titus wrote it?' For a moment her concern for her sister was overshadowed by the fear that her husband could end up in trouble again.

Hannah shook her head. 'I covered up for him. I hope he appreciates it.'

'But how did they find out? After all this time?'

Hannah shrugged. 'I don't know. Mrs Feilden said someone had told them no one from Sudells' got a character. They compared the signature with a real one, and of course it were different.'

Jennet suddenly remembered her encounter with Mrs Pickering. Surely the woman couldn't have been so vindictive as to do this? It was a bit out of proportion over just a burned blouse, although she wouldn't put it past her.

They were still sitting drinking tea when Titus came in for his dinner.

'What's she done now?' he asked.

'She's done nowt, Titus Eastwood!' Jennet told him. 'It's what tha's done that needs some explaining! Hannah's been dismissed and it's all thy fault! I asked thee about her character reference and tha said tha knew nowt about it.'

As she drew breath he pulled off his cap and sat down at the table. He looked shocked and worried. And so he should, thought Jennet. He'd let her down badly this time.

'Did tha tell 'em it were me that wrote it?' he asked Hannah.

She shook her head. 'No.'

'Well, that's all right then.'

'All right for thee, tha means!' Jennet said. 'It's not all right for Hannah. She's takin' all the blame, and how's she supposed to get another job after this?'

'I thought she were set to marry James Hindle. She'll not need another job.'

'And does tha really think he'll want to wed her now?' Jennet slammed his dinner down on the table.

'Is that all there is?' he asked, looking at the plate of cold oatcakes and cheese.

'Tha's lucky to get that,' she told him. 'I'm behind with my work as it is.' She watched him eat for a moment. 'Perhaps tha could go and explain it to them,' she said. 'If tha could make it right they might take her back.'

'I wouldn't go back!' said Hannah.

'What good would it do?' asked Titus. 'They'll just think I'm covering up for her. Besides, I've to get back to work in a minute.'

Jennet watched in exasperation as he pulled his cap back on and went out. Hannah was crying again and the wet washing was still waiting to be pegged out to dry. Bessie was sitting in the corner sucking her thumb, upset by all the arguing, and Jennet knew that Molly next door would have had her ear pressed up to the wall to hear every word and that before teatime everyone on the street would know that Hannah had been sent home in disgrace.

Chapter Twenty-Five

Mary was peeling potatoes in the kitchen when William Hart came into the Star.

'Anyone would think tha didn't have a job of work to do,' she told him as he stood in the doorway twisting his cap.

'I've just slipped out for a moment. I have summat to tell thee.'

'What?' she asked, hoping he wasn't going to press her for an answer to his proposal.

'There's a maid's job going at the Feildens' house. I've just heard that Hannah Chadwick's been let go.'

'Let go?' asked Mary, turning to face him. 'Does tha mean she's been sacked? Why? What for?' She couldn't think of anything that her friend might have done wrong to warrant such an outcome.

'It doesn't matter why,' he said. 'Thing is they'll need a new maid. I know as tha wants a better job, so tha needs to get round there straight away and enquire about it. Tha doesn't mind if she slips out for half an hour, does tha?' he asked Mrs Hall.

'Nay. I'll be glad to see t' lass wi' a better position.'

Mary let the half-peeled potato slip back into the water and dried her hands on a rough towel. Maybe this was the opportunity she'd been waiting for.

'But what about a character reference?' she asked him. 'I never had one from Woodfold.'

'Mrs Hall will write one for thee. Put that down,' he urged as she continued to wipe her hands on the towel. 'Go and put thy best frock on. I'll walk with thee, if tha likes. I'll have time if tha's quick.'

She shook her head. 'No. Get back to work,' she told him.

'But tha'll go straight away?'

'Aye. I'll go,' she promised. It would be better than staying here, she thought as she went upstairs to get changed. Although she suspected that it wasn't just her own interests that he had in mind. If he could take her home and introduce her to his parents as someone who worked for Mr Feilden then they'd be much more amenable to a marriage, and she wondered if she wasn't playing into his hands by agreeing to go. On the other hand, he might not have considered that if she got the job she would have a wage and a place to live and wouldn't have to marry him at all.

She changed into a clean blouse and put on her coat and her plain bonnet. She hoped that it would make the right impression. When she went back down, Mrs Hall had written a letter of recommendation.

'I've told 'em tha's honest and a hard worker,' she said as she blotted it dry. 'I hope tha gets it,' she added, 'although I'll be sorry to lose thee. Tha's a good little worker,' she added.

The morning was cold with a fresh wind that had blown away the stench of the gunpowder from the dragoons' guns. The workers had gone back to their jobs, afraid of being put out without pay, and on the face of it, Blackburn had returned to normal. Mary walked briskly down to King Street. She hesitated for only a moment at the gate before she went in, closed it behind her and followed the path to the back door. She knocked and waited, hoping that it wouldn't be answered by the surly butler. She really didn't fancy having to work for him, but if he kept his hands to himself then she would put up with him.

'Yes?' A red-headed lass stared at her curiously. 'What does tha want?' she asked.

'I were told there was a vacancy for a maid.'

'Well, tha heard wrong.'

Mary felt a weight of disappointment fall on to her shoulders. It was almost physical and she reached out to steady herself on the doorpost. William must have been misinformed.

'Is Hannah here?' she asked.

'Hannah Chadwick? No.'

'But she does work here?'

'Not any more.' So maybe it was true that she'd been dismissed.

'Who is it, Jane?' called a voice.

'Someone asking for Hannah.'

'Hannah's gone, love,' said a plump woman with flour dusted across her bare forearms. 'She's been let go.'

'So there is a vacancy for a maid? I were told there was.'

'No.' The woman shook her head. 'Jane here's come back to fill the place. Tha's heard wrong. I'm sorry.'

A moment later Mary found herself staring at the closed door. The letter from Mrs Hall was still in her hand. She crumpled it into a ball in her frustration. For just a short while she'd thought that she'd been given an option, but now she was left with no choice but to agree to marry William Hart, and probably without the blessing of his family.

*

'Already taken?' he asked suspiciously that evening when she told him what had happened.

'Aye. I did go!' she added. 'It would have been a good job for me. I would have had a safe place to stay an' all and I wouldn't have to ...' She didn't finish. She saw from his face that he understood her meaning.

'But tha'll say aye to me now?'

'I don't have much choice, do I?' There, she thought, it was said. She'd agreed to marry him and she would have to make the best of it. 'If tha'll still have me,' she added.

'Of course I'll have thee. It doesn't bother me what tha is. It's just that it would have been easier to introduce thee to my family as a maid, rather than a ...'

'Prostitute,' she finished for him.

'Aye.' He took a drink of his beer. 'It'll be all right,' he said. 'I'll make sure of it. We'll get that house on Penny Street and we'll be happy. I promise.'

Mary was less sure, but if she had to take this man to her bed at least she would be able to do it with a ring on her finger.

'I'll take thee to meet them,' he said. 'Then they can see that tha's a decent sort of lass and they need have no qualms. It'll be all right,' he repeated.

Mary wasn't so sure.

*

Hannah was sitting at the table helping Jennet with some darning. It was dark outside by late afternoon now and it meant there was less daylight for intricate work. They both looked up when there was a knock on the door. No one called out and came in, so Jennet got up and went to answer it, tidying her hair as she did, knowing that it must be someone important.

Hannah was astounded when James Hindle stepped inside, taking off his hat and running his fingers through his hair to push it back from his face.

'Hannah,' he greeted her.

'Come and sit where it's warm,' said Titus from his chair by the fire. 'Jennet'll make thee some tea.'

'It was Hannah I wanted to talk to,' James told him. 'Would you like to walk for a bit?' he asked her. 'It's cold outside but you'll be all right if you wrap up warm.'

'I'll get my shawl,' she said, reaching it down from the peg. She wished that she was wearing her best clothes rather than the shabby blouse and skirt that she had on, but it would look too obvious that she was trying to impress him if she went running up the stairs to get changed.

James told Titus and Jennet that he wouldn't keep her out long and would see her safely back.

Then they went out on to the street. She'd thought that she would never see him again, but here he was asking her to walk out with him. To be seen with him in public. She could scarcely believe it. Unless, of course, he hadn't heard about her dismissal. In that case she would have to explain it to him herself and she dreaded what might happen then. To have him ignore her was one thing, but to have him deliberately walk away and tell her that he wanted nothing more to do with her would be devastating.

She pulled the shawl around her head and shoulders and he offered her his arm.

'Dost tha know what's happened?' she asked tentatively, hardly daring to look up at him.

'I've heard all sorts,' he said. 'That's why I want to get it straight from you.' They set off in the direction of the town centre. 'I heard you'd been dismissed.'

'It's true,' she said, avoiding his glance.

'What for?' he asked. 'Did Mrs Feilden catch you writing again?'

'No. It were more serious than that.'

'More serious? What happened?' he asked. And as they walked she related the tale of the letter that Titus had written for her. He said nothing all the time she spun the sorry tale and even when she'd finished he stayed silent. Hannah was afraid. She thought that at any moment he would pull away from the hand she had tucked inside his elbow and march off without a word or a backwards glance.

'I never told them it was Titus that wrote it, and tha mustn't breathe a word,' she warned him, suddenly afraid that he might reveal the truth and the magistrate might send someone to arrest her brother-in-law. 'I don't want him to get into trouble. I don't think our Jennet would manage if he were sent back to prison.'

'I never had Titus Eastwood down as dishonest,' said James. 'I'm surprised at him.'

'He thought he were doing me a good turn,' she said, wondering why she felt compelled to defend him. 'I'd never have got the job otherwise.'

'But it was dishonest,' he said. 'And it's a serious thing to do – to forge another man's name.'

'I know. That's why I don't want to get him into trouble.'

'But what about you?' he asked.

'I doubt they'll send the magistrate after me. They dismissed me and that's probably the end of it.'

'Even so,' he said. 'I hope you'd tell the truth if it came to it. What made you agree to do it in the first place? You must have known it was wrong!'

'I know. But he left me with no choice. He wanted me to have a job so as I wouldn't be a burden to them.'

'We always have a choice, Hannah,' James told her and she could hear the tone of the schoolmaster in his voice. This must be how he spoke to his pupils when they'd transgressed, she thought. She was sorry that he seemed angry with her, even though she'd explained it as best she could. He really didn't understand what Titus was like when his mind was set on something.

'Well, I could have chosen to go with Mary,' she told James. 'Maybe that Mr Starkie would have bought me some fancy frocks as well, in exchange for favours.'

'I'm sorry,' he said. 'I didn't mean to be harsh. I thought Mrs Feilden had dismissed you over the writing and I was going to offer to go and speak to her about it. But now ...' He was quiet for a few more minutes. 'I can't fault the Feildens for dismissing you over this,' he said at last. 'I don't think there's anything I can do to help.'

'Well, I never asked thee to do owt.'

'I know.' They walked on in silence. 'What will you do now?' he asked at last.

'I don't rightly know. I can never work as a maid again. Word will have got round. And none of the mills are taking on. Maybe I will have do t' same as Mary after all.'

'Don't talk nonsense!' he replied. 'There must be jobs you can do.'

Hannah shook her head. She couldn't think of any, especially if people had heard that she was untrustworthy.

'Perhaps I *should* go and speak to them,' he said. 'I could try to explain that it wasn't entirely your fault. That you were coerced into giving them the letter. I could speak for you. They might take some notice.'

'Only if I put the blame on someone else. They'd never believe it otherwise,' Hannah told him. 'Anyway, it's too late. I went round to see Jane and her house is all locked up. I think she must have gone back.'

'I see.'

They'd reached the edge of the town and they stood looking out at the bleak moorland that surrounded the valley. It was growing dark and a huge full moon was sitting on the horizon just above the distant hills.

'My parents live up there, at Ramsgreave,' she told him. 'I know they'd welcome me home, but there's no call for hand spinners any more. I'd only be a burden to them if I went back. I'm a burden wherever I am. Nobody wants me.'

'Don't say that, Hannah.'

'But it's true. Isn't it? Maybe I should just set off walking, and walk and walk until I can't go no further ...'

'Now you're just being dramatic.' He put an arm around her shoulders. 'I know you're not dishonest, Hannah. I'm sorry if you thought I was judging you. I was just taken by surprise. If I'm angry with anyone, then it's Titus. He really should have known better.'

She leaned against his warm, solid body. He hadn't walked away from her and she was thankful for that, but something had changed between them and she wasn't sure what was going to happen now.

'Come to the poets' corner with me,' he said suddenly. 'We can sit down and have a think about what to do. And it'll be a sight warmer than standing out here.'

They turned back towards the town. The lamps were being lit and they flickered in the wind, casting eerie shadows and filling the streets with a smell of gas. James led the way towards a small beerhouse on the corner of Bradshaw Street and Nab Lane. He held the door open for her and she went in, wishing that he'd gone first as she heard the lull in the conversation as people looked at her. A group of serious-looking men were gathered around the fire and one of them was reading out his poem. She and James stood and listened, and when he was finished James ushered her forward and one of the men stood up to give her his place on a polished chair. She eased the shawl from her head and let it lie over her arms as James introduced her.

'This is Hannah. She's a bit of a writer herself.'

'Dost tha write poetry?' asked one.

'No. I've not tried. I write stories,' she said. 'I like to listen to poetry though,' she added, hoping they wouldn't think she wasn't a real writer if she didn't pen verse.

'Aye, good.'

James handed her a half-pint of beer and squeezed a stool into the gap next to her. A man with a luxurious beard, and spectacles perched on the end of his nose, stood up to read from the sheet of paper in his hand.

There was applause when he'd finished. As James had promised, it was warm and although the room quickly filled with smoke, for once Hannah didn't pine for fresh air. She felt safe here. No one knew her secret except for James, and although she could see that her confession had troubled him, he hadn't sent her away.

After a while some hotpot was passed around in dishes and Hannah ate. She'd brought no money so she hoped that James had paid for it. She'd pay him back as soon as she could, she thought.

As it approached ten o'clock the men began to make their excuses and head for home.

'I'd better get you back,' said James. 'Jennet'll be wondering where we've got to.'

She pulled the shawl around her again and took his arm as they made their way back to Water Street.

'What did you make of the poets?' he asked.

'I enjoyed hearing them,' she said. 'I might have a go at a poem or two myself now that I'm free to write again.' She frowned as she remembered that she'd left her paper and pencils hidden at the Feildens' house. 'Tha didn't read owt out,' she said.

'I hadn't brought anything with me. And I always seem to get muddled if I try to recite from memory.'

'Maybe next time?' she ventured, hoping that he might agree to take her again.

'Aye, maybe.'

'Will tha come in?' she asked as they reached the door.

He shook his head. 'Not tonight. It's late.'

She could see that it was because he didn't want to speak to Titus and knew that it was going to make things difficult. 'Will tha call for me again?' She heard her voice waver as she asked.

He didn't answer straight away.

'I don't know,' he said at last. 'What Titus did was wrong ...'

'Aye. I understand,' she said as her hopes plummeted. 'A schoolmaster has to be above reproach.'

'I'm sorry, Hannah,' he said. 'Goodnight.' And he turned and walked away from her, back down the street.

'What's to do with him tonight?' Titus had grumbled after James and Hannah had gone out.

'He's probably heard all sorts about our Hannah getting dismissed,' Jennet told him as she turned the sock she'd darned right side out and examined the mended patch. 'I just hope it doesn't spoil things between them.'

'Why should it spoil owt?'

'Because he has a position in society as a schoolmaster. He can't go hobnobbin' with the criminal classes.'

'What's tha talkin' about? We're none of us criminals.'

'Forgery's criminal – and tha's already served one prison sentence,' she reminded him. 'I just hope Mr Feilden doesn't discover it were thee that wrote that letter and decide to press charges.'

'He'll not,' said Titus, filling the bowl of his pipe with more tobacco. 'Tha worries too much.'

'What possessed thee to do it?' she asked as she folded the sock with its pair and closed her work basket. 'It were a stupid idea.'

'It didn't seem so at the time. She needed a character to get a job and Sudell had gone off without giving her one when he should have done. It weren't fair on her. I just made amends. That's all.'

He made it sound so reasonable, thought Jennet. Sudell's thoughtlessness *had* been unfair on Hannah. But two wrongs don't make a right, she told herself. And in the end it had all been for nothing because Hannah was without a job again and had even less prospect of finding another. She just hoped that Titus wouldn't start grumbling about her staying with them.

'It were still dishonest,' she reminded him.

'Aye. Happen so.'

She threw more coal on the fire and watched it smoke. 'It'd be a cryin' shame if James decided not to marry her because of this,' she said.

'Don't talk daft. It'll work itself out.'

Jennet looked down at him, puffing on his pipe and reading yet another pamphlet. She wanted to grab both items and toss them on to the fire to make him look up and acknowledge the serious-ness of what he'd done. Because it was affecting Hannah rather than him he seemed to think it was of no consequence and she itched to force him to face up to his actions. Instead she said nothing and went upstairs. Peggy and Bessie were both fast asleep in the bed they had to share with Hannah and Peggy would grumble in her sleep when Hannah came in and shoved her up. They needed to get another bed from somewhere if Hannah was to stay, she thought as she eased Bessie's thumb from her mouth. The child moaned and then slipped it back in and sucked on it in her sleep. She was such a good lass, thought Jennet as she crouched down beside her. So like George. It was at times like these that she wondered if she'd made the wrong decision when she'd let him go to America alone.

It hadn't been an easy choice, but in the end loyalty to her husband had won. Now she couldn't help but ask herself if he deserved that loyalty. He should have realised that if he was found out, it would make people question his trustworthiness. Since he'd come back from prison he'd campaigned tirelessly for Reform and he'd won the respect of many of the townsfolk and some of the gentry. Even the vicar's wife would give him the time of day although he rarely graced a pew. And Mr Feilden had trusted his judgement enough to mention the maid's job to him. Why couldn't he just have been honest and explained why Hannah didn't have a character? They might have overlooked it and taken her on anyway. But no, he had to try to be clever and show off his writing skills, never thinking where it might lead. Maybe she should have just gone with George, taken Peggy with them and sailed off across that ocean to a new world. She might have been happy, she thought. And little Bessie would surely have been happier with her real father instead of being the target of Titus's resentment. It was a shame. He'd promised to treat the child as his own, and he probably thought he'd kept his word, but it didn't take much to see that Peggy was his favourite.

She heard the door and Hannah came up the stairs. 'Tha's been a while?' Jennet was hoping it was a good sign.

'Aye. I explained it all to him.'

'Everything?' Her sister nodded. She looked close to tears. 'And what did he say?'

'Not a lot. He's furious with Titus.'

'I can't blame him for that. I'm furious with him an' all. But how was he with thee?' she asked.

'I don't rightly know.' Hannah sat down on the bed to unfasten her boots. 'He took me to the poets' corner and he bought me a drink and some supper. But it wasn't the same. I'm worried that it were his way of saying goodbye. I think he's concerned for his own reputation and I don't know if he'll come again.'

'I'm sorry, Hannah. I thought that, in time, he might have asked thee to marry him.'

'Aye.' She wiped away a tear and tried to pretend that she didn't care, but Jennet could see that she was badly upset by it. 'I don't know what I'm going to do,' she said after a moment.

'Tha could always help out with t' laundry.'

'Aye. I could.'

Jennet knew that it wasn't a real answer to what was troubling her sister, but she was at a loss to know what else to suggest. 'Happen he'll come round,' she said.

Hannah was glad when Jennet left her alone and went to her own bed. She undressed and slipped between the sheets next to Peggy. One good thing about sharing a bed with her nieces was that it was already warmed when she got in.

She lay awake for a long time thinking about what had happened. She went over the things that James had said again and again in her head, trying to tease the meaning out of them. It had been a shock for him. He'd been all fired up to protest on her behalf when he thought she'd been dismissed over her writing, but the truth had extinguished that. There was nothing he could protest to the Feildens about. She turned over in bed, making Peggy mutter, and thumped at her pillow to try to get comfy. But sleep wouldn't come and she cried quietly. She'd thought that she would get her happy ending, but now it was all spoiled and there was nothing at all she could do to change it.

Chapter Twenty-Six

Mary put on a clean, ironed blouse and brushed her hair carefully before pinning it up. Her reflection in the little mirror still looked pale and she pinched her cheeks with her fingers to bring some colour to them. It was Sunday afternoon and William was taking her to meet his parents. She was terrified. She knew that they would judge her and not want her to have anything to do with their son. In a way it would be a relief. If they forbade him to see her again, then she would be free of him. But all her attempts to find work had come to nothing and she knew that if he didn't give her the money for her rent she would have to go to the workhouse because, even though there were plenty of Mrs Hall's customers who she knew would pay her for her services, she couldn't do that again.

She put on a plain bonnet and a little jacket. Both were old-fashioned now that the new London styles had reached the north, but it didn't matter. The thing was to look clean and respectable. She picked up her little reticule and hung it over her wrist and then went down the stairs to the parlour. He was already there, waiting for her.

'Ready?' he asked.

'I think so.' Her stomach was dancing a jig and she thought she'd never been so afraid of anything in her life.

'It'll be fine,' he told her. 'Tha looks lovely and I'm sure they'll like thee.'

Out on Shorrock Fold he gave her his arm and after a glance towards the pawnbroker's to check that there was no sign of Mr Starkie, she took it and they walked down Church Street to his parents' house. The shops were all closed up and it was quiet. No one was allowed to work on a Sunday although there were a few who were out and about, looking furtive as they carried tools in their hands.

The Harts' house was larger than the workers' cottages but not on such a grand scale as the houses of the gentry. William opened the door himself rather than knocking and waiting for the maid to let them in. They entered a small flagged hallway. Beyond it was a staircase and a couple of closed doors. He led the way upstairs to a room at the front of the house where the door was ajar.

'We're here,' he said and pushed it wider for her to go in.

Mr and Mrs Hart were sitting on either side of the fireplace. It was an open fire, not a range like the ones in the cottages. They would have an oven downstairs for cooking, she thought, and a servant to clean and blacklead it. They both looked at her curiously. Mr Hart, with his thinning hairline and neatly trimmed beard, had been reading a book and he closed it and put it down on a side table to study her. His wife had some embroidery on her lap and she too scrutinised her.

'This is Mary Sharples,' said William.

'How do you do,' said Mary and gave a slight curtsey.

'Come and sit down,' said Mrs Hart. She was a fierce-looking woman with sharp eyes and angular features. William clearly took after his father in looks. 'William, call down to Mrs Threlfall and ask her to bring up some tea.'

Mary went forward and perched on the edge of the horsehair sofa. She could feel it prickling her legs through the cloth of her skirt.

'William hasn't told us much about you,' said Mrs Hart. 'Are you a Blackburn lass?'

349

'Not originally,' she said. 'I came here when my parents moved to work in the mill. I was in the Dandy Mill myself for a while, then at Woodfold House until Mr Sudell went away.'

'And what's tha been doin' since then?' asked Mr Hart.

'I've been working for Mrs Hall at the Star,' she said, thinking that she might as well be honest. She didn't know what William had told them, but she wouldn't be surprised if they'd already made enquiries about her. Everybody knew everybody else in Blackburn and it was hard to keep anything a secret.

Mr Hart glanced at his wife. 'It has a bit of a reputation,' he said.

'It's where the Reformers meet,' she explained. 'That's how I met William.'

'Aye, so he said.'

Mary was glad when William came back in and sat down next to her. His parents had begun to ask her more about what she did at the beerhouse and she was trying to make her work sound respectable.

'I help in the kitchen, preparing the food. And I wait on the customers a bit in the parlour.' She met Mrs Hart's eyes and sensed her hostility even though the woman was superficially polite. It was clear that she knew what other sort of work went on in the beerhouse.

'I hear you were friendly with Mr Starkie, the pawnbroker,' she said.

'He was a customer,' said Mary. 'But he doesn't come in now.'

It was clear what they thought, even though they wouldn't say it out loud. The disapproval on their faces couldn't be hidden.

She was glad when a stout woman came panting in with a tea tray and put it on the table. Mrs Hart thanked the maid and said that she would pour. She handed Mary a china cup and saucer and offered the sugar bowl. Mary took a small piece with the little tongs and tried to drop it into the cup without making a splash before she stirred it.

'So have thy parents both passed on?' asked Mr Hart.

'No!' The question took her by surprise and her spoon clattered on to the saucer. She'd never mentioned her family to William. In truth they hadn't talked about much at all. They hardly knew one another.

'Do they live locally?' asked Mrs Hart.

Mary could feel her cheeks flaming. She needn't have worried about looking pale, she thought.

'They live on Paradise Lane,' she explained. 'But I don't have anything to do with them. I see my brother though, and my sisters sometimes … but I don't get on with my father.'

'Hast tha spoken to him about asking for t' lass's hand?' Mr Hart asked his son.

'No. Not yet.' It was clear that the existence of her parents was news to William as well. Mary cursed herself for not having made things clearer to him sooner. It had never occurred to her that they needed to be involved.

'Well, tha knows tha must. If tha's serious about this marryin' lark,' Mr Hart told his son. 'She's not over twenty-one, is she?' He looked at Mary.

'I'm nearly twenty,' she said.

'Then tha'll need thy father's permission,' he said.

'But I don't have anything to do with them,' Mary told him again.

'Even so, tha'll need his permission to be wed,' he told her and she detected a glimmer of hope that his son might not be able to go through with a marriage after all. It was a complication that Mary hadn't considered and she very much doubted that her father would give his permission for her to be married. He would refuse just to spite her.

They all sipped their tea in awkward silence and Mary wondered how long she would have to endure their censure before William decided it was time for them to leave. Surely he could see that they would never approve of her, and now that she realised she would need her father's agreement to a wedding she knew that the whole visit was pointless anyway.

'They didn't like me,' she said as she and William came down the stairs after an interminable time of polite but stilted conversation.

'I'm sure they did really.'

'Tha's foolin' thyself!' she told him as they got out on to the street. She wished he would see reason. His grand gesture could never be. His parents wouldn't allow it, and her father certainly wouldn't agree. 'Besides,' she told him. 'I'd forgotten about needin' to ask my father.'

'We could go round to see him now,' William suggested. 'Will he be in on a Sunday afternoon?'

'No! He'll not speak to me. They'll not let me in!' protested Mary.

'I'm sure they will. He can't be that bad,' insisted William. 'Lots of families have a falling-out, but they make up again. Perhaps it's time to make peace with them. This could be the best opportunity.'

'But tha doesn't know what they're like! They're not like thy parents!' She wondered what on earth William would make of her family. His parents seemed genuinely fond of him, even willing to meet her and be polite to her when it was obvious they were dead set against her becoming his wife. He'd probably never known anything like hers with their shouting and their arguing and their picking fights with all and sundry. Besides, she didn't even want him to meet them. She'd told him nothing about what her father had done to her – and she never would. It was bad enough him knowing about Mr Starkie.

'Where do they live?'

'Paradise Lane. Opposite t' mill.' She knew there was no point lying.

'Come on then,' he said as he grasped hold of her hand. 'We'll go to see them too and tell 'em as we mean to get wed.'

She walked with him reluctantly, wondering how she could persuade him that it wasn't a good idea, that it would only cause more trouble.

They turned on to Paradise Lane and as she approached number eight she could hear them arguing with one another even though the door was shut.

'This is it,' she said. 'It doesn't sound like it's a good time though. Maybe we should come back later.'

'But we're here now,' said William as he knocked on the door.

A moment later Mary found herself face-to-face with her mother. Her expression was grim. There was a fading bruise in pale yellow and lavender around her eye.

'What's tha want?' she asked. She looked at William with suspicion. 'Who's this tha's brought with thee?'

'This is William Hart,' she said. 'We're meanin' to get wed, but I need my father's permission.'

Her mother hesitated, glancing up and down the street. 'Tha'd best come in then,' she said after a moment. It seemed that although she didn't want Mary in her house again, she was reluctant to have a scene on the doorstep.

Her father was smoking his pipe with his feet up on the fender. His big toe was poking through a hole in one of his socks. John was sitting at the table, a pamphlet open in front of him. Susan was mending a shirt. The yard door slammed and Esther came in and stood in the doorway to the back kitchen, staring at William who was so tall he seemed to fill the small parlour.

'Tha's a cheek showin' thy face here after up and leavin' us without a word,' Mary's father told her.

'What does tha mean? Tha knew I'd gone to work for Mr Sudell.'

'Aye, and a fat lot of good that did thee. Don't think tha can start beggin' to come back home again. There's no place for thee here any more.'

'I'd rather starve on the street than come back here. And tha knows why!' She glared at him and he didn't even look contrite.

'Who's this?' he asked, turning his attention to William.

'I'm William Hart.' He held out a hand in greeting. Her father ignored it and blew a cloud of smoke from his pipe. 'My father has the rope-maker's,' added William as his hand fell to his side.

'Aye, and what's tha doin' here?' he asked.

'I'd like to ask your permission to marry Mary.'

Her father took the pipe from his mouth and burst out laughing. *'I'd like to ask your permission,'* he repeated in a singsong voice, mocking William. 'What makes tha think I'd agree to that?'

'Why wouldn't tha?' asked Mary.

'Because tha's no child of mine no more. Not after tha walked out without a word, leavin' us to struggle without thy wages. Thy sisters went hungry,' he told her.

'If they went hungry it were because of thy drinkin'!' she told him. 'It weren't my responsibility to provide for 'em!'

'It's up to family to work together,' he replied. 'Tha knew we were strugglin' but tha couldn't care less. Tha always were a selfish lass, thinkin' of nothin' but thyself.'

'That's not true!'

'I heard as tha's been back in Blackburn for months, but tha's never come to see us before. And now tha's only here because tha wants summat. Didst tha even know that our John were home?'

'Of course I knew. Who dost tha think gave him money for his new clothes? It weren't thee!' She glanced at her brother who looked uncomfortable. She hoped he wouldn't take the brunt of it after she'd gone.

'We're not asking for money or owt,' William tried to reassure him. 'It'll not cost thee a penny. All we need is a mark on the licence to say that you agree.'

Her father spat into the fire, making it sizzle. 'Like I said. She's no daughter of mine. Tha can do as tha likes. It's nowt to do wi' me.'

'See?' said Mary to William. 'I knew it'd be a waste of time. Let's go.' She grasped his sleeve and pulled him back out of the door, anxious to get away.

'I didn't really think he'd be so awkward about it,' admitted William as they reached the end of the street. 'I thought tha were exaggerating.' He seemed shaken by the experience.

'He hates me,' said Mary. 'Just like thy parents hated me.'

'They didn't!'

'Of course they did. It was clear as a bell on their faces. They know what I am and they'd never let tha marry me even if it were possible, which it isn't. So tha might as well forget it!'

They reached the Star and he followed her into the deserted parlour and sat down. She unfastened the ribbons on her bonnet. There was no way out for her, no way at all. She'd been prepared to marry him as a last resort and now even that had been snatched away from her.

William sat, glum-faced. She could see that he was bitterly disappointed that all his plans had come to nothing.

'I will marry thee, when tha's old enough,' he told her after a moment. 'I will wait.'

'And what am I expected to do in the meantime?'

'I'll think of summat.'

She shook her head. 'Tha'd best forget it, William,' she told him. 'It were a kindly gesture, but it can't be. Find some other place to drink and forget about me,' she advised before she left him to his brooding and went upstairs to her room to try to think of another way of leaving the beerhouse for good.

Chapter Twenty-Seven

Hannah sat in church between Jennet and Peggy. Bessie was on her sister's knee and Peggy was holding a little prayer book where she followed the prayers with a finger, keeping her place under each word. As Mr Whittaker's voice droned on, Hannah glanced up and found her eyes drawn to the familiar figure sitting in the pew a few rows in front. It was the first time she'd seen James since the night they went to the poets' corner. He'd been missing from church the previous Sunday and although Hannah had been to all the Reform meetings with Titus, held in the Assembly Rooms now, James Hindle had never attended. She thought that he was avoiding her.

She knew that he needed time to think about whether he wanted to continue their courtship, and she didn't want to pressure him, but not knowing whether he would even give her the time of day if she caught his eye after the service was agonising.

He'd had his hair trimmed, she noticed, and his shirt was new. In a moment of jealousy she wondered where he'd been the week before and who'd sewn it for him, thinking that she could probably have made him a better one.

She frowned and tried to concentrate on the vicar's lengthy prayers for the sick and the needy. There were still plenty of those despite the Reform. And Mr Turner was showing little enthusiasm for representing the town in Parliament. He hadn't even gone to London yet, saying that he was far too busy with his mills. Titus was right when he said the fight was far from over.

After the last hymn the congregation spilled out into the churchyard. It had turned very cold and there'd been a first frost on the Friday morning. Folk welcomed it. They said it would kill off the last of the cholera. Her family had been lucky, she thought as she glanced at all the extra graves the illness had brought about. Peggy could easily have been buried in one of them and she wondered how much her survival had been owing to Titus insisting that she had something to drink when she was so thirsty. Perhaps his disrespect for authority was sometimes a good thing.

'Hannah!' She looked behind her as James called her name. 'May I talk to you?'

'Aye, of course.' Her heart soared as he took her elbow and led her away from where Jennet was waiting to speak to the vicar's wife. She was still hoping for a favourable decision about her washhouse, although it seemed more and more like a lost cause.

'How are you?' he asked.

'I'm fine,' she lied, noticing that his cravat was coming loose. She longed to reach out and tidy it for him.

'How's the writing?'

She shook her head. 'I've not done any more.'

'Not even a poem?'

'No.' It was untrue. Her new notebook, that she kept hidden in a drawer under her petticoats away from little Peggy's prying eyes, was filled with page after page of verses into which she'd poured out her sadness and heartbreak.

'I'm sorry I've not seen much of you lately.'

'I've been to all the Reform meetings.'

'Aye. I couldn't bring myself to come,' he admitted. 'I was so furious with Titus that I was afraid of what I might say.'

Out of the corner of her eye she saw Jennet grasp Peggy and Bessie by the hand and set off for home. She was grateful that she hadn't walked across to tell her to hurry up.

'He meant it for the best,' she said. 'And I think he's sorry. He's been nice to me ever since and there's been no hinting about me outstaying my welcome.'

'But you don't want to stay there for ever, do you?'

'No. They're good to me, but they do have a tendency to treat me like a child, and after a taste of independence it can be hard. I've been helping Jennet with the washing, but it's not much of a job.' She was glad she was wearing gloves. She would have hated him to see the state of her hands from scrubbing with the lye soap. 'I need to find summat better,' she said.

'Hannah?' He hesitated and looked embarrassed. 'Did you say your parents lived up at Ramsgreave?'

'Aye, that's right. Why?'

'I wondered if we could walk up there this afternoon?'

'We could,' she said, thrilled that he was asking her, but wondering at his reason.

'I think it's time I met your parents,' he said. 'I'd like to ask your father if he'll give me permission to propose to you.' Hannah stared at him. 'Would you, Hannah?' he asked. 'Would you marry me?'

'I thought tha wanted nothing more to do with me!' she confessed. 'I thought tha were too concerned about thy position.' She could scarcely believe what he was asking her. It seemed too good to be true.

'I was for a while,' he admitted. 'But I went home to see my own parents last Sunday and I talked it through with them. They helped me see that what other folk think isn't the most important thing in the world. There's bound to be gossip. Folk always like to gossip, but in the end if they think I'm wrong then that's their affair. And if I lose this job, we'll go somewhere else and I'll find another. There's a need for good teachers now that more and more schools are opening.' He paused for breath and reached out to take her hand. 'Will you marry me?' he asked again.

'Aye, of course I will,' she said. She'd never imagined it would happen like this. All the stories she'd written down and all the ones she'd simply imagined had always ended with him proposing to her, but none of them had the scene taking place on a cold Sunday morning in the graveyard with her hands chapped and his cravat come undone.

'So shall we go to see your parents?'

'Aye, we will,' said Hannah, imagining their surprise and astonishment when she came in with the schoolmaster and told them that he wanted to marry her.

'Where's Hannah?' asked Titus, looking up from his paper when Jennet came in and told the lasses to run upstairs and change out of their Sunday best before dinner.

'Talking to James Hindle! I didn't like to interrupt so I left 'em to it.'

'Why? Were they talkin' about summat important?'

'I really hope so,' said Jennet. 'He had the look of a man set on proposing marriage.'

'Oh, aye. And what does that look like?'

'Tha's a fool, our Titus,' she told him. 'Tha wants to take thy nose out of thy paper for a while and see what's going on around thee.'

'I thought he were keeping well out of her way. He's never been to any more meetings.'

'Perhaps it's thee he's avoiding,' she told him and saw from the look on his face that he hadn't considered that.

Moments later Hannah came in, looking fit to burst with excitement. 'He wants to marry me! We're going up to Ramsgreave so he can meet Mam and Dad and ask permission!'

'Hannah! I'm that glad!' Jennet pulled her sister into her arms and hugged her. 'I knew it would turn out all right in the end. He's lucky to have thee.'

'I need to go and tell Mary,' said Hannah. 'I can't go now, but I'll go tomorrow if tha can spare me for an hour or so. I want to make it right with her before I get wed. I want her to be at the wedding.'

'Aye,' said Jennet. 'This falling out has gone on for far too long. And I know that Mary wants to make up with thee as well. She were lookin' for thee at the hustings, and she's told me how grateful she is for what tha did that night. She might not have lived otherwise.'

'Aye, but she did say some nasty things to me,' Hannah reminded her.

'Put it behind thee,' advised Jennet. 'Tha were such good friends with Mary for a long time, despite her family. Go and make it up with her tomorrow.'

That afternoon, Hannah walked hand in hand with James up to Ramsgreave. It was the first time in many months that she'd been home and she realised how much she missed the fresh air and the wind that whistled down from the hills.

As they approached the cottage she increased her pace. 'Come on,' she said. 'I can't wait to see their faces when we tell them!'

When she pushed open the door everything was the same. Her father's handloom stood idle for the Sabbath but a length of woven cloth was hanging from it ready to be finished the next day and her mother's spinning wheel stood close to the hearth with a bobbin of cotton half spun. Her parents looked up in surprise when she swept in, smiles lighting their faces as she rushed to kiss them.

'What's all this?' asked her father, noticing the stranger in the doorway.

'This is James Hindle,' said Hannah, taking his hand to pull him further into the room. 'He's the schoolmaster on Thunder Alley. He wants to marry me.'

Hannah heard her mother squeal in delight before she got up from her chair to hug her, then she gathered herself and began to hunt in her pantry for something special to offer them to eat.

'Well I never!' she kept exclaiming as Mr Chadwick got to his feet and shook James by the hand.

'Sit thee down,' said Mr Chadwick, offering James his rocking chair.

'No. No.' James urged him back to his seat. 'I'm fine here,' he said, bringing one of the upright chairs over from the table.

'So tha's a schoolmaster?' Her father sounded impressed.

'That's right.'

'And tha wants to marry our Hannah?' She wished he didn't sound so surprised.

'If you'll give me your permission to ask her,' said James.

'Aye, tha can have that, lad, and no mistake. I never thought I'd see our Hannah wed to a schoolmaster, though she always were determined to go up in the world.'

'Well, don't mistake me for a man of importance,' James told him. 'My family are only ordinary folk like you. My father's a silk weaver and my mother's a seamstress, but they wanted me to move up in the world too, so they made sure I was educated and I was lucky enough to do well and become a teacher. It's a good job and there's a little schoolhouse to go with it, so Hannah will be well cared for.'

'She'll have to give up her job in service.'

'That's all arranged,' Hannah told him. Neither of them revealed that she'd been dismissed. Her parents both looked so pleased that Hannah wouldn't have spoiled their joy for the world.

'Will tha come to the wedding?' she asked. 'It'll be at the parish church once we've had the banns read out.'

'Of course we'll come,' said her mother. 'I wouldn't miss it for anything, and happen our

Jennet'll let us stop the night so we don't have to walk back in the dark.'

'I'm sure she will,' said Hannah. There would be room at Jennet's once she was wed, and the thought that on that night she would be sharing a bed with her new husband made her blush at the prospect.

'I'll gather the last of the flowers for a posy,' promised her mother, 'and I'll bring eggs and jam and we'll have a special tea afterwards.'

Hannah hugged her mother. 'That would be wonderful,' she said.

'Will tha come in when we get back?' asked Hannah as she and James approached the outskirts of Blackburn. She felt him tense up although his expression didn't change and he said nothing. 'Tha'll have to forgive him,' she said, meaning Titus. 'I can't begin married life with my husband at odds with my brother-in-law. Besides, it was me that came off worst.'

'Aye. That's what makes me so angry,' he said. 'I hate the thought of you being dismissed from your job because of him.'

'He meant well,' Hannah told him, not for the first time.

They reached Water Street and she asked him again. 'Come in for a bit?'

'Aye, all right.'

Hannah pushed open the door and stepped inside, holding it open for him to follow. Jennet was doing her mending and Titus had a pamphlet on his lap and his pipe in his mouth. Bessie was playing on the rug and Peggy was busy with some knitting.

'How were they?' asked Jennet, getting up to fill the kettle.

'They seemed well,' said Hannah, taking off her bonnet. 'They said they'll come to the wedding. And they seemed to like James.'

'So they should!' Jennet smiled at him. She looked pleased that he'd come in. 'Come and get warm,' she said. 'It's turned cold.'

'What are you reading?' James asked Titus as he sat opposite him and Jennet drew Hannah into the back kitchen.

'Leave 'em be for a minute,' she advised.

'I hope they can settle their differences,' said Hannah.

'Well, I think that was done as soon as James stepped through the door. He made the first move and I'm not even sure that Titus knows he were mad with him. Not that I can blame him – James, I mean. I were madder than he'll ever be when I found out what Titus had done.'

'He thought he was helping me.'

'His trouble is he doesn't think things through,' said Jennet. 'He just does them without considering the consequences. It makes me so angry.'

'But tha forgives him.'

'I don't know about that. I puts up with him,' she said.

Hannah watched her sister butter some oatcakes and place them carefully on a plate. 'Dost tha ever regret it?' she asked. 'Not going to America with George?'

Jennet was silent for a while. 'Sometimes,' she admitted at last. 'On occasion I think I should have gone for our Bessie's sake, if not for my own. But it's too late now.' She handed the plate to Hannah. 'Take that through,' she said.

When Hannah went back into the parlour Titus was showing James the pamphlet he'd been reading. 'Chartism,' he was telling him. 'That's the new thing. I think we should begin a movement here in Blackburn. Carry on the fight.'

James looked up at her and smiled. He might not have forgiven Titus any more than Jennet had, but she was glad that he was willing to talk to him again.

Chapter Twenty-Eight

Mary was in the parlour, sweeping up the remains of the previous night's detritus, when there was a tentative knock at the door.

'It's not opening time yet!' she called.

'Mary? Can I talk to thee?'

She recognised her friend's voice straight away and propped the brush against the wall to hurry over and lift the sneck. 'Come in,' she said. 'Mrs Hall's not here.'

Hannah stepped inside and Mary locked the door again behind her. For a moment they stood looking at one another awkwardly until Mary broke the silence.

'I came to see thee, but they wouldn't let me in. I wanted to thank thee. If tha hadn't made 'em send for Dr Barlow that night, I don't know what would have happened to me.'

'Jennet said tha'd tried to see me, though no one at the house told me tha'd been.'

'I heard as they'd dismissed thee.'

'Aye. Tha heard right. I'm back at our Jennet's again.'

'What did tha do?' asked Mary. 'I heard that it were over a stolen book, but I know tha's not a thief.'

'It were because of how I got the job,' Hannah told her. 'Tha knows I never had a letter of character. But Titus wrote one for me. That's why I couldn't tell thee about it, because he would never have written one for thee. I think he only did it to get me out of the house. I'm sorry,' she said. 'Tha knows I were worried about thee stoppin' here, but there was nowt I could do.'

'Aye. I can see that,' said Mary, although she wasn't sure that she really forgave Hannah. She should have been honest with her from the start. 'How did they find out?'

'Someone told Mr Feilden that no one from Woodfold had been given a character and so they checked and saw mine were a forgery.'

'And do they know it were Titus that wrote it?'

'No. I couldn't get 'im in bother again.'

Mary stared at her friend. So much had changed over the past months and she knew that things could never be the same between them.

'So what will tha do now?' she asked her.

'I'm to be married. James Hindle has asked me.'

So, everything was working out for Hannah again, thought Mary. She had a charmed life. Unlike hers, where everything seemed to go wrong.

'I wanted to tell thee myself,' said Hannah. 'I wanted to ask thee to come to the wedding.'

'When will it be?'

'In a few weeks. We need to get the banns read first, but James doesn't want to wait long and neither do I!'

She looked excited. Her cheeks were glowing pink and Mary knew that she should congratulate her, but she couldn't.

'Will tha come?' asked Hannah. She seemed anxious at Mary's lack of enthusiasm.

'Aye, I suppose so, unless I've moved on.'

'Moved on? Where to?'

'I heard as Mr Fowden is opening up Woodfold Hall again. I were planning to go up and ask after a maid's job. I thought maybe our John could come with me. He's home now.'

'Aye. I've seen him at the stables on Thunder Alley.'

'He's good with horses. I thought they might take him on as a groom. It would get him away from Paradise Lane.'

'It's not definite then?'

Mary shook her head. 'It's a long walk,' she said. 'I need to wait until I feel strong enough.'

'But tha's feelin' better now?'

'Aye. I'm all right.' She wondered whether to tell Hannah about William Hart and his proposal of marriage. She didn't want Hannah to think that she was the only one who could get a chap with a bit of money. But she said nothing. There was no point, because she couldn't marry him anyway, and although he insisted that he would wait for her it would be over a year before she turned twenty-one and a lot could happen in that time.

'Well, if tha's still here tha must come to the wedding. Bring John as well. There's to be a bit of tea after. Tha'd both be welcome.'

'Aye. Thanks.'

They looked at one another in silence and Mary could see how awkward it was for Hannah. Mary knew it was her own fault, but she couldn't help how she felt. She was jealous. She'd done her duty and thanked Hannah for her help, but she was finding it hard to remember how close they'd once been. Before, they would have hugged one another but now Hannah simply turned towards the door.

'I'd best be off then,' she said.

'Aye.' Mary unlocked the door.

'But tha will come?' asked Hannah again and Mary felt herself softening.

'Aye. Of course I will.'

Hannah leaned towards her and brushed her lips against her cheek. 'Take care of thyself,' she said. 'I'll let thee know what day when it's settled.' And then she was gone, off to meet up with the schoolteacher probably, thought Mary as she watched her hurry away up Shorrock Fold.

She was just about to shut the door again when she saw William Hart on his way down. She wished that he would stay away. The way he kept on coming round was only taunting her now that it was impossible for them to be married and she hated to know that he was still paying Mrs Hall for her room. She knew that sooner or later he would want something in return.

She was tempted to shut the door in his face, but he waved his hand when he saw her and snatched off his hat as he came in.

'We're not open. I'll catch it from Mrs Hall if she sees thee.'

'She's not here,' he said. 'I've just seen her in the marketplace. Shut the door. I need to talk to thee. She told me as tha were planning on going away.' He sounded distraught and Mary felt a bit sorry for him.

'It's for the best,' she said as she resumed sweeping the floor. 'Thy parents'll soon have some nice lass lined up for thee,' she told him. 'And what would I do then? It's best if I go, William. I'm grateful. Tha knows that. But I won't be indebted to thee any more. I prefer to make my own way, even if it means movin' on from this town altogether. I'm sorry,' she added when she saw the anguish in his eyes.

'No!' He grabbed the brush from her and let it fall to the floor with a clatter. 'Mary, sit down and listen to me. It's important.' He pulled out a chair and almost pushed her into it. 'I've had an idea,' he said.

'What about?' she asked.

'About going to America.'

'America?' She might have known that it would be another hare-brained scheme. 'What's brought that on?' she asked him.

'I've heard of a few people who've gone and done really well.'

'Aye. The chap that had the house on Paradise Lane before us went there. George Anderton, I think he were called. Hannah reckoned he'd asked their Jennet to go with him, but she wouldn't.' She could see that William wasn't listening to her.

'Would tha go?' he asked her.

'What? To America? I haven't even the fare to get to Preston.'

'I mean would tha come with me?' He was watching her with a pleading look. 'I've been finding out about it,' he explained. 'We can get a coach from the marketplace that'll take us right into Liverpool and we can buy tickets there for passage on a ship. We needn't be fussy. Any ship'll do.'

'And what will we do when we get there?' she asked. She had no idea what America was like and she doubted that he had either.

'Find work. Get a place to live. We can get married later.' He held her gaze. 'I will marry thee,' he promised. 'As soon as I can.'

'Tell him *aye* and don't be a fool,' advised Mrs Hall from the doorway. Mary hadn't heard her come in, but she must have overheard them, or else William had already told her what he was going to propose. 'There's nowt left for thee here,' she said, putting her baskets down on the table.

But there was, thought Mary. There was John. She couldn't just go off and leave him. She couldn't bear to think that he might get into trouble again without her to look out for him.

William was watching her, waiting for an answer.

'What work will tha get?' she asked.

'Same as now. Ropemaking. There's more and more mills opening over there and they all need workers.'

Perhaps John could go with them, she thought. Nobody there would even need to know that he'd been in prison. He might be able to get a job where he could use his numbers.

'Do the tickets cost a lot?' she asked, wondering if she could find the money from somewhere. Perhaps she could sell the dresses and bonnets that Mr Starkie had given her.

'Tha doesn't need to worry about that,' said William. 'I'll pay thy passage. I've a bit put by.'

'I was wondering if our John could come,' she said. If there was work to be had in America she could save up to pay William back, she thought. In fact, it struck her that if she was able to get work that paid enough to keep herself she might not have to go through with a marriage at all. Perhaps she and John could make a new life together.

'John?'

'My little brother,' she told him. 'He were at the house that day.' William looked doubtful. Mary knew that he wanted it to be just the two of them and it was hard to explain that she felt responsible for her brother. 'A fresh start could be the makin' of 'im,' she said. 'He fell in with a bad lad and got into a bit o' trouble. He'll never be given the chance to make owt of himself in this town.'

William frowned. 'I were thinking of it just being me and thee.'

'I'll not go without John,' she told him, trying to force his hand even though she could see Mrs Hall shaking her head at her.

William bit his lip, but Mary held out, her expression firm.

'All right,' he said after a moment. 'If it means that much to thee then John can come with us.'

That afternoon, Mary went up to Thunder Alley to look for her brother. He was in one of the stalls, rubbing down a steaming horse that had come in from the mail coach. He looked smart in his new clothes. They were good quality and although the trousers were a little thin at the knees the jacket hadn't been patched at all and should last him for a while.

'Dost tha fancy going to America?' she asked him.

'Where?'

'America!'

He paused and stared at her as if she'd taken leave of her senses. 'I can't say as I've ever thought about it,' he said as he threw a rug over the horse's back and patted its neck.

'I might be able to get thee passage on a ship.'

'Why would tha do that?' He looked hurt, as if he thought she wanted to get rid of him.

'Not just thee,' she said, glancing over her shoulder to check no one was listening. William had warned her not to say a word to anyone. He didn't want his parents to get wind of his plans because he knew that they'd try to stop him. She pulled on John's sleeve and led him to the back of the stall. 'William Hart has asked me to go to America with him. He said we could take thee an' all, but tha mustn't breathe a word of it to anyone.'

'I don't want to go to America,' he said. 'And I certainly don't want to be playing gooseberry between you and him.'

'But it's not like that,' she told him. 'I don't want to be married to him. Once we get there we can find work and when we've paid him back we wouldn't need to have anything more to do with him. We could make our own life, away from here.'

John looked doubtful. 'What work?'

'Tha could maybe find work as a clerk. It'd be better than this.'

The horse pushed its nose against John and he stroked it thoughtfully. 'I like the horses,' he said.

Mary sighed, exasperated. 'Tha could make summat of thyself,' she told him. 'Say as tha'll come and then William can make the arrangements.'

Her brother shook his head. 'No, Mary,' he told her. 'Tha's chasing a dream. I'm best off stayin' put.'

No matter how much she pleaded and argued, John wouldn't change his mind and in the end she stormed out of the stable, angry and disappointed. If he wouldn't go then she couldn't go cither. She'd have to go back to her first plan and see if she could persuade him to go to Woodfold with her.

'I can't go,' she told William later as they sat in the kitchen at the Star. 'Our John doesn't want to come.'

'That's his choice. It's not stoppin' thee,' said William. He looked pleased that her brother had refused and it annoyed Mary.

'I'll not go without him,' she said. 'He needs me. My father takes all his wages and he's nowt for clothes and such unless I help him out.'

'I'll not keep payin' thy bed and board if tha stops here,' he warned her. 'And tha's not been able to get any other work.' She knew it was meant to be a threat.

'I'm going to Woodfold tomorrow to ask there.'

'They're not takin' on. I heard Mr Fowden himself say he had all the staff he needed.'

She wasn't sure that she believed him. They glared at one another and William was the first to look away.

'What if John had a better job?' he asked after a moment. 'One where there was a decent wage, enough to pay for lodgings. Would tha be willing to leave him then?'

'What sort of job?'

'I could try to get him summat in our office, as a clerk. And I'd enquire about lodgings if tha's worried about him livin' at home. Would tha promise to come with me if I managed it?'

'He might not want it,' she said, thinking how stubborn he'd been. 'I'd have to ask him.'

'But will tha promise to come with me if it can be arranged?'

'Aye, I suppose so,' she said at last, knowing that there wasn't much of a choice.

Chapter Twenty-Nine

Hannah sat beside James at morning service in the parish church. They'd been to see the vicar to ask him if he would marry them and this morning was the first reading of the banns. They were to be married in three weeks' time on the Sunday afternoon and Hannah would move into the schoolhouse. She could scarcely believe that it was really happening – the happy ending she had so wanted and which she'd thought had been out of her reach so many times.

James smiled at her as Mr Whittaker read out their names: *James Herbert Hindle, bachelor of this parish, and Hannah Margaret Chadwick, spinster of this parish.* It gave her a warm feeling inside and she was surprised at the number of people who came up to them in the churchyard afterwards to offer their best wishes. She saw Mr and Mrs

Feilden and their daughters, but they hurried away without even looking at them.

'They'll not be asking thee to supper any more,' she said to James, wishing that things could have turned out differently.

She looked around for Mary, although she didn't really expect to see her. Her friend had always preferred evensong. She'd go down to the Star tomorrow, she thought, to let her know that it was all settled and tell her again that she really did want her to come to the wedding.

It was still dark when Mary came down the stairs the next morning with her bag packed, ready to catch the early-morning coach to Liverpool. She was surprised to see that Mrs Hall was up before her and had made hot tea and toast.

'Here. Take these,' she said, pushing a bundle with some pies wrapped in a cloth into her hands. 'For the journey,' she added.

Mary felt a wave of emotion overcome her and she hugged the woman. 'Thank you,' she said. 'For everythin' tha's done for me.'

'I've done nowt,' replied Mrs Hall, her chin quivering. 'It were a cryin' shame that tha ever fetched up on my doorstep to begin with. Now, get off with thee. Don't keep him waiting. He's a good man, so be good to him,' she advised as she unbarred the door.

Mary stepped outside and her breath caught on the cold morning air, sending a cloud of vapour around her. One or two engines were starting up and she could hear the knocker-up making his way down one of the side streets, but it was mostly still quiet.

William was waiting for her with his bag in his hand. He took hers and gave Mrs Hall a nod of gratitude. Then they hurried to the Bird in Hand on Darwen Street where the Royal Union would leave for Liverpool, promptly at half past six.

The coach was waiting when they arrived, the coachman yawning sleepily, and the horses snorting and filling the air with their breath. Mary wondered if John had fetched them down from the stables. He hadn't waited to say goodbye if he had. Maybe he didn't want a public farewell, she thought. She'd seen him the day before and given him the letter from William and his instructions to report to the office of the ropeworks on Monday morning to begin his new job as a desk clerk, and then to go to the lodging house on Northgate where there was a room on the top floor with the rent paid for the next month.

William ushered her forwards as she hesitated, glancing about for her brother.

'Come on,' he urged, probably hoping she wasn't about to change her mind.

There were some folk already inside the coach – men going to do business at the port – but none that seemed to recognise them. William threw up their bags and then helped her climb to one of the outside seats at the back. He got up beside her and pulled her close to keep her warm and safe.

'This is it,' he said as the driver flicked the reins and they rolled out of town. 'Our new life together.'

Mary looked down at the low-lying mist in the valley as they reached the brow of the hill and turned on to the road to Preston. There was no turning back now, she thought as they passed Dr Barlow's house and heard the screech of his peacocks as they were roused from their sleep. William held her close and she leaned against him as they bumped over ruts in the road. Now that the time had come, she wasn't entirely sorry to be leaving. This town had done nothing for her and she would be well rid of it. She regretted leaving her brother behind. John had been adamant that America was not for him, but he'd been grateful for William's offer of better employment and Mary knew that it was the best she could do for him. It was up to him to make some-thing of himself now. She was sorry to miss Hannah's wedding too. She hoped her friend wouldn't be too disappointed when she found her gone, but William had warned her to tell no one in case his parents tried to stop them.

At Preston, William took her into the Old Dog and they ate bacon and eggs, with as much bread and butter as they required and pots of strong, fresh tea. Then they were off again, until, in the early afternoon, she smelled the sea air as they approached Liverpool.

Mary had never seen so many people in one place. If she'd thought that Blackburn had grown into a large town this place seemed a hundred times bigger. The streets were filled with coaches, and wagons laden with all manner of goods. There were people everywhere – gentleman with tall hats, businessmen like the ones who'd travelled with them, families carrying everything they possessed down to the docks on handcarts, and filthy beggars and street urchins with barely enough clothing to cover their scrawny bodies.

William caught their bags as they were thrown from the roof of the coach and then they walked up and down the crowded streets until they found a lodging house that had rooms. William paid for one small room. The owner never questioned that they were husband and wife, and didn't look as if he cared anyway.

'Stay here and watch our stuff,' said William. 'I'll go and enquire about boats and get tickets.'

Mary sat on the edge of the bed. It looked none too clean but she hoped they wouldn't be there for long. From the tiny attic window she could see the masts of the sailing ships in the harbour and she wondered which one might take them to their new life.

William was gone a while but returned with a smile of triumph and showed her the tickets. 'We can sail tomorrow on a packet ship!' he said. 'We couldn't have planned it better.'

He went out and bought more pies from a street vendor. They weren't as good as the ones they'd eaten earlier, baked by Mrs Hall, and for a moment Mary felt a wrench of homesickness. Did she really want to go? She wasn't sure. But it was too late to change her mind now. She had no way of getting home.

Even though she was weary and aching from the journey, she allowed William to make love to her for the first time before they slept. He was clumsy and unsure and she didn't have the patience to guide him. She was just glad when he was finished and hoped that it wasn't enough to get her with child again. She must try to find a druggist before they got on the boat tomorrow, she reminded herself as she drifted off to sleep with the sound of rumbling wheels and strident voices rising from the streets below.

That same morning, Hannah insisted on walking Peggy to school, just so that she could smile at her future husband. Peggy was put out about it.

'I don't need you to take me,' she kept telling her as they made their way up to Thunder Alley. She'd understand why one day, thought Hannah, when she fell in love herself.

James was ringing the bell and he grinned across the street when he saw her. One or two of the boys nudged each other and smirked. Hannah smiled back and stood until the girls had gone in. Then she tore herself away as the doors thudded shut and she went down to the Star to see Mary.

She knocked timidly on the door and called out to say who it was when she heard Mrs Hall bellow that she wasn't open yet.

'Come in,' Mrs Hall said when she'd unbarred the door. Hannah stepped into the familiar parlour, empty now, where Mrs Hall had been wiping down the tables. 'Tha's just missed her,' she said.

'Oh, has she gone out? I don't mind waiting.'

Mrs Hall shook her head. 'She's gone for good,' she told Hannah.

'What? Where? Has she got work at Woodfold?' Hannah felt let down again that her friend had left without telling her.

'No.' Mrs Hall waved towards a chair. 'Sit down,' she said. 'I'm not supposed to say owt, so tha must swear as tha can keep it secret.'

'Of course I can,' said Hannah, wondering what she was about to be told.

'She's gone with William Hart. They caught the early coach to Liverpool. They're off to America.'

Hannah stared at her. 'William Hart?' she repeated. 'I thought she hated him.'

'Well, she were never that keen on him,' admitted Mrs Hall.

'So why did she go with him?'

'She were indebted to him,' Mrs Hall told her. 'He's the one who's been paying for her to stay here. It were him that paid Dr Barlow too. He's soft on her,' she added.

Hannah remembered the night that Mary had been ill and how keen William had been to rush for the doctor, but Jennet had told her about the day of the hustings when Mary had been trying her best to avoid him and she couldn't imagine why she would have agreed to go with him.

'She's not expectin' again, is she?' she asked.

Mrs Hall shook her head. 'I don't think so.'

'But why didn't he just marry her? Why go all that way?' asked Hannah, suddenly realising that she would never see her friend again.

'Her father wouldn't give his permission.'

Hannah wished that Mary had confided in her. She must have known she was going the last time she'd seen her and she'd never breathed a word.

'Mind tha keeps it to thyself,' warned Mrs Hall. 'I shouldn't have said owt really and they'll not be properly safe until their ship has sailed.'

'Why? What are they running from?' asked Hannah, hoping that William Hart hadn't committed some crime.

'His parents,' said Mrs Hall. 'If they get wind of it they'll fetch him back. And where would that leave poor Mary? If tha's as good a friend as tha says then tha'll never breathe a word of what's been said here.'

Next morning, Mary woke early. William was still sleeping beside her and she watched him. He looked younger as he slept, more vulnerable. His long lashes flickered a little before he finally woke and smiled up at her. He reached for her hand and raised it to his lips to kiss.

'I'm so glad you decided to come,' he said. She didn't remind him that all the other options had been worse.

'Aye,' she said as she pulled her hand away. 'We'd best be making a move if we're to get to the docks on time.'

They walked down the busy streets, following others towards the ships. There were several lined up and William enquired which one was theirs.

It was the *Pacific*. The sails were still furled on the towering masts, but Mary could see the sailors climbing up high into the rigging to loose them ready to sail. There was a gangplank propped against the side of the ship and passengers were making their way aboard, carrying bags and boxes between them.

'Come on!' urged William. 'Time to get on!'

She hurried after him, afraid of losing him in the crush. Perhaps they would come back one day, she thought. Or maybe she'd never see her home again. It was a poignant thought and she fought back the threat of tears. She didn't want William to see her crying because, like Mrs Hall had said, he was a good man and maybe that was enough, for now at least.

Chapter Thirty

The following Sunday, Hannah was walking through the marketplace with James. They were on their way to catch a coach to Bolton so she could meet his family and she was feeling nervous.

A group of men were stopping every passer-by and questioning them although everyone shook their heads and moved on. Hannah was wondering what it was about. They didn't look like beggars. Maybe they were from the temperance movement, she thought, asking men and women to sign the pledge.

One approached her and James and she felt him tighten his grip on her arm.

'Mornin'!' the man greeted them, touching his cap. 'I wonder if tha can help us. We're looking for young William Hart, son of the ropemaker. He's not been seen for days and his family's right worried about him. Dost tha know him? Hast tha seen him about at all?'

'I know him,' said James. 'He was a regular at the Reform meetings at the Star. I saw him at the hustings, and on Election Day. But I can't think that I've seen him since.'

'What about thee, miss? Hast tha seen him anywhere? His mother's that upset she won't stop crying.'

Hannah hesitated. Should she tell them where he was? Reassure them that he was safe and that no harm had come to him? She couldn't bear to think of his mother suffering so much grief. But she'd made a promise to Mrs Hall and the land-lady might get into trouble if it was revealed that she'd helped him. Besides, she didn't know if they would have sailed yet. His parents might go to look for him, and Mary would never forgive her a second time if she found out who'd betrayed them.

'I'm sorry,' she said after a moment. 'I haven't seen him.' And it was true, although she knew that it was a lie by omission. But she'd done it for Mary, she told herself as they walked on. She wouldn't spoil her friend's chance of happiness again.

*

394

Hannah had sewn herself a new frock for the wedding, hiding it away every time James called round so that he wouldn't see it. Over it she wore her jacket and her best bonnet, with a new feather.

At five to two in the afternoon, Jennet and Titus went into the church ahead of her, with her two nieces and her mother. Her father, in his Sunday best, waited with her in the porch. He smiled at her.

'I'm right glad tha's found such a nice man to wed,' he told her. 'Tha's done well for thyself!'

'I know,' she said as she peeled off her gloves. Her hands were soft and white now that she'd begun to rub them every night with lanolin. Jennet had forbidden her to do any more washing until the wedding, although she'd helped with the mending and the pressing.

Her father pulled her arm through his, patted her hand, and took her inside. James was waiting for her and his family had come over from Bolton. They were nice people, just ordinary folk, and they'd welcomed her warmly. She walked up the aisle to the altar rail where her father put her hand in James's. He smiled at her and they turned to Mr Whittaker, who was waiting with his prayer book open to bless the plain gold band that James had bought for her to wear.

After they'd both signed the register, they walked back to Water Street. There was quite a crowd of people there and Hannah was worried that not everyone would fit into the house, especially when she saw how the table had been filled to overflowing with food by Molly and some of the other neighbours whilst they'd been in church. She needn't have worried about there not being enough for everyone.

Titus was going around filling up everyone's cups with ale. He'd found the money from somewhere to buy a barrel and James had helped him to roll it down the street the day before. Everyone was hugging her, congratulating her and kissing her cheeks.

After a while James came to find her. 'Shall we go home?' he asked. 'Shall we just slip away whilst no one's looking?'

Hannah nodded. It seemed a good idea. The only person she wanted to be with was him. They went out of the door unnoticed and walked across town together. As they turned the corner into Thunder Alley, James took the key to the schoolhouse from his pocket. He went ahead of her to unlock the door; then he lifted her in his arms and carried her over the threshold.

'We don't want any bad luck!' He laughed. 'So we'd better do things right.'

He set her down on the floor and Hannah glanced about as he got the fire going. *New curtains*, she thought, *cushions, a nice tablecloth.* She'd get the stuff from the market and sew and stitch until she made this bare room into a home. And then, who knew? Clothes for a baby maybe?

She watched his broad shoulders as he coaxed up a blaze and then went to stand beside him as they both warmed their hands.

'Welcome home, Mrs Hindle,' he said.

Welcome to

Penny Street

where your favourite authors and stories live.

Meet casts of characters you'll never forget,
create memories you'll treasure forever,
and discover places that will stay with
you long after the last page.

Turn the page to step into the home of

Libby Ashworth

and discover more about

A
LANCASHIRE
Lass

Dear Reader,

I hope that you enjoyed reading about Hannah and Mary in *A Lancashire Lass* now that they are a few years older than when we left them in *The Cotton Spinner*. In the previous book they managed to escape the smoke and grime of the mill town when they went to work as maids at Henry Sudell's manor in the nearby countryside at Mellor. I don't suppose their lives there were easy. They would have worked hard for long hours, but at least the air would have been clean, they would have a decent bed to sleep in and adequate food. It must have been very hard for them to lose their jobs and have to return to Blackburn just as a cholera outbreak took hold.

Keen-eyed historians may have spotted one or two discrepancies in the dates when compared to the actual historical timeline. Although it's true that Henry Sudell did lose a huge amount of money speculating on the cotton market, his flight from Woodfold Hall took place in 1827, whereas *A Lancashire Lass* is set in 1832. But I thought the story of what happened to Henry Sudell was too interesting not to use. It was an ideal way of forcing Hannah and Mary back into Blackburn when they thought they had escaped the worst of the poverty and hardship that was still apparent there, and it shows that even the gentry were not safe from the fluctuations of the cotton trade.

Blackburn's first election following the Representation of the People Act took place in December 1832. The book doesn't specify a date and it may seem that the election was earlier in the year. I hope that these small changes didn't spoil anyone's enjoyment of the story.

The outbreak of cholera, which was a real event, gave me an ideal way to bring Jennet back into the story with her fight for a washhouse for the town. I took inspiration for this from the real story of Kitty Wilkinson, who lived in Liverpool in 1832, and who, like Jennet, was a washerwoman. It was a story that my late father told me and one that has stayed with me. Kitty Wilkinson was eventually successful and some years later became the superintendent of a public washhouse on Frederick Street in Liverpool. If you ever visit Liverpool Anglican Cathedral you will find her memorialised in a stained-glass window in the Lady Chapel. Do go and see it if you can. There aren't many memorials to ordinary working-class women who made a difference to society.

Another real person who was mentioned in the book is Mrs Kitchen. She founded the first Female Reform Union in Blackburn and was present at the Peterloo Massacre in Manchester. Although you will find her named as Kitchen in almost all online sources, my research shows she was actually named Alice Mitchard Hitchen. She was a widow with at least one daughter and went on to marry George Dewhurst, who was mentioned as a reformer in *The Cotton Spinner*. George is an interesting character. He served time in Lancaster Castle for his efforts to win the vote for the ordinary working man. He made such an impression that his friends and admirers presented him with a silver cup, which was recently discovered by a descendant of George's in an antique shop in Bristol. With the help of a fundraising page, the cup was brought back to Blackburn and is now on display in Blackburn Museum, where you can also see a painting that depicts the 1832 election.

I think you've probably guessed by now how passionate I am about the history of my home town! I hope you'll join me for book three and continue to follow the story of Jennet and her family and to learn more about Blackburn in the mid-19th century.

Libby x

The Representation of the People Act 1832

The changes brought about by the Industrial Revolution meant that so many people had flocked into the towns to live and work that there needed to be a reform of the way Members of Parliament were chosen. Some boroughs, sometimes called 'rotten boroughs', were sending one, or even two, members to Parliament when there were only a handful of people to vote for them – and those electors were often forced or bribed to vote for the man their patron chose. On the other hand, places like Manchester and Blackburn that had rapidly growing populations returned no MPs at all.

The Act created 67 new constituencies of which Blackburn was one. The vote was also broadened to include small landowners, tenant farmers, shopkeepers and householders who paid a yearly rental of £10 or more. However this still left the majority of working men without a vote, and, as a voter was defined in the Act as a male person, it was the first time that women were formally excluded from voting in Parliamentary elections. Before 1832 there were occasional, although rare, instances of women voting.

By 1832 Blackburn had a population of over 27,000 although only 627 of them were electors. This entitled the town to two seats in Parliament. Four candidates were in the field for the two seats: William Feilden of Feniscowles, John Fowden Hindle of Woodfold Park (who withdrew on the evening before the first vote), John Bowring of London, and William Turner of Mill Hill. William Feilden and John Bowring appeared to be the favourite candidates and it was expected that they would be returned together. But William Turner brought his local influence to bear – the story of his rolling out the barrels in the churchyard is true. Voting took place over two days and the electors had two votes. The result of the first day's vote was: Feilden 346; Bowring 324; Turner 314. The second day's poll ended with Feilden 376; Turner 347; Bowring 334. The narrow defeat of John Bowring resulting in rioting and disturbances in the town.

The 1832 Cholera outbreak

The summer of 1832 brought an outbreak of Asiatic cholera to Blackburn. It had been gradually spreading across the country since the first cases were reported in November 1831, despite efforts to quarantine ships coming from the Baltic. The first cases were in Sunderland and the disease seems to have spread to London on board coal ships from the Tyne. The victims' extremities appeared to take on a blue tinge shortly before death, confirming that this was the feared 'Asiatic' or 'blue' cholera. The spread of disease was not properly understood and most doctors clung to the belief that cholera was spread by a miasma, a poisonous vapour which held particles of decaying matter and was characterised by its foul smell. In 1832, the advice given to patients was to eat and drink nothing until the sickness and diarrhoea had passed, and as it was also still common for patients to be bled, it's possible that many of the deaths were actually caused by dehydration. There was an awareness that cleanliness was important and homes were cleaned and limewashed after cases were diagnosed, but it wasn't until 1849 that Dr John Snow stated that cholera was spread through contaminated drinking water. It then took until 1854, when there was another cholera outbreak, for him to be able to begin to prove his theory by pointing to a single water pump on Broad Street in London that had poisoned hundreds of people. However it took many more years before his theory was taken seriously and it was not until sewers and drains and clean drinking water became commonplace that cholera was prevented.

Contraception in
Victorian Britain

Whilst I was writing Mary's story I began to research what forms of contraception were available to women in the 1800s. As well as douching, washing yourself out, one of the most popular methods seems to have been a sponge, as I've described in the book. If the sponge failed, as it often did, then women might turn to a version of Ma Critchley's little pills, which were promoted as an aid to regulating monthly flow. Some were even called Pennyroyal Pills. Pennyroyal is a herb of the mint family, which like tansy and rue, has been used for a long time by wisewomen and herbalists to induce an abortion. Pennyroyal is a poison and taken in excess it can damage the liver. Many women died after taking it. I recently discovered that my great-grandmother died after a back-street abortion. I don't know the details, but I have dedicated this book to her memory.

If you enjoyed *A Lancashire Lass*, read on for an exclusive extract from Libby Ashworth's next book in The Mill Town Lasses series.

A
FAMILY
Secret

Coming February 2021

Available to pre-order now

Chapter One

It was still dark when she woke, but Bessie could hear the knocker-up making his way down the street, rapping on the windows until he heard an answer from the sleepy occupants inside. She pulled the blankets tight around her neck and hoped for a few more minutes' sleep.

Beside her, Peggy was breathing deeply as she lay with one hand tucked under the flock bolster and the other curled into a tight fist near her face. She'd slept like that for as long as Bessie could remember and since they were children.

It was no use, she thought, she couldn't wait a moment longer. Not needing a candle or rushlight to find her way, Bessie swung her feet over the edge of the mattress and felt for her clogs with her toes. They were icy cold and a shiver ran through her. She reached for her shawl from the bedpost and pulled it around herself, over her red-flannel nightgown. She was bursting for a wee and she knew that it would be perishing cold outside. She went down the steep stairs, resting her hand on the wall where they curved midway, glancing back as she heard her mother getting up. She'd be in trouble if she was caught going out in her night clothes. Her mother didn't approve of her going down the yard until she was properly dressed, but Bessie couldn't wait and she hated using the chamber pot.

She unbarred the door slowly, trying not to let it squeak and wake Grandma Chadwick who had her bed in the parlour now that she couldn't climb the stairs any more. Bessie could hear her snoring and knew that she'd be lying on her back with her mouth wide open, and probably a dribble of spittle running down her chin. She hated that her grandma had grown old. She remembered her when she lived in the cottage at Ramsgreave, when they would walk up there to see her and Grandad Chadwick. Bessie had always enjoyed that. She'd liked the way that the skies cleared to let the sun shine through and the scent of the air changed as they left the town and its dozens of smoking chimneys behind. The stench of the Blakewater was replaced by the clear streams that ran down from the hills, and the incessant noise of the engines gave way to the sound of sheep calling to their lambs and the gentle thud of the handloom weavers at work.

Her grandad had been a handloom weaver. She remembered watching him as he sat at his loom, working the treadle with his feet, as the shuttle flew back and forth. He'd tried to teach her to weave, but her legs hadn't been long enough and her feet wouldn't reach the pedals, even when she was sitting in his lap. He would laugh and kiss the top of her head and call her his grand little lass. She missed him.

It was cold in the house and there were frost patterns on the inside of the back kitchen window, but the chill that struck her as she stepped outside was even more fierce. Her feet slipped on the ice as she went down to the little brick building at the bottom of the yard that housed the privy. She lifted the latch, pushed open the door and put the flickering lantern down on the stone floor. Then sat down with relief on the wooden board, her teeth chattering as she emptied her bladder.

The knocker-up had moved on to the next street and in the distance she heard the noise of the engines starting up in the mills for another day's work. Her day began at six and it would be six this evening before she was finished – and her father would work another couple of hours after that. She supposed they were lucky. The mills were working full-time at the moment and the money was welcome, although there was always the fear that they would be put on short-time again if the mill owners decided they had more cloth than they could sell.

When she went back inside, her mother was up and had lit the fire. She was helping Grandma Chadwick get up and Bessie managed to close the door quietly and creep back up the stairs unseen. Her teeth were still chattering as she took off the nightgown and replaced it with a petticoat, followed by her skirt and blouse with an indoor shawl crossed at the front and fastened around her waist. She'd take it off later because even if she was cold now it would be hot in the mill. She welcomed the thought of beginning her work, even though it would be difficult to mend the threads at first until she got the feeling back into her fingers.

Peggy was still in bed. She didn't begin her work at the school until eight o'clock and Bessie often felt jealous of what she regarded as the privileges her elder sister had. But, she reminded herself, her sister didn't bring home the wages that she did as a four-loom weaver at the Brookhouse Mill.

She went back down to get her breakfast. The parlour was growing warmer and she tried to keep near to the fire, even though her mother kept calling her into the back kitchen to carry through the bowls and cups to put on the table for their porridge and tea.

Her father appeared yawning loudly, scratching his head, and sat in his rocking chair by the hearth.

'It's a cold 'un this morning,' he observed. 'They say as when the day lengthens, the cold strengthens. And it's true.'

'I'll be glad when it comes lighter in the mornings,' said Bessie as her mother dished out the oatmeal. 'I hate starting work in the dark and finishing in the dark. And the smell of the gaslight makes me feel sick.'

'It's better than oil lamps and candles,' her father told her. 'In my day that's all we had, and there's many a mill gone up in flames because of it. Lives lost too,' he added as he blew on his tea to cool it before taking a long sup from his pint pot. 'Thing's have changed a lot since I were a lad. But not always for the better.' He frowned. 'The Chartists are right when they say we should have a fair day's pay for our work every day instead of being subject to the whims of yon mill owners.'

'Don't be startin' on politics at this time of the morning,' her mother warned him. 'We've heard it all before anyroad.' She sliced him a thick crust off the end of a precious loaf of bread and spread it with butter for him. 'Let that stop tha mouth for a bit,' she said.

Her father was always talking politics, thought Bessie as she ate. And he was always out at some club or meeting after he'd come home from work and had his tea. Her mother sometimes complained that they hardly saw him, but Bessie preferred it when he was out. She liked it best when it was just her and her mother. Her father – well she found him difficult, and he'd never made any secret of his favouritism for Peggy, who, if it was to be believed, never did a thing wrong – unlike her who never seemed able to please him.

Her mother poured a cup of tea for Grandma Chadwick and took it to her. She was sitting up in bed with a couple of pillows propped behind her, and her shawl tight around her shoulders. Her mother would move her to the rocking chair by the fire once her father had gone to work and she'd sit there all day, nursing a little rag doll that used to be Peggy's and singing it lullabies as if it were a real babe. They were the same songs that her grandma used to sing to her and it made Bessie feel sad. Grandma Chadwick had never been the same since Grandad died. It was the shock, her mother said, that had done something to her mind.

'Time we were off,' said her father and drained his cup. He took his jacket and cap from the peg by the door and Bessie got her outdoor shawl and put it over her head and shoulders. She kissed her mother goodbye and followed her father out on to the dark street to join the other workers who were coming out and slamming their doors behind them before making their way to the mills – some to the Dandy Mill, some to Quarry Street, but most to the Brookhouse Mill.

'Good morning!' The street was filled with early greetings. Some heartfelt, but most still sleepy as folk trudged to their jobs. Her father soon fell in with his friends and Bessie walked behind until they reached the gates. As the hooter blared across the town, joined by the other mills until it sounded like a fanfare, her father and the other men clattered up the iron stairs to the spinning rooms and she followed the women into the weaving shed. She hung up her shawl, slipped her feet out of her clogs, checked the looms and set them running. Two were weaving Blackburn Check for shirts and the other two were weaving a fine calico that would be sent up to Darwen to be printed in bright colours for summer frocks.

Her friend Ruth, who worked beside her, greeted her with a smile. It was too noisy to hold any conversation but they managed to convey their thoughts with sign language, Ruth making it plain she was cold, tired and wished it was time to go home already.

Bessie had worked hard to progress to being a four-loom weaver, but running four looms took a lot of concentration and she was kept busy all day knowing that the cost of any mistakes or flaws would be docked from her wages and make her father cross. It was very different from her grandfather's handloom that she'd been thinking about earlier. There was no chance here to take ten minutes for a breath of fresh air and a cup of tea. Once the engines began to turn, the looms worked without stopping until dinner time.

Bessie was a conscientious worker and she prided herself on her skills. She found it difficult to hide her jealousy of her sister though. All her life she'd seemed to live in Peggy's shadow, with their father telling everyone that Peggy was the clever one, the quick one, the pretty one. There'd been no question of Peggy leaving school at thirteen to work a twelve hour day in the mill. Their father had been adamant about that. No, Peggy was to be a schoolteacher and so she'd stayed on at the Girls' School as a pupil-teacher. At first Bessie had enjoyed the reflected esteem. The other girls had admired her for having a big sister who was their teacher even if Peggy had sometimes been intolerably bossy. Bessie had hoped that her father would do the same for her. But as her thirteenth birthday had approached, he'd made it very clear that she was to go into the mill to learn to weave.

'Book learnin' won't suit her,' he'd told her mother as she'd hidden behind the kitchen door listening to them discuss her future. 'She's good with her hands. Weavin'll suit her better.'

Her mother hadn't argued. Not much anyway. And no one had asked her what she wanted. Once she was old enough, she'd had no choice but to leave the calm of the classroom for the frantic, deafening world of the cotton mill.

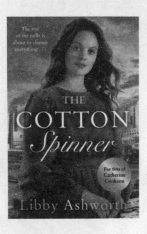

Lancashire, 1826

When Jennet and Titus Eastwood are forced to move from their idyllic cottage into the centre of Blackburn to find work in the cotton mills, their lives are changed in ways they could never have imagined and their new home on Paradise Lane is anything but . . .

Then Titus is arrested and sent to prison for attending a Reform meeting. Jennet is left to fend for herself and things go from bad to worse as she finds herself pregnant and alone – with another man's child . . .

'An engrossing tale of hardship, struggles, love and family. Well researched, perfect for fans of Catherine Cookson.'
Kitty Neale

AVAILABLE NOW

Hear more from

Libby Ashworth